DARK KING

SEA FAE SERIES — BOOK ONE

C.N. CRAWFORD

CHAPTER 1

"*H*e's here to kill me."

I stared at the image reflected in the scrying mirror. The assassin stood aboveground: a beautiful fae with sun-kissed skin and hair the color of flames. Death had arrived in one handsome golden package. Within an hour, he would have a knife to my throat. Twenty minutes later, my dead body would be swinging from the bough of a hawthorn tree.

Gina stood next to me in our cluttered shop, her hands in her pockets. "Don't overreact. Americans are always overreacting about everything."

I chewed my gum and blew a pink bubble. It popped. "I'm not American."

"You *sound* American. And anyway, the whole point of living literally underground is that the assassins can't find you, right? He doesn't know where the trapdoor is. We're fine."

"Maybe." A pulse of fae magic made me shiver. His power was intensifying.

The fae assassin had about a dozen blades strapped to his

body. The only thing stopping him from killing me was that he had no idea how to find us.

"How do you even know he's here for you?"

"Because he's directly above our shop, and I'm the only illegal supernatural in this part of London."

Gina blew one of her dark curls out of her eyes. "I'll tell you what, though; he does look bloody terrifying."

"Yep."

I should have known this would happen.

At some point, the assassins came for *all* us supernaturals. They hunted down the witches and fae, the demons and shifters. They delivered death from glamoured palaces. Only the assassins—the elite fae--were allowed to use magic.

The rest of us? We hid in tunnels, pretending not to exist.

Pacing on the earth above our shop, the assassin pulled out his sword.

My breath quickened, and I narrowed my eyes at him. "I need to stop him before he finds us."

"Can you do some kind of magic from here?"

"I don't think so." I rushed for the spell books anyway. I wasn't wealthy enough to have books of powerful spells—nothing for making armies burst into flames or reaping souls out of bodies. I had many agricultural spells that had no point whatsoever in modern London, and a really nice book of curses, but those generally took a long time to get going.

I pulled it off the shelf anyway, flipping through the pages as fast as I could. At the back, many of the curses had been damaged by water, but I found one that could turn someone's thoughts into gibberish. Not the *best* spell in a life-or-death situation, but maybe it would confuse him enough that he'd just wander away, no longer able to remember why he'd come.

"I've got one," I said, hope blooming. "I'm going to make him go insane."

"Good. Just—don't aim it at me."

I began chanting the spell, but the ink smudges over the words made it hard. I wasn't sure if I was reading the spell correctly. Then, to my horror, the letters rearranged themselves on the page, until they made no sense at all. I whirled, finding that the books around me now all had gibberish writing on the spines.

I hadn't made him go insane. I'd made the books go insane. *Son of a gun.* I'd have to fix that later. "That didn't work, Gina."

"What else do you know?"

I slammed the book shut. "I mean, I can make him hear music. I don't think that will scare him away."

"It's worth a shot. It would be creepy."

"Guess I'll try anything right now." I crossed back to the scrying mirror.

Standing before it, I closed my eyes, singing Miley Cyrus's *Wrecking Ball* in my eeriest voice. The sound wended through the enchanted glass, all the way to the warrior above us. This was Gina's favorite song—at least the way I sang it. When she got upset or couldn't sleep, I sang it to her like a lullaby. I'd been doing that since I found her on the streets two years ago—when she was only fourteen, living rough. She'd been with me ever since.

But singing Miley probably wasn't going to scare the killer away. After a few verses, I let the song fade out.

The intruder still stood above us, gripping his sword.

"It appears he still wants to kill me," I said. "Probably more violently, after that song. I'm going to have to face him head-on before he kills us both."

"I have an idea," said Gina. "How about you just—don't go above ground? We've got Pot Noodle and custard creams in here. That's basically all we need for at least two days. And there are zero fae assassins inside the shop, so that's a win for staying in here."

I lifted my sea-green eyes to her. "He's not going to go away."

"He *might*. Don't be such a pessimist." She stared at the mirror again. "Wait, he's writing something on a piece of paper. Maybe this is a good sign. He's open to communication."

"I know you like to see the best in people, Gina, but I don't think the armed assassin is a nice person."

"Maybe he's seen you around and he's here to ask you on a date. You could use one. Look at his big manly arms! And you're both fae, right? He's a fae, you're a fae. You both have magic. Perfect. You'll have beautiful fae babies."

My gum was losing its flavor. "We're both fae, but we're not on the same side here, Gina. My magic is illegal, and his isn't. He's going to snap my neck in a hasty execution, and then he's going to drink beer in a castle to unwind."

"Or maybe he's lonely? You know, a bit of romance might help you enjoy life a bit more, maybe a walk by the Thames at sunset, get a Cornetto from the ice cream van. Get you out of the ol' dirt hole a bit more."

Gina was a people person. I was not.

"I like our dirt hole," I snapped. "It helps me avoid people, and particularly men. Also, I prefer the term *natural earthen domicile* to dirt hole."

"There are nice people out there. Even men. The old man who works at Pizza Express gave me a free meatball yesterday."

Gods have mercy. It was fairly clear to me at this point that Gina did not understand the gravity of the situation. "But this man is not here to give me a free meatball. He's here to cut my head off. Do you get where I'm coming from with my concerns?"

In the scrying mirror, the fae held up the paper. In perfectly formed, elegant letters, he'd written: *Aenor, Drowner of Islands, Surrender or Die a Painful Death.*

I spat my gum into the trash. "Well then. Doesn't he seem like a catch? I'll just put on my best dress for when I let him murder me by the Thames after our Cornettos and meatballs."

"Shit." Her forehead crinkled. "Drowner of Islands? What's that about?"

"No idea. Swear to gods I never did that. But it's an amazing nickname, isn't it? I might adopt it." I pointed at the scrying mirror. "Look at that sign. Do you see it? Not only is he threatening to kill me in a painful manner, but he did a weird thing with capitalizing all the words. That alone tells me he's the worst sort of psychopath."

"Is that blood on his sword?" Gina asked, apparently no longer charmed by him.

"It is, yes. Not ideal."

"He didn't even wash it off before showing up here. That bit seems a bit off, you know? I mean, give it a good rinse first, at least. Showing up to a kill with other people's blood is just not on."

It creeped me the hells out that he knew my first name. Also, yes, the fresh blood wasn't endearing him to me.

"How did he know he was being scryed on?" Gina asked.

"You can feel it," I said. "On the back of your neck, like someone's watching, you know?"

Gina ran her fingers over the magical glass. "So he's here to kill you. But what exactly are you gonna do about it? You can't fight him. He's trained to kill outlaws within seconds."

A powerful pulse of his magic vibrated through the walls. My stomach clenched at the dark music of his magic. What exactly was he brewing up there on the surface? Whatever it was, it wouldn't be pleasant.

Goosebumps rose all over my skin. "Have some faith in me. I can kill him." I pointed to the dried demon hearts nailed to our rickety underground walls. Demon body parts, crammed between shelves of potions and magical amulets. "Look. You see that? I've killed before. Plenty of times. That's why I'm known as Aenor, Flayer of Skins, Scourge of the Wicked. Boom."

Gina gave me a sympathetic look that was frankly patronizing coming from a sixteen-year-old. "First of all, you gave yourself that name. Second of all, those guys you scourged weren't as scary as this blood-sword motherfucker."

"Language!" Perhaps I carved out hearts and broke bones, but I had some standards for proper behavior. Or at least I expected those under eighteen to follow them.

"Fucking hell, Aenor." She pressed her hands on either side of the mirror, ignoring my admonition. "He's, like, eight feet tall and well...murdery. Third of all—was I on point three? Your demon kills were extreme circumstances. You didn't have a choice. Those were demons beating their girl-friends. Or vampires hunting teenage girls through the streets. You intervened to save lives. There's no, like... imme-diate emergency right now. As long as we stay in the shop, no one has to die. Like I said. Zero assassins inside the shop. We're perfectly safe underground."

She was reassuring herself more than she was making a coherent argument.

The magic intensified around me, setting my teeth on edge. "You're wrong, Gina. If I don't act, we both die. He's fixing to do something nasty."

"I don't see it that way. You could stay in here and wait till he gets bored enough to leave. He'll slink off home to watch *Doctor Who* at some point and have a spliff or something."

"That's not how this works. Assassins don't get bored and

leave." I stood, my body buzzing with adrenaline, and crossed to the desk behind the counter. I rolled it open and pulled out a handgun. "And anyway, I have a little advantage. They'll be expecting me to use an attack spell, not a gun. Traditional fae like him never use modern weapons. It's a whole taboo thing for no good reason whatsoever. Lucky for us, I don't care a lick about tradition, so I'll just shoot him in the heart with iron bullets. Unlike lead, they actually kill the fae. Job done."

"But he has magic."

"So do I."

"Right," she countered. "But you just have sad dirt-hole magic, and he looks like his would be better."

"*Anyway*," I said a little too sharply. "Waiting until an assassin gets bored enough to wander home isn't a real solution."

"What will I do if you die, Aenor? I'd have no one to take care of me. I get scared at night, and I can't run the shop on my own."

Sometimes, Gina seemed surprisingly worldly. And at other times—like now—she seemed more like the sixteen-year-old human that she was.

From above, the killer's magic grew stronger, thrumming over my skin in a dangerous warning. I breathed in the heavy, sea-smelling air, and my heart started pounding harder against my ribs.

He was going to hit us with an attack at any moment. Then—our bodies would sway from the hawthorn tree.

I had to stop this murderer before he got the chance.

CHAPTER 2

*C*old, wet magic skimmed through my cluttered shop, growing so powerful it rattled the floorboards beneath my feet. Gina's dark eyes went wide, and she stared at me, looking lost.

Suddenly, I wanted to protect her with a fierce intensity. Humans could break so easily.

Gina gripped the mirror tighter, staring into it. "Oh, bloody hell. There's a second one, Aenor. At least I think I saw him? He sort of glowed from the shadows for a moment, like a... I don't know, a creepy angel. There's no way you can go fight both of them." She looked up, her forehead creased. "Maybe we can escape through the underground tunnel. It goes to the river, right?"

It wasn't the *worst* idea. We couldn't go straight up through the hatch in the ceiling, but there was a second route out of here. An old tunnel led south from here to the Thames, carving underground through the most ancient parts of London.

I threaded my fingers into my blue hair, pacing now. "We

might be able to get to the river. I'll have more power there anyway."

That's when it hit me—the heavy scent of the river, slamming into me like a fist. When I looked down at the old floorboards, my stomach dropped. Dark water seeped through the cracks, pooling in my shop.

"Change of plan," I said. "They want to drown us. They're going to flood us out. They're flooding the tunnel as we speak."

These creeps wanted to destroy my home, my livelihood.

And this was exactly why I had a gun loaded with iron bullets.

"Bollocks. Bollocks!" Gina looked frantic. "Let's run. Now."

"No. You stay here for a few more minutes. You'll drown if you go further down that tunnel. Unlike me, you can't breathe underwater."

Dark river water pooled beneath my feet, soaking the bottoms of my high heels. My teeth chattered from the cold.

I shoved my hand into my pocket, running my fingertips over a mother-of-pearl comb.

The gun was one of my most useful weapons. Believe it or not, the comb was the other. It would help lure the assassins to me. Then, I'd simply shoot them.

"I've got this, Gina," I said. "Just keep the doors shut. If the water fills up too fast, you can escape through the hatch in the roof. I'll lure the assassins away from that opening, so they won't notice you. Sneak out from the ceiling hatch and make a run for it. In five minutes, they'll be totally gone. They're not after you, anyway. They just want me."

"Please be careful." She pulled a plastic ring off her finger and shoved it at me. "Take this for good luck."

"Thanks." I slid the gun into the belt on my shorts, then the ring onto my finger. A cartoon donkey on the top grinned at me. I was pretty sure it had been a prize from a Happy Meal, but I'd take all the luck I could get.

Now the water had risen up to my toes, and powerful magic skimmed over my body.

I crossed though the silk curtains that hid the tunnel door. Then, I pulled open the door into an ancient, earthen tunnel. Here, dirt particles filled the air, and I couldn't see a thing. Already, the water was turning the dirt walls to mud. In another life, I'd once had total power over water. Not anymore.

Magic electrified the air. I broke into a fast run, pumping my arms as I sprinted through the tunnel, my feet splashing in the rising water. I might be crap at powerful magic, but I was *great* at running in heels.

If I could kill the assassins fast, maybe I could save the shop.

Long ago, priests had used these tunnels to escape Henry VIII, sneaking down to the Thames to flee the city. Now, I was using it to save my own rear.

Water streamed in heavier now, and running was getting harder. Still, the river called to me.

If I ended this fast, I'd keep Gina safe. I'd promised years ago to keep her from harm.

It had been two years since I'd found her running from a demon predator. He was about three hundred years older than her and rotten down to his bones. He'd broken her jawbone and nearly choked her to death behind a dumpster. I'd put him out of her misery.

Gina had lived with me since.

The icy water was flowing faster now, chilling my calves.

I was one minute away from the Thames. One minute till I could lure the assassins to me.

My breath grew ragged in my throat as I fought my way

through the rising water. Another powerful wave of magic set my teeth on edge. The water rushed up to my hips now.

When the water reached my ribs, I dove under, sinking into its cold embrace. The water was my home, and I moved through it swiftly. I held my breath, and the river rushed over my skin as I swam, faster and faster, moving toward my target.

The assassins were fae like me, but they had struck a deal with the humans long ago. They could live in the world, in exchange for killing all the other supernaturals.

But why come for me when there were demons far more dangerous roaming London's streets? Demons who could make your blood drain from your body on sight.

Moonlight pierced the water's surface.

I kicked my legs, moving higher and higher, until my head reached the top. I took a deep breath of spring air.

Icy water soaked my clothes, and my teeth chattered as I hoisted myself up onto the river walkway. The moon and streetlamp cast faint light over the empty pavement.

I shivered, pulling my comb from my pocket. Tonight, mist hung thick and low over the Thames.

All magic had certain properties—smells, sounds, textures. I mostly listened to the sounds—like music that every magical being possessed. It was a thread of magic connecting two people.

I tuned into the vibrations of the assassin. He'd come for blood and it sounded like a drumbeat, a pounding in my blood.

Once I'd found him, I pulled the comb through my sodden blue hair, and I launched into a low, ancient song— the song of the Morgens. In the night air above London, my magic called to my target.

This was my magic—my sad dirt-hole magic. I lured men

to me with a comb and a song. And if they were bad men, I killed them.

Admittedly, this wasn't the most effective magic in a battle. I needed a body of water for this to work, and then I had to sit by the water while singing and combing my hair. There were very few battle situations that provided this kind of opportunity.

Once, I'd been jumped by a gang of six demons near Fenchurch Street. They'd beaten me within an inch of my life, burned my skin with their names. They'd left me for dead. My particular skillset had done me not a lick of good in that moment. "Sorry, fellas, but could you just pause the torture for a bit while I get my comb out and make my way to the Thames? Give a girl a fair chance, will you?"

But I'd found them in the end. I'd lured them to me. Then, I'd ripped out their hearts, dried them, and sold their bones in my shop.

The way I saw it, I *was* the scourge of the wicked, and I did a darn good job of it.

A shiver of connection skimmed over my skin as my magic found the rhythmic vibrations of my target. By the time this guy found his way to me, he'd be too mesmerized to fight.

Then, I tuned into a second sound. Gina had been right— there were two of them. The second was melodic and sad— like a dirge. Beautiful, really. Too bad I had to end it.

Soon, this would all be over, and I could go back to my shop.

I pulled the comb through my hair, chanting the ancient song. I could feel them drawing closer.

I felt my magic wending through the air, slipping around my victim.

In theory, Morgens were supposed to be seductive, and sometimes I looked the part. But right now, I was wearing an old T-shirt drenched in river water and cutoff shorts, my bare legs streaked with mud. Still, it wouldn't matter.

When I felt the magic humming more powerfully along my bones, I turned and saw the flame-haired fae standing behind me, trying to catch his breath. Enormous, he cast a long shadow over me. Moonlight glinted off his weapons, and swathes of silvery fog curled around him. His cheeks were flushed, sweating. He'd run to get to me like his life depended on it.

In his amber eyes, I could see my spell had already taken hold. Entranced, his gaze swept over my body, taking in the wet clothes that clung to the curves of my hips and the swell of my breasts.

A strange sort of mental shift happened when I enchanted people. I could see how I looked to them, how they felt about me—like a bubble in my mind, giving me a clear view of their warped image of me.

And right now, this assassin's vision of me was downright pornographic.

In his mind, my wet blue hair draped over my bare breasts, nipples hard in the night wind. I was wearing nothing but a white thong, practically transparent from the river water—one hand thrust in my knickers. My other fingers were by my mouth. I *think* that was honey I was licking off my fingertips, but the gods only knew. In his vision, my eyelashes fluttered at him. He envisioned me pulling the thong aside and smiling at him seductively. *Men.*

What he did not see was the reality—an angry, mud-spattered chick in a Joy Division T-shirt pointing a gun at him.

It almost felt like a sin to shoot someone as helpless as him, but my time was running out, and what's more, his fantasies were filthy and disturbing. And in any case, he wouldn't be helpless for long, and then he'd kill me in a frenzied rage of lust and violence.

He reached out for me like I was his long-lost lover, an ecstatic smile on his lips, hand straining for my breasts.

My heart felt heavy as I squeezed the trigger and shot him in the chest. Iron ripped right through his aorta, ending his life. He fell hard to the pavement, and I wiped a shaking hand over my forehead. At least he died happy, I guess.

Exhaling, I scanned the shadows by the river's edge, quiet in the dead of night. Why wasn't the other one here?

I was sure I'd lured him also.

When I turned around, I saw him, and my heart skipped a beat.

There he was, towering over me. The second fae. He glowed with the cold, unearthly light of an angelic king.

His beauty was devastating. Unfortunately for me, he did not look the least bit enchanted. In fact, he looked like he wanted to rip my head off.

CHAPTER 3

*H*e smelled like almonds and sea-swept stones. The wind toyed with his pale hair—so light it nearly looked silver. His deep blue eyes pierced me. He had the cold perfection of an angel—sculpted cheekbones, a perfect mouth, straight, dark eyebrows—and the arrogant stance to match. Masculine beauty that could have been carved by Michelangelo himself.

With his tightly coiled muscles, he gave the impression of being a warrior. But the crown on his head told me he wasn't an ordinary foot soldier in the assassin crew. At first glance, it looked like thorny wildflowers.

On closer inspection, it was clearly dark, spiky gold.

It took me a moment to realize he *was* enchanted—a little.

I was getting an image of how I looked to him, and it was much like reality—pale blue hair, soaked with river water. No transparent thong for him—instead, it was skin-tight shorts that hugged my curves and red high heels. He liked the heels more than he wanted to.

He saw my big green eyes, heart-shaped face, pink lips. I'd look innocent if it weren't for the gun, and the sharp-lined tattoos curling over my tan skin. He *liked* the innocence, but reminded himself it was a lie. His gaze took in my breasts, peaked in the cold air, headlights engaged.

I glanced down for a second. That was all real. He saw the real me—slight, curvy, and dirty. And cold, it seemed.

But the overwhelming feeling emanating from him was disdain.

Deep under the surface, desire flickered as he took in the shape of my legs in my tiny shorts, eyes lingering at the apex of my thighs. But it felt kind of like that lust only made him hate me more. For whatever reason, I was someone he'd spent a lot of time thinking about. And I didn't even know who he was.

This had never happened with an enchantment before, and it was throwing me off. I couldn't get a good read on him at all. It was like he wanted me and hated me in equal measure.

But despite the warning bells ringing in my mind, he was stirring something in me, a buried energy. He intrigued me.

Why, though? In my long life, I'd learned that men were generally just trouble not worth your time. Even if they looked like gods.

I gripped the gun hard. *Shoot him, Aenor. Before he kills you.*

But my eyes strayed down to his perfect mouth again, and an image blazed in my mind of the two of us against a tree trunk—him shirtless, me in only that white thong, pulling it down for him. My pulse raced in the heated air.

Was *he* enchanting *me*? He must be, because I didn't even like sex. And if I did, this shiny-haired jerk would not be my type.

Shoot him, you idiot.

This was the thing about the fae. We had the power to make people feel things—rage, sadness, *lust*. And while this beautiful man stood before me, I felt his magic stroking my skin, a strange and powerful pulse. I had an overwhelming urge to get closer to him, to feel his body against mine.

River water slicked my hands as I gripped the gun, fingers wet.

His gaze slid down me, taking in the filthy clothes that clung to my body, and they suddenly felt too small and tight on me. Once again, I felt his disdain. My muscles tensed as I tried to focus.

This was all backwards. *I* was supposed to entrance *him*. I wasn't supposed to be imagining him grabbing me and stripping the clothes off my body.

With the gun still trained on him, I took a step back. A shiver danced up my spine. Something about his deep blue eyes looked strangely familiar, but I couldn't put my finger on it. The power of his magic overwhelmed me, and for just a moment, my knees felt weak. I felt strangely inadequate before him, painfully conscious of my dirty little clothes. What *was* he?

"Aenor." The quiet way he spoke my name sounded like an ancient curse. "Using a gun. Iron bullets, I suppose?"

I nodded, my finger on the trigger. Why in the gods' names didn't he look scared? He was about to die. And how did he know I had iron bullets? It's not like they were easy to come by. Everything about this was bizarre.

His lip curled away from his teeth, baring his canines, and he snarled. He seemed part divine, part beast. Like a beautiful god dredged up from a grave of moss and soil.

"Why am I not surprised?" Disdain laced his voice.

My skin felt hot. Why hadn't I shot him yet? Something about him made me want to drop to my knees. To worship him. To stick out my tongue and—

"I'm pointing an iron weapon at your heart," I said, interrupting my own fevered thoughts. "Why aren't you scared?"

"IT DOESN'T MATTER." He prowled closer, and I took a step back, my legs shaking. "You won't escape me, Aenor. I will find you again, and I will make you suffer."

"No. You won't."

I gritted my teeth, then unleashed two iron bullets into his heart.

Tendrils of dark magic burst from his body, transforming into shapes that looked like ravens flying away into the night sky. My enemy fell to the ground, and the pavement trembled at the impact of his fall.

"You should have modernized." It was a whisper, my voice shaking.

Everything about this felt wrong, but I didn't linger over his corpse. These fae had come to kill me, so they had to die. It was as simple as that.

I let out a long breath. Now, I had to make sure Gina was okay.

Already, I was diving back into the Thames, heading back to Gina. I plunged deep into the river, swimming until I found the tunnel's entrance. My body undulated in the water.

As I moved further through the tunnel, the water level grew lower. When it became too shallow to swim, I trudged through it until at last I could run.

With burning lungs, I burst through the door into my shop, cold mud streaking my body.

I found Gina standing on the countertop, staring down at the filthy water that had flooded half the room. I heaved a sigh of relief. She was fine.

"Are you okay?"

She beamed at me. "You're alive!"

"Of course I'm freaking alive. I'm a major badass. Scourge of the Wicked."

"Right."

Gina hugged herself, shivering. "Shop's totally wrecked. The dried herbs and demon hearts aren't so dried anymore, and everything stinks. Can you still sell them? Those hearts are worth hundreds."

I rubbed my eyes. "We can fix it. We're both alive, that's the important part."

"What happened to the assassins?"

"I killed them. I told you, I'm Aenor, Flayer of Skins, Scourge of the Wicked." I'd meant it to sound light and fun, but I just sounded sad.

Gina was only a teenager. I needed to stop her from thinking about the supernatural chaos. She shouldn't worry about iron bullets or fae corpses, or how she almost drowned in Thames water. She should be thinking about normal teenage things.

I took a deep breath. "What happened to your stuff? Is it all wrecked?"

"Yep."

"Even your schoolbooks?"

Gina shrugged. "Everything's online now. But my computer's dead, so... You know what? Who cares. I don't need to know how to graph linear equations."

Gina's school grades had been plummeting recently. I had no idea what linear equations were, but apparently they were important. "Is that accurate, though?"

"Do you know that some girls make a hundred thousand pounds a month dressing up in Lolita outfits on Snapchat?"

"Oh my gods, you are not doing that."

"Why? It's just a lacy dress with ribbons. You don't take the dress off or anything."

"You can't do that because the creepy men who watch those—"

"How do you know it's creepy men? It's not, like, the *book* Lolita. It's an anime thing."

"That is not a long-term life option for you. And you are human and don't have to live in a tunnel like I do. You can live in a house! So you need to talk to your teachers first thing in the morning about your computer situation."

"Fine."

It smelled awful in there. I wasn't sure if it was the bottom of the river or the dried demon parts that were no longer dry.

Gina's brow furrowed, like it always did when she was upset. "All our food is gone. All the Pot Noodle." She made this sound like an absolute tragedy. "The custard creams…"

I could tell she was hungry. She got emotional when she was hungry. "I'll get more. Look, the water's receding already. No harm done." The place was a stinking mess right now, and I sounded much more optimistic than I felt. "I'll run out and pick up a few things. We might not be able to stay here tomorrow, but I can make it habitable for tonight."

My heart sank when I looked at our shelf of ancient, magical texts. The river had soaked them entirely. I wouldn't be able to fix the gibberish situation, because the ink no longer formed letters at all.

I pulled one of the leather-bound tomes from the shelf and opened the pages to find that the words had turned to tiny rivers of black.

I hadn't memorized most of the spells, or really paid them much attention. Except for one book—the ancient and rare book of curses. I'd memorized every single page. I'd scoured it from top to bottom, searching for a way to reverse what had happened to me long ago. The ancient words were now midnight streaks on muddy paper.

All that magical knowledge—gone.

Gina was still looking at me. "Don't suppose you know a cleaning spell?"

I closed the sodden book, surveying the shop. Sadly, it

wasn't just a shop. It was our home, too. We lived in little rooms just down the hall. At one point, there had been a few more witches here, but we were always broke, and they'd moved on.

Now, pungent sludge covered everything we owned. The washer and dryer probably didn't work. I actually had no idea how to fix this. "No, I don't know a cleaning spell."

"Why not?"

"Mainly because I don't care if things are clean? And I never really learned spells. Magic memorization was never my strong suit. I mostly get by on my charm."

"Right. The Flayer of Skins is definitely known for her charm." Gina sat on the countertop, still hugging herself. "How are you going to pay for new food and stuff? Aren't we broke?"

"I have some money stored away." Total lie. There just weren't many witches around anymore, since the assassins killed them all. And the ones that had stayed in London couldn't find our shop, given that we were literally hiding underground.

Things were bad now, and they would only get worse.

Gina's stomach rumbled so loudly I could hear it. We'd missed dinner.

"Sit tight," I said. "I'm going to fix this."

I had twenty-four quid and seventeen pence left to my name, and I'd have to see exactly how far that would get me in Tesco.

CHAPTER 4

The value-brand section was my friend. They purposefully made the labels look off-putting— just plain white with black text, like they wanted you to feel bad about the situation. But as the Scourge of the Wicked, I wasn't going to worry about the graphics on my tins of beans. My boots left muddy footprints on the floor as I walked through the supermarket.

At the self-checkout machine, I stuffed my plastic bags with canned corn and peas. Beans and eggs for protein, whole wheat bread.

Gina had food restrictions—she couldn't eat any nuts without going into anaphylactic shock. I always checked the labels on everything and made sure nothing was contaminated with peanut dust from the factories. We ate total garbage most of the time—chips and candy—but it was all perfectly safe for her.

The cans of vegetables were for vitamins and fiber, the stuff humans needed. I wasn't sure exactly why I was worrying about vitamins now, but after the shop disaster I felt a sudden and overwhelming drive to act responsibly.

The woman bagging her groceries to my right shook her head at me, tutting loudly. I looked very much like I'd just crawled out of a sewer. I mean, I basically had.

I stuffed a roll of trash bags into my haul. The trash bags were the centerpiece of my cleaning plan. Admittedly, it was not an excellent cleaning plan. It involved sleeping on plastic bags to stay dry, washing our clothes in the bath, and letting them hang to dry overnight.

And as for what we would sleep in? Lucky for us, Tesco now sold value-brand underwear, size large. Anyway, the important part was that it was clean.

Please remove item from the bagging area.

I snarled at the robotic voice. Right now, I wished I had enough money to take a bottle of wine home with me as well. My mood darkened when I thought of the two assassins, hunting me down. Now they were both dead, and my life had gotten a whole lot more grim.

Item removed from the bagging area. Please place item in the bagging area.

My temper was ready to rip this place apart. I clenched my jaw tight, trying to scan the trash bags again. Didn't the robot understand these were crucial to my cleaning plan?

Please remove item from the bagging area.

"Go to the sea hell, you robotic tyrant!" I shouted. "I'm just trying to buy some freaking nut-free vitamin corn for my human!"

No one looked up. In a city of nine million, watching dirty people scream at the automated checkout was just part of life.

After a few more tries, I was on my way home again, muddy footprints trailing behind me. I clutched my little bag of food and cleaning products, feeling a bit pathetic. I called myself Flayer of Skins, Scourge of the Wicked. But my life was possibly a bit sad. I'd been a princess once. Now what did I have? No money, no family. Basically no friends, except the teenage human I looked after.

Perhaps I'd spent too long isolating myself, hunting down the wicked and living under the dirt.

As I walked home, an image flashed in my mind—of that angelically beautiful fae. I felt a strange pang, like a loss. I had no idea why. I'd had to kill him to protect myself.

When I reached the rough patch of land above our shop, I thrust my hand into the soil, looking for the roof hatch. I felt around until my fingers brushed against the copper handle. I pulled it up, and the shop's stench hit me.

I frowned as I slipped into the passage. Maybe my life was slightly sad, but it was *my* life, and I'd worked to make things fun. I had my record player, my movie nights with Gina. I'd put a life together here in my dark little corner of London.

It just would take a *lot* of work to get it smelling nice again.

I walked through the dark tunnel that led to the shop. This was the more direct route—unlike the long river pathway I'd taken earlier.

Karen, our phantom guardian, sat outside the door watching soaps on her TV. She stroked the cat in her lap. "Smells a bit off in here," she said as I approached.

"We were attacked earlier by two sea fae. The river water flooded us."

"Nasty business." She shuddered. She wasn't a particularly good phantom guardian. "Did you pick up any Victoria sponge cake?"

"No. We're doing healthy stuff now. Like corn."

"Corn?" she snorted. "What, just on its own?"

"It's got vitamins. So Gina won't get scurvy."

I crossed to the door, and her hand shot out and grabbed me. "Come pay us another visit in a bit, will ya?"

Karen was deeply lonely, so I tried to visit a few times a day.

"Sure, Karen." I pushed through the door into our shop, my heart sinking at the sight of it. I had nothing left to sell—the potions and herbs had all been ruined.

My heart squeezed. I'd be starting from scrap.

Gina was still sitting on the countertop. "The microwave's not working."

I hadn't even thought of that. How much did microwaves cost these days?

I dropped the plastic bags on the counter, regretting my attempts to buy healthy food. Should have gone for the Victoria sponge, or maybe McDonald's. We needed something to liven up the atmosphere a bit.

"We're going to have food, and a cleaning party," I declared.

Gina brightened. "Sounds fun. Can we invite some fit blokes?"

"It's not really that kind of party." I began scaling one of the old bookshelves, knocking over a mason jar of basil as I did. The basil was supposed to protect us from scrying, but somehow, the assassins had found us anyway.

"Why not?"

"Um, because we don't know any, and also we're basically fugitives trying to lay low, and also the shop smells like a corpse. But maybe I could conjure some visions of party-goers while we start scrubbing everything down. Illusions. It can look like a real party."

On the top shelf, the battery-powered record player was unscathed by the flood.

She cocked her head. "Illusions of fit blokes. Is that how you've managed to stay single all these years? You just conjure up a delicious piece of arse to drool over when you're feeling lonely?"

I pulled the record player off the top shelf, holding it carefully as I climbed down. I'd grabbed an old Elvis album—probably not Gina's favorite, but she didn't yet understand that music from the nineteen-sixties and seventies was the pinnacle of human achievement. Some of my best years were spent in Nashville, Tennessee, listening to the amazing music.

"No, Gina. That's not how I've managed to stay single. I've managed to stay single because I have come to realize that nearly all men are garbage. Also, I think I scare them."

"Your attitude towards men is because of your mum, isn't it?" she asked. "Your mum screwed you up."

I narrowed my eyes at her. "No, she was plenty wise, and she did not screw me up. I am not screwed up. And that's the end of that discussion. It's time for Elvis." I slid the record player onto the countertop, and loaded up the record. I turned it on and placed the needle onto *Suspicious Minds*. The music crackled through the air, and I closed my eyes, trying not to think about how I'd pay for food next week. I had to focus on the problems I could actually fix.

As the music lit up the room, I pulled out the haul of food onto the countertop. "We've got good tunes, food, and a bit of magic. And clean underwear. Everything we need."

"Luxury. Couldn't ask for more." Gina pulled out a plain piece of bread and started chewing on it with a half grin. "Delicious meal you've put together."

I closed my eyes and conjured up a spell for illusion. My magic hummed and vibrated around the place, and images flickered around us... My subconscious was projecting images of my home—distant memories from a place that no longer existed. They were images from a ball by the seaside, of fae draped in silks and jewels—harvested from my oldest memories.

And others from my more recent memories shimmered

into view alongside them—the woman who sold crepes from a food truck nearby, who always made me laugh with her complicated handshakes. The local Jack the Ripper tour guide, who lingered a little too long on the phrase *ripped from vagina to breastbone.* The elderly woman who pulled pints in the nearby pub, the one who amused herself by saying "Fancy a lap dance?" to horrified customers.

Gina beamed at me, her mouth half full of plain bread. "Who are these lovely people?"

"Just random people from my memories."

"I recognize some of them, but not the ones in the long gowns." She whistled. "You knew some super posh people, didn't you? In your old life?"

"Like, a hundred years ago." No idea why they were popping up now. They were from a life I'd long since abandoned. My mind had just sort of produced them on autopilot.

I crossed behind the counter into the hallway and made my way to the bathroom. The mirror was still untouched by the water, and I caught a glimpse of myself—my blue hair caked with mud, streaks of dirt on my face. My green eyes shone out brightly from all the muck.

I did what I could to wash off my face and hair in the sink.

Then, I turned to the tub. With the tap on, I washed off my face and my hands, my legs. I did what I could to clean off my body. Then I got to work on scrubbing down the ceramic. This would be ground zero for the cleaning effort. Everything would go in and out of the tub to rinse off the muck.

When the tub was clean enough, I crossed back into my room to change into the clean value-brand undies and tank top. The baggy cotton hung off me.

I glanced at a blue hula-hoop hanging on the wall, still

clean. The record player started playing *A Little Less Conversation,* and I had to take the hula-hoop down, just for a second. I put it around my hips, then started swinging them for a moment. Ahhhh... normalcy again. If hula-hooping in baggy underwear to Elvis could be considered normalcy.

"Ooooh... this bloke is lovely." Gina's voice floated over Elvis's melodious singing. "Who's he? Please tell me you got off with him."

I pulled off the hula-hoop, and I popped my head around the corner. "It's unlikely I got off with anyone, Gina. I've hardly gotten off with—"

I froze at the image.

There, flickering in our filthy little shop, was the fae I'd killed earlier—the one who'd glowed with the unearthly light of an angelic king, his skin burning gold like a lantern. All the other images seemed to fade into the shadows around him. The music seemed to slow down and grow deeper, reverberating over my skin. It was like Elvis was melding with the assassin's sad song.

"Who is he?" Gina repeated. "Wouldn't kick him out of bed for eating cereal."

"That's not the phrase, and you're too young to have anyone in bed."

"I'm not that young," Gina protested.

Perhaps in the human world, seventeen was nearly grown up. But for a fae like me, seventeen was a baby.

"So who is he?" She asked.

I grabbed a packet of strawberry gum off the countertop, popping a piece into my mouth. "That's one of the assassins I killed tonight."

"Oh, shit. And you knew him?"

My entire body felt cold. "I hardly spoke to him. Not sure why my mind conjured him." This image felt like a slap in the face from my unconscious, two men I wanted to forget.

My stomach tightened, and I crossed out of the room, unwilling to dwell on these thoughts any more.

I'd done what I needed to do. Just like I always had. I had to look out for myself and Gina, and it was as simple as that.

She frowned at me. "What the fuck are you wearing?"

"Language! And I'm wearing our temporary wardrobe. I got you some."

"Lucky me."

I turned to head back to my room, when Gina's voice stopped me. "Aenor? Thanks."

A smile curled my lips as I crossed into my filthy room.

CHAPTER 5

*D*eep into the night, I lay on a plastic bag on the floor in my stinking bedroom.

The mattresses couldn't be salvaged, and it had come to this—sleeping on rubbish bags on the floor, feeling the cold damp, even through the bin liners.

I still wore the giant discount underwear. We had no dry blankets, so Gina and I had just covered ourselves in more underwear for warmth.

Unsurprisingly, I was having a hard time falling asleep in these conditions. I lay awake for hours, listening to the crinkling of the plastic beneath me every time I rolled over. I was just about getting used to the smell.

It must have been around three a.m. when I finally drifted off, and I dreamt of the seaside by Cornwall. Starlight glimmered over the ocean and glinted off the frothing sea like pearls. I wore a gown, sheer as the sea-foam itself.

A man rose from the waves—the divine face of the man I'd killed. He moved, fluid as the water, and seawater flowed down his powerful body in glistening rivulets. Ancient fae runes glowed on his chest with the light of the gods. I licked my lips, and I crossed to him—

A hand around my throat woke me from my dream, and my heart froze.

I couldn't see much in here. I had a *Betty Boop* nightlight plugged in, but my intruder was in the shadows. All I knew was that a powerful body pressed against me—one hand around my throat, the other pinning my wrists to the ground with a viselike grip.

"Don't move." A deep, quiet command from a voice I recognized. One I'd heard earlier today. The crowned assassin I'd *killed*. Except now he sounded kind of like an animal.

My pulse pounded out of control as I struggled under his grip. How was this possible? He was *dead*.

He pressed in closer, sniffing my throat, like some kind of beast. His muscled body pressed against me.

He moved back a little into the golden glow of my nightlight.

It *was* the fae I'd killed earlier, but death had changed him. His crown now glowed with golden light, and it had grown longer, more spiky. His eyes gleamed with gold instead of blue—a pale gold, a sharp contrast to his black eyelashes and straight, dark eyebrows.

His canines had elongated. He no longer wore a shirt, and strangest of all, his tattoos moved across his skin, writhing like golden snakes on his muscles. The effect was disturbing —terrifying and oddly beautiful at the same time. In fact, beautiful as he was, his whole appearance scared the bejesus out of me. It was like a vision of divine wrath no mortal was supposed to behold. A pit opened in my stomach, and I felt like I was falling.

My enemy's fingers were crushing my wrists where he held me down. His lip curled, and the look in his eyes was wild—so different from the cool, composed man I'd met earlier.

Gina.

What had he done to her?

"Where's Gina?" I tugged at my wrists, getting nowhere.

His hand tightened just a little around my neck—a warning. I stilled my movements and went quiet.

His breath warmed the shell of my ear. "You killed me." The dark power in his voice rushed over my skin. "With iron. Fucking... shot me." Animal rage imbued his words.

I tried to get my knee into his groin, but the weight of his body pressed me down.

Son of a gun. How did he even get in here? No—scratch that. How was he *alive?* What the hells was he, some sort of god?

I racked my brain to think of how to get out of this one. Most of the time, I'd use an attack spell—harnessing what little sea magic I had. But a powerful sea fae like him would simply absorb it. Gina was kind of right—my magic wasn't amazing.

My enemy loosened his grip on my neck a little, and I gasped for air. "You were here to kill me. Self-defense. Don't get your panties in a bunch about it."

"No." One simple word, as if that alone were a sufficient refutation of my point.

Another deep breath. "Your friend said *surrender or die.* You said you would make me suffer. I killed you in self-defense."

"Vile creature. You should have surrendered."

"I didn't want to surrender." My mind was still reeling from this situation. "How are you alive? I don't understand. And where—"

"You fucking shot us in cold blood." His voice had a deep,

powerful timbre that slid along my skin and made my breath catch. "A black hole in my heart. I will punish you."

Anger started to simmer. Surrender or die—like that was a reasonable choice? He was only proving my deepest belief —most men were garbage.

God of the deep, give me power.

Fury rippled through my body, giving me strength. Lightning-fast, I thrust my hips upward, gripping him by the back of his hair. With all the strength I could muster, I pulled him off me, and he slammed down on the wet ground next to where I'd been sleeping. In the next second, I was on top of him, straddling his taut waist. I punched him hard in the face, and the impact of the strike stung my knuckles.

I caught my breath, waiting to see if he'd react. In the glow of the nightlight, I could see that he looked strangely comfortable with me straddling him. He didn't look the least bit bothered by my attack.

"What do you want?" I asked. "You came to find me. Why?"

A burst of magic radiated out from his body, skimming over my exposed skin, making me shiver. I felt something twining around my hands and arms—thorny ropes that bound my wrists together behind my back. I nearly toppled over, but I held onto him with my thighs. The jerk was using his magic to tie me up, the tendrils of magic scratching at my skin.

"Gina!" My blood was roaring in my ears now. "Gina!"

The intruder sat up, then pressed a finger against my lips. "The human sleeps."

"What are you?"

"I'm the Ankou, and I need to use you."

If wild beasts could talk, this is what they'd sound like.

And yet... the word *Ankou* was like a distant bell ringing in the hollows of my mind. It was a calling of sorts. Something to do with gods or death. I hadn't heard it since I was a child.

Now, we were inches from each other, my bare legs still wrapped around him.

"You're going to *use* me?" The phrase was… disturbing.

"To find what I need. To track something."

This dude was deranged, and I was sitting in his lap, tied up in my underwear. I hated feeling this vulnerable.

I narrowed my eyes at him. "I can't help you track anything. I don't have any powerful magic. I hardly have any magic except the Morgen song. Not good for tracking. So can you buzz off now?" I nearly used saltier language, but I managed to gain control.

"I don't believe I have the wrong person, Aenor Dahut, disgraced princess from the House of Meriadoc." A shiver rippled over my skin. He knew my full name. "I know exactly who you are."

"And what is it you think I can help you find?"

"That's not your concern right now. You just need to do as I tell you to."

I quirked an eyebrow at him. "I'm not inclined to do as I'm told, given that you showed up at my home, threatened to kill me, flooded us, and then tied me up in the dark. Wearing only underwear. Perv."

"*I'm* not the pervert, princess." He rose abruptly, knocking me off him onto the muddy floor. I landed face down, ungracefully.

Then, the creep yanked me up by the bindings around my wrists, jerking me onto my feet.

"Ow!" The way he'd said *I'm not the pervert* made it sound like he thought I was.

I scrambled to try to stand, to regain a *little* of my dignity, but the bindings made it hard.

"And you don't get a choice about what happens next," he

said. "You have broken fae laws. You destroyed your own kingdom. The only reason you're still alive is that I need something from you."

"I absolutely did not destroy my kingdom. Are you high? What kind of idiot would do that?" Someone had destroyed my kingdom over a century ago—but it wasn't me.

He was still holding me by the binding from behind, like a trainer holding the reins of a wild animal.

He leaned down and spoke in a low voice, his breath warming the shell of my ear once more. "You don't have the skill or the decency to fight like a fae. You're the Flayer of Skins, an iron-user. You hammer body parts to the wall with *iron nails.*" Something particularly enraged him about this last part—like he wasn't angry about the severed body parts. Just the material that I used to secure them to the wall.

"Men's body parts," I retorted. "You know what men are like. Selfish, murderous, abusive assholes who break into your house and tie you up in thorns." I looked back at him over my shoulder. "Case in point. I kill the bad ones, and I simply repurpose their organic material for other uses. Everyone wins. Except the people who deserve to die."

From behind me, he gripped the ropes of magic so tight they cut into my wrists. "You killed the prince of the Court of Lyonesse with iron. You slaughtered him without mercy after luring him into a helpless state." Everything he was saying was factually correct, I'd give him that, but he made it all sound so *wrong.* "You are worthless."

"You say I'm worthless, and yet you obviously need me." Now, I *really* wanted to hurt him. "Look, I am a good person. Or at the worst I am morally gray. You're clearly the monster in this situation."

I'd simply refuse to comply, considering he was obviously a sadistic beast. What was the worst he could do? I could withstand torture if I had to. "You may not realize you're asking for my help, but you are. And the answer is no. I won't help you track whatever it is you want, because I despise you, and your desiccated heart will someday decorate my wall. With *iron* in it."

Silence filled the room—somehow more terrifying than his growling or his threats.

From behind me, heat radiated from my attacker's body as he clutched the bindings.

At last, he spoke, in a deep and quiet voice. "I could threaten to kill you, but I'm not sure you care sufficiently about your life. Given the state of it, I can understand why. Hating yourself is likely the one sensible thing you're capable of."

My lip curled. "I'm not sure I like the tone you're taking."

"You live in filth."

Was he serious? *"You* caused the filth when you flooded us."

"You don't care about your own life, but you care about that little human. Do as I ask, and she will have food and shelter. Refuse, and she will be forced to wander the streets on her own."

I fell silent, desperately wishing I had the power to crush him for good. Whatever happened, I had to keep Gina safe. She was just a kid, really, and this had nothing to do with her. This was elite fae business, and the elite fae were basically monsters.

"How do I know you're telling the truth?" I asked. "About giving her food and shelter."

He dropped his grip on the bindings behind me, and I struggled to stabilize myself.

He slowly prowled around to stand in front of me, his movements precise. He stared down at me, and the eerie look in his gold eyes made me shiver. "I give you my sacred oath as the Ankou."

In general, the fae could lie. But when we uttered a sacred oath, we were bound to it for good. It was simply impossible to break it.

I flexed my wrists in their bindings, silently simmering with fury. If I helped him track whatever he wanted, at least Gina would be fed and safe.

But I needed to get specific, because the fae could get tricky with their oaths. "When I say shelter, I mean specifically she needs a hotel room at the Savoy." Why not? Everyone knew the assassins had tons of money. "All of her meals will be covered by room service, whatever she wants to eat, whenever she wants to eat it."

"You have my oath that those specific conditions will be met."

"And she'll need cab rides to school in the morning, and a computer. But block access to YouTube."

"I have no idea what you're talking about at this point."

"Forget about YouTube. But she needs rides to and from school in a cab."

"Fine."

"I need your oath for that, too."

"You have my sacred oath that she will remain in a room at the Savoy Hotel, served room service at her whim, with cab rides to and from school, until you help me track the object I need."

"And I'll need an oath that once I help you find your thing, you will let me go free, and not harm me."

"You make a lot of demands for someone who sleeps on rubbish bags."

"Oath or no deal," I said.

"You have my oath that I will let you go without harm once you help me find the object I seek."

I let out a long breath. Okay. So perhaps this wasn't the

worst turn of events. Except for the part where I had to spend more time with this maniac.

"Will someone tell Gina where I've gone, and that I'll be back?" I asked.

"Yes."

"I'm in. Let's find your… whatever it is. But I need more clothes."

He ignored that request, and he gripped me around the waist. His magic whispered around me—a seductive, sea-tinged power. It felt as if I were being lulled under the ocean waves…

A sharp stab of regret pierced my chest. This was all happening rather quickly. Had I been too quick to agree to him?

"Wait—wait." I fought to keep my eyes open. "What's the catch? I know there's a—"

The words fluttered away as images of ocean waves filled my mind, the pounding of foamy water against a rocky shore. Pressed against his strong body, I felt myself fall into freezing waters, my arms still wrenched behind my back.

CHAPTER 6

I woke still bound in ropes of sharp magic, arms twisted behind my back. I seemed to be in a freezing dungeon, still wearing nothing but the baggy underwear, which was now soaked with cold water. I lay on a damp sandstone floor, its surface coated in a freezing sludge. Wherever I was, it smelled like rotting fish.

The cell I found myself in was about eight feet by six feet, and faintly illuminated by a torch. Light shone through the iron gate, flecking the dungeon cell with squares of gold. Through the gate, I had a view of a dim sandstone hall lit by torches.

The magical bindings cut into my skin. A bitter taste coated my tongue. I think that at some point during my time here, I'd thrown up the toast in my system. *Gross.*

Was I the only one in here? "Hello?"

The sound of dripping water greeted me.

I'd come in here stinking of sewage, and now I smelled of pee. Possibly my own. *Hopefully* my own.

This wasn't quite what I'd been picturing when the Ankou had suggested I join him on his mission. Then again, there was a reason I didn't trust men. Especially not the beautiful ones.

"Hello?" I tried again.

"Oh you're awake now, hah? You were snoring for hours. Kept me awake," a woman brayed in an American accent. "I can't see you, honey. What did they throw you in for?"

I wet my lips, then swallowed. Gods, I needed water. "Nothing, really. Well, apart from that I shot them."

"Oh yeah, that'll do it. What kind of creature are you? Demon of some kind?"

"I'm a fae."

"Me too! You don't really smell fae, you smell like… You know what it is? It's like when you leave the flowers in the vase too long and they get moldy, and then you finally have to throw them out and you just want to retch at the stench. I threw up in the sink once from that. That's what you smell like."

"Thanks."

"You're American."

"No. Not really. I mean, I lived there for a very long time."

"Southern," she added.

"Tennessee. Okay, can you tell me what's happening? Are we in America by any chance?"

"We're in a dungeon. Hang on, I didn't tell you my name. My name is Debbie. Dungeon Debbie *hahahahaha!* Gods, you know, I'll tell you something, I have been making myself laugh over the years. Just me and the rats. Havin' a good time."

I tried to move my face away from the part of the floor where I'd puked. "How long have you been in here?"

"I don't know. Couple of years maybe. Could be forty." She coughed. "Give or take. It's hard to keep track of time in a dark hole of your own filth, you know what I mean? And to be honest I really have no idea where we are.

Dungeon seems kinda old for America though. Could be China."

"Does the Ankou ever come down here?"

"The what? I don't even know what you're talking about."

"The big man with the crown. Does he come down here?"

"Oh, I'd remember that if he had. I've been getting mighty lonely in here. He's a big man, you said? Like are we talking muscular or what? Does he have meaty hands? I like meaty hands. Get a good grip on your haunches."

"Never mind."

Something was dripping on my forehead, and I inched my body back, away from the gate. My back brushed against a rough, slimy wall.

I'd made sure the Ankou was pretty clear on the Gina oath, but I'd been less demanding of the other oath. I'd demanded safety *after* I helped him find what he was looking for, but I'd said nothing about the living conditions before.

"What are you in for?" I asked.

"Well, you know it was the funniest thing. I was in a bar, right, like a real dive bar in Boston with a bunch of old men, and this woman spilled her beer right down my shirt. And it was my favorite shirt, like it has a green shamrock on it, and it says *Irish today, hungover tomorrow.* And I just thought that was a hoot. You know, I do like drinking, and as fae we all come from Ireland originally, right?"

"We come from the British Isles," I corrected her. The fae were fallen angels who'd ended up in Ireland, Scotland, Great Britain, and the islands. Long ago, we were angels who'd decided we actually kind of *liked* the pleasures of earth better than heaven, and we indulged in enchanted food and dance. Over the centuries, most of us had lost our wings—but not everyone.

"Right. Whatever. So as an Irishwoman, I feel pretty proud on St. Patrick's Day, even though I actually have no idea who the hells he was. Some snake guy. So anyways, I had the shirt on, and some college girl spilled a beer on it. And I got kinda mad, right? So I enchanted the bitch to stab herself in the eye, right into her brain. Eye popped right out, she dropped to the floor." My new friend broke into howling laughter. "You shoulda seen it. She was like *AHHHHHHHH.* It was hilarious. But I guess people got kinda mad. The humans were weirded out by eyes coming out or whatever. Called the knights to come get me. Anyway. Now I'm here! Hoping to meet this guy you said had meaty hands."

What was a polite way to say, "I wish I'd never begun this conversation and I would vastly prefer silence?"

"Thank you for that." I cleared my throat. "I'm going to go to sleep now."

My skin itched as a bug crawled up my thigh, but with my hands bound, there was nothing I could do about it. It was mingling with the cold sweat on my back and tickling me uncomfortably.

I shut my eyes again, trying to imagine Gina. I'd never been in the Savoy Hotel, so I had no idea what it was like inside. In my mind, it was a grand place with gold-rimmed mirrors and four-poster beds, and probably celebrities swanning around a ballroom. Gina would be able to phone for room service, tell them about the nut situation, and they'd bring her what she needed. Then she'd wake up in the mornings, get her cab to school, and she'd show up well-rested enough to bring up all her grades. She'd pass chemistry. She'd get into college! I could picture her now, sitting in an ancient Oxford hall, the sun streaming in, a stack of books on her desk as she chewed the end of her pencil and wrote something brilliant.

Maybe not entirely realistic, but I needed fantasies right now. This was fine. I could pretend.

That's what I needed to focus on right now. Not the bug

that had now worked its way into my little undershirt, and was crawling over my left breast toward my nipple. *Ugh.*

Sadly, in my pocketless ensemble, the comb I needed wasn't with me. Not that I was near a river, anyway. I had no power here.

"Gods!" I tried to yank my wrists out of their bindings to get the thing off me, but I only tore at the skin more, and scraped my arm against the rocks.

I deeply regretted that the Ankou hadn't *stayed* dead. I'd figure out how to destroy him at some point.

As the bug scampered over my breast, I let the image I'd conjured of the Savoy Hotel bloom in my mind again. I was pretty sure it was near a park of some kind. Maybe the Thames.

When I opened my eyes again, a bit of movement in the corner of the cell caught my eye. A rat scuttled around on the damp stone.

Then, the hairy thing turned to look at me. Its dark, beady eyes fixed right on me, and it *ran* for me. It scampered over my face, and I gagged, rolling onto my front for a moment to knock it off. I rolled back to my side and glared at it.

The rat was now staring at me from a dark corner of the cell. I had the distinct impression that he wanted to eat me, but I wasn't sure if that was possible. I bared my canines, snarling at him. He did not seem impressed.

A pile of rat bones lay in another part of the cell. I had the unsettling feeling that this larger rat had eaten his brother.

With my arms wrenched behind my back, my shoulders ached. First thing I needed to do was find a way to get myself out of these restraints. They were made from magic, but that didn't mean I couldn't break through them with enough effort.

In the dim light, I spotted a jagged bit of stone protruding from the walls. I scooted my bottom across the floor until I sat closer to it.

Then, I started dragging the bindings up and down against the jagged edge. Slowly, the friction started eating away at the ropes as I moved my wrists faster. My arms burned with the effort, and my mind started to wander again. I felt myself back in the island of Ys, once my home. The kingdom's bells chimed over the rocky landscape. My mother stood on a cliff in the distance, her pearly crown gleaming on her head. I wanted to run to her.

Gods, I was losing it in here. I tried not to think of anything at all as I wore down the ropes.

I felt something scamper over my feet, and I yelped and kicked at the rat. I thought the thing hissed at me, but I was probably delirious.

By the time the last bit of fiber snapped in the bindings, it felt like three hours had passed. It could have been twenty minutes for all I knew, but the pain in my arms told a different story. Relief washed through me as soon as I got my arms free, and I heaved an enormous sigh.

At last, I could move my shoulders again. I stretched my arms out, rubbing my shoulders, fingers kneading the muscles. I'd really taken free movement of my arms for granted in the past one hundred and seventy-six years of my life. Never again would I fail to appreciate this freedom.

Next, I needed to get the heck out of Dodge. My throat felt like it was coated with sand. How long had I gone without water?

What I needed was something sharp to pick the lock. It was a simple, old-fashioned skeleton-key lock.

All I had to do was find two thin instruments to flip the deadbolt inside it.

And this is why every girl should carry a pile of rat bones in her purse at all times. One needed to be curved, the other straight. I snapped a rib off the ribcage, then picked up a femur. I slid the bones into the keyhole, and I used the straight one to lift the lever, the curved one to push at the deadbolt. Any second now...

The lock clicked, and I grinned as the cell door creaked open. I'd just started to slip out when magic slammed into me, knocking me back into my cell.

I didn't see anyone coming—didn't hear their footsteps or feel magic moving closer. I just felt the impact as I shot back into the wall, and I heard the cell door slam shut.

Then I heard the sound of footfalls moving closer.

Was there a guard? I shifted my body a bit to move upright into a sitting position. Maybe the Ankou was coming back for me.

Whatever the case, I'd face my attacker with dignity instead of lying on the filthy ground. Or at least, what dignity I could muster, given that I was in mud-streaked, baggy underwear reeking of piss.

Still, you could pull off anything if you had the right attitude about it, right?

When three figures came into view, my heart sank a little. None of them were the Ankou, and I knew only that the Ankou was the key to my freedom.

In the dungeon passageway just outside the gate stood three tall fae.

A female knight with midnight hair and eyes the color of jade stood at the front. She wore a silver cloak that blended to deep blue at the end, and a necklace of spiky silver branches.

She was one of the few fae with wings—a sign of the most ancient fae nobility. Slits in the cape allowed her wings to swoop down her back—ginger wings, flecked with gold and black. Like a monarch butterfly. She smelled of orange blossoms.

She belonged here, among the fae, wielding power like she was born to it. For one painful moment, I felt envy so deep it seemed my heart was splitting in two. I didn't envy beauty, but I did envy power.

The elegant winged female sniffed the air, then grimaced. "Seneschals, is this *thing* the prince-killer? She looks like something dredged from the sewers. Is that how she *dresses?*" She held her hand over her mouth like she was about to be sick. "Did you see this thing trying to escape her cage? Gods, we'd all die of the stench."

I did my best to flash a smile at her. "I *was* dredged from the sewers, as it happens." Might as well just own it. "You lot turned my home into one. And the Ankou pulled me out of it."

One of the males stepped forward. Torchlight danced over his deep brown skin. "*This* dirtling killed Irdion, heir to the Isle of Lyonesse?"

My throat was sandpaper, and I tried licking my lips again. "Who are you, exactly?"

"Gwydion, seneschal of the Sea Court of Acre." A thin wreath of seaweed rested on Gwydion's close-cropped hair, and a sea-green cloak draped off his shoulders.

It took me a moment to process the word. "Acre…" I repeated, mentally reviewing my history. *An ancient city on the coast, something about crusaders.* No wonder this place looked medieval. "Israel."

The woman clapped. "Very good! She knows a basic fact about the world."

"Well, friends," I said hoarsely. "Irdion didn't mention he was a prince when he showed up threatening to kill me."

The other male stared at me, his vibrant crimson hair a stark contrast to his somber clothing. He stood rod-straight, and his silver epaulets gleamed in the light. His eyes were dark as the bottom of an ocean. "Iron," he said through gritted teeth. "You slaughtered him with iron."

Then, he flicked his wrist, and those magical bindings wrapped around my arms again, wrenching them together behind my back. I fell forward on my knees, struggling to stay upright as the bindings slid around me. This time, the ropes felt strong as iron.

Finally, he sealed up the keyhole with another flick of his wrist. "There. The thing won't be getting out again anytime soon." His voice was eerily calm.

The disappointment of finding myself bound again was crushing, but I forced myself to look up at him. "And you are?"

"Midir, the other seneschal, not that it's any of your concern."

Gwydion nodded at the female next to him. "And this is Melisande, one of our lady knights. But we're not done with introductions yet, are we? Because you haven't been informed of our skills yet."

What in the world...? "Your skills? Do I need to know?"

Gwydion smiled. "Midir, the lovely ginger seneschal, is skilled at slow torture and skin removal. I once watched him rip out a man's spine, keeping him alive for a full hour after that. And that's the first thing you need to know about us."

My stomach lurched. Oh *gods*.

CHAPTER 7

I could withstand torture if I had to, but it's not like I relished the thought. I wasn't a masochist.

"As for me," Gwydion went on, "I'm an expert at curses, so I could condemn you to rot from the inside out or something like that. I once replaced a woman's hair with infected molar teeth." He laughed delightedly. "Do you remember that, Midir? She was so upset. *My beautiful blond hair!*" He was in fits of laughter. "Her dental bill must've been insane. Anyway, I just wanted to make sure you were up to speed on everything."

Midir glowered at him. No one that dour should have had hair that festive. "Is our divine Grand Master *really* going to let this one live? Does he really need this filthy thing? I'm surprised he didn't kill her long ago."

I desperately wanted to ask them for water, but it didn't seem like they were inclined to help me. "How long will I be in the dungeon for?"

Melisande shrugged her perfect shoulders, and her wings lifted up and down. "You should probably stay here forever in filth, atoning for your crimes."

The rough wall behind me scratched my skin. "You all kill people also, and you kill them just for having magical powers. I only kill the bad guys." Why was I bothering arguing with them? They were obviously insane.

"You *are* the bad guys," said Midir, his red hair gleaming like blood. "You kill unlawfully for your own benefit. You make your living selling body parts to witches. You're a creepy hole-dwelling sadist."

I tried to swallow and failed. "I'm the sadist, and you all just finished telling me how amazing you are at torture. That's literally how you introduce yourselves. *Hi, we're seneschals and we're super great at torture.*"

Midir glared at me. "The disgraced princess from Ys thinks she's clever."

It was jarring to run into people who had heard of Ys. The island kingdom, ruled by my family, had been a secret when it still existed.

Melisande's lip curled back from her teeth, and she flashed her canines. "Here's the thing, tunnel swine. Our actions are lawfully conducted. We serve the greater good. We follow the divine orders of our Grand Master, the Ankou. We keep order in the world, we follow the fae laws, and we consecrate souls to the sea god so their deaths serve a purpose."

Divine. That clawed maniac who broke into my apartment *was* divine.

"You've been disgraced." Melisande went on. Then, she reached back and stroked one of her wings. "Do you know how kings and queens came to be called monarchs? It was after my ancestors, the ancient House of Marc'h, whose wings looked like monarch butterflies. We were always seen as the true rulers of the Sea Court."

I frowned at her. She might be resplendent, but she was

wrong. "That's... not what happened. American Puritans named monarch butterflies after William of Orange—"

Midir let out a loud groan. "Bored now. I thought tormenting a disgraced princess would be more amusing, and now she's lecturing us about Puritans. It seems the tables have turned."

Melisande looked furious that I'd corrected her, her lips pressed into a line.

I licked my dry lips. "About your divine Grand Master, he said he wanted me to help him with something. When will that happen?"

Midir, the spine remover, didn't look inclined to answer my question. "Did she really compare her kills with ours? But she serves only her own bestial desires, not the rule of law. I doubt she's capable of understanding the distinction."

"You're all making a lot of assumptions about me." I could feel another bug crawling into my shirt, working its way under my right breast. "And do you know what they say about people who make assumptions? You make an ass of you and... umptions." I'd butchered the saying, and I tried to clear my throat. "Which is a valid human expression."

Gwydion tapped his finger against his lips. "Former Princess of Ys. I must say, I imagined the daughter of Queen Malgven would look a bit more formidable. This is all just... sad."

Melisande was lifting the hem of her cape so she wouldn't trail it in the filth around her. "Under the grime and shamefulness she's pretty enough, I suppose, for a dirtling, but hardly looks like fae royalty." A grimace. "I mean, *look* at her. I suppose it's fitting, given her disgrace."

"Are you all going to keep calling me *dirtling*?" I asked. "Can you just leave me to repent in silence or whatever it was you had in mind?"

"We have other names for your class," said Gwydion. "Soil

snakes, ground dwellers, filth misers, groundlings, tunnel swine, fuck pigeons—"

"That doesn't even make sense," I interrupted.

"But it has a nice sound to it," Gwydion smiled. "Doesn't it? *Fuck pigeon.* I can't quite explain it. It just rolls off the tongue."

Did I really have to *talk* to these people? "Sooo... it's been nice meeting you, but I'm afraid I'm very busy right now. I was in the middle of an important meeting with my rat friend and the bugs crawling under my shirt, so if you'll forgive me, I'd like to return to that."

Melisande's lip curled. "Why do you sound so... American?"

"I lived there for, oh... eighty years," I said.

Melisande cocked her head. "You know what? I don't think I care. In any case, our divine Grand Master will return for you when the time has come for your trial."

Finally, a useful bit of information. "What trial?" I rasped.

"You'll find out." Melisande looked at Gwydion pointedly. "You know, before we go, I feel I should point out that you skipped over me when you told her about everyone's skills."

Gwydion's smile faded. "Oh, so I did. Melisande is skilled at enchantment. She can ensorcell people to do what she wants. *Even* other fae."

"Would you like to see?" she beamed.

"Absolutely not." I'd rather let the rat crawl all over my face again.

She knelt down anyway, her eyes darkening to the lurid violet and oranges of a sunrise. I couldn't tear my gaze away from her, even though I knew I needed to. The others faded away. Now, it was only darkness and the beautiful light in her eyes.

A delicious power whispered over my skin. I felt tingles running over my body. Lightheadedness made me giddy. But most of all, I felt *desperate* to impress the beautiful goddess in front of me. I had to make her happy.

"Are you impressed by me?" she asked.

Of course I was. Who wouldn't worship such a stunning creature? She was born to be adored. "Yes. I live to serve you."

This made her smile. "And you'll do as I say, little dirtling?"

Her sunset eyes lit me up with joy. The goddess Melisande made me happy. My life depended on her. Did anyone else even exist? Of *course* I'd do as she asked. "Anything," I breathed.

"Tell me again that you worship me."

She was the beginning and the end of the universe. "I worship you, of course I do."

"Tell me that you're a filthy little dirtling."

"I'm a..." I hesitated. Something about this wasn't quite right, was it? A sense of *wrongness* was building in my chest at what she asked of me.

She tilted her chin down, and her eyes blazed brighter. Joy erupted in my mind that she was blessing me with her attention.

"Say it to make your goddess happy," she repeated. "As loud as you can, so the whole fortress can hear!"

Who was I to deny the will of the gods?

"I'm a filthy little dirtling!" I shouted.

Laughter echoed off the rock, but I wasn't sure where it was coming from. Was my goddess laughing at me? That made me feel terrible.

"There's a good girl," said the goddess. "Now hit your head on the wall, hard."

No no no...

Something in the back of my mind was trying to stop me from doing what she asked.

But another wave of her magic rocked into me, making my body tingle. "Goddess Melisande." I whispered her name with reverence.

With her eyes locked on me, she repeated her command. "Hit your head, dirtling. Hard as you can."

I slammed my head back into the wall. It didn't hurt as much as it should have, and it seemed like it had delighted her. She was positively beaming with joy. My eyes were still locked on hers.

"Again," said the goddess.

I couldn't refuse, and I slammed my head into the rock once more.

Delirium started to cloud my mind, my vision blurring a bit. This was all wrong. "Please," I said. I actually had no idea what I was asking for. I just knew something wasn't right.

"Aw, she's begging," she cooed. "Should I make things really fun?"

At that moment, something ripped her attention from me, and she pulled her gaze away. All at once, pain shot into my skull, so intense I thought I might throw up again. Wincing, I tried to reach for my head, but I realized my arms were still bound.

The three knights were standing at attention, watching something further down the prison passage.

Gwydion smoothed his green cape. "We were just paying a visit to our captive."

Howling laughter filled the hall, and it took me a moment to recognize it as the other captive's. "Oh she gotcha good, Tennessee! She gotcha really good."

Shut up, Debbie.

Silence fell, followed by slow, deliberate footfalls that echoed off the stone.

The three knights stepped away from the cell, moving further into the hall.

Then, the Ankou appeared, peering at me through the cell bars. He looked once more like the angelic fae I'd seen by the riverside. His tattoos no longer snaked and moved around his body. But he still had a black hole in his heart where I'd shot him. It looked like the iron had started to poison his flesh, turning it dark.

He folded his arms, staring at me. His face betrayed no emotion.

"What happened to her head?" he asked in a quiet voice. "Did she do that to herself?"

The sudden stillness of the other knights unnerved me.

Then, Melisande sidled up to him. She draped her elegant arms around his neck and gazed into his eyes. "I wanted to demonstrate my skills of enchantment," she purred, "to our new little plaything."

The Ankou stared at her impassively and pulled her arms from his neck. He didn't look thrilled with her, but I had no doubt at this point they were lovers. Of *course* they were—they were both beautiful and vile.

"I think you've done enough," he said. Shadows climbed around the Ankou. "I need the fallen princess to be mentally functioning for her mission. Otherwise there is no point in all of this."

The Ankou glanced at the other knights. "Leave her now. She needs to be conscious for her trial."

The pain in my skull was mitigated only by a vivid image of my hands ripping Melisande's wings from her back.

I blocked out the rest of their conversation, mentally retreating into a hazy world of memory. I saw my mother sitting at the head of a table before me. She looked resplendent in the afternoon light, even though her white gown had yellowed over time, and deep brown stains darkened the front. She picked up a silver chalice and smiled at me. "The world is full of wolves, Aenor. If you show weakness, they'll tear out your belly. Don't let them get that close. Keep your distance. Show no mercy."

The swinging of the iron gate knocked the vision right out of my head, and the sharp pain in the back of my skull came rushing back. Suddenly I missed Mama so much it was like an ache in my chest. I missed her like a four-year-old misses her mother, not like someone over a century old.

The Ankou looked blurry as he stood above me, only his eyes clear. The other knights had left.

"What am I doing here?" I asked. When the time came, I would show him no mercy.

He crouched down before me, blue eyes burning like heavenly fire.

He reached through the bars and touched the side of my temple. My muscles went limp. A deep, heavy sleep washed over me.

CHAPTER 8

When I woke, I found myself lying on my side on the slimy dungeon floor, with my arms still wrenched behind my back. My shoulders ached. A bug scuttled up my back, under my shirt.

With no windows, I had no idea what time it was.

It took me a moment or two to realize that I could no longer feel the deep cut on the back of my head, and the headache was gone. Had I lost all feeling in the back of my head?

"Hey! You awake yet?" The American woman's voice boomed through the hall.

My mouth tasted like cotton—dry, sandy cotton. "It seems I am."

"Hey, how do you like your pillow?"

Only at that moment did I realize my head was resting on something soft. I shifted to sit up and look at it. A black cloak lay beneath my head. *Where did that come from?*

The torchlight dimly illuminated a symbol stitched into the cloak with gold thread. It looked like a triangle with a seashell embroidered in the center. If my hands hadn't been bound behind my back, I would have touched it.

"How did you get this in here?" I asked.

"I thought you'd like it."

"Wait, how did you get it in here? This is important. How did you get out of your cell?"

Silence followed, then footfalls down the hallway. When the Ankou appeared outside my cell, a fresh wave of hatred practically blinded me.

"You were right, Tennessee!" Debbie shouted. "He does have meaty hands. Good for holding on to your ass, like you said."

My cheeks flamed hot. "I never said that."

Given my current situation, I wasn't sure why denying the "meaty hands" claim was the most important thing. It was just that even when covered in baggy piss-stained underwear and bugs, you had to maintain some dignity.

He whispered a spell, low under his breath, and the door unlocked.

It swung open. The Ankou stepped inside and put his hands around my waist to help me up.

"Don't touch me," I snarled. "I can stand up on my own."

He took a step back, watching me closely. He'd come for me unarmed, except for a leather arm sheath around his enormous bicep that held a dagger.

I no longer felt my head injury at all, even though I was starving and dehydrated and smelled like a moldy flower vase.

I took a tentative step, slightly dizzy. Then another, through the threshold of the cell door. I'd just be walking at my own, slow place.

"Hey Ankou!" Debbie shouted. "I'll tell you what, Ankou, you could grind me into a fine dust and I'd die happy!"

When I shuffled past her cell, I glanced over at her. I was

shocked to see she was a delicate little thing with wide, green eyes and pale pink hair that looked like cotton candy. Her body glowed with a silver light, and she smiled at me. Gorgeous. Then, her gaze flicked back to the Ankou.

"Seriously, I will mount you and ride you like a drunk centaur!" she called out, her voice echoing.

The Ankou ignored her completely.

It *definitely* concerned me a little that I couldn't feel the wound in the back of my head. I'd been certain that I'd cracked my skull. Was it gaping open, but I had brain damage and couldn't feel it?

"You put me to sleep last night," I said. "Or whatever time that was."

"You and the other prisoner were making too much noise. I could hear it through the fortress."

"Name's Debbie!" she called out from behind us.

"And you healed my head, too? After your girlfriend forced me to crack my skull open for her own amusement."

"I'll need your cognitive functioning to remain intact for our task."

"I think I'll be needing that, too. Look at how much we have in common already. Where are we going?"

"The Winter Witch is ready for you."

"The Winter Witch?"

"Do not make me repeat myself."

I'd heard of her, of course. I just had no idea she was real.

As far as I'd known, she was a story to scare children—Lady Beira had once been a princess of the Unseelie kingdom, until her cruel husband threw her in an ice dungeon. The story went that her mind had become twisted and warped over time, turning her into the Winter Witch. She stole bones and hearts as prizes.

"Why will I be facing a trial with Beira?" I asked.

"She's a prophetess. If I'm going to use your help for this upcoming task, I need her to approve of it."

My throat burned. Gods, I wanted water. "What happens during the trial?"

"You'll find out," he said in a casual tone. He pushed through a door into a stairwell. The light from a window burned my eyes.

The concept of witches and trials together didn't inspire a ton of confidence that my next few hours would be pleasant. My upcoming schedule wouldn't involve tea and a chat around a table. In fact, the words *trial* and *witches* evoked images of intentional drownings. Death in flames. A million tons of rocks crushing Old Man Corey's ribs in Salem. That kind of thing.

I followed the Ankou onto the winding stairwell, struggling to keep my balance with my arms bound. Truthfully, my legs were shaking with fatigue and dehydration, but I'd be darned if I gave in and asked for water.

What had old Giles Corey done when the Salem judges had pressed him to death for witchcraft? He'd asked for more weight.

I'd ask for more dehydration.

Less poetic but still noble.

I leaned against the slimy wall for balance as I followed him up the stairs. "What does the trial involve?" I tried again.

He shot me an irritated look, like any idiot would know the answer. "I asked her a specific question. The question was 'should I use Aenor for my task?' Your trial is simple. All you have to do is meet her. If she deems you acceptable, you will help me with my task."

"That's it?" My legs juddered up and down as I dragged myself up the stairs. *More dehydration.* "I just meet her? Trials are usually unpleasant."

"It will be very cold."

I snorted. I could take a bit of cold. Although, the fact that I was still wearing nothing but baggy, damp underwear ate away at my bravado a little.

"Also," he added, "if the Queen of Misery decides that I should not use you for my task, she will kill you by piercing your heart with her iron claws."

"What?"

He pushed through a door into a towering hall of golden sandstone.

"You heard what I said," he said quietly. "Why are you so determined to make me repeat myself?"

I gritted my teeth, a vivid image blooming in my mind of two more iron bullets slamming into the Ankou's heart. It warmed my cockles.

"You said I'd be safe," I said.

"Did I?"

"You swore an oath." I stumbled in the hall trying to remember the exact wording of the oath. "I'd help you with your task and you would let me go free without harm."

He shot me another sharp 'are you thick' look. "You haven't yet helped me with my task. I have no obligation to keep you safe at this point."

"And how does this witch—"

"Please stop talking. It's grating on my nerves."

He stopped in front of a towering oak door, its surface covered in dark, spiked metal. When he held up his hand, the door swung open.

The room it revealed was enormous. Towering vaults of golden stone arched high above us. Ruddy sunlight slanted in through arched windows. And through them, the scent of the ocean floated on the air, and the sound of waves crashing outside. I shivered a little. The sea air kissed my skin, raising goosebumps all over my body.

A large bed stood against one wall, the dark blankets

neatly tucked.

"What's this?"

"My bedroom."

I breathed in the humid air.

Israel—so far from home. Once, the fae lived only in the British Isles. Now? The elite fae ruled from fortresses all over the world, their glamour and magic offering protection.

The Ankou turned to look at me, examining me. He took a step closer, and I felt like his gaze was cutting right through me. He'd been so determined on our march here, and now I had the sense he was hesitating. He looked almost... unsure of himself.

For the first time since he'd hauled me out of the prison, I got a good look at him. Sunlight beamed over his sharp cheekbones. His eyes were the shocking blue of the sky over the Mediterranean. If I weren't totally dead inside to the charms of men, I might have been distracted by his heart-breaking beauty.

Was it just me, or were the worst people also the most beautiful?

A skeleton key hung around his neck. He wasn't wearing a shirt, which gave me a view of his chest—a hole right in his heart. Not to mention his thickly corded muscles, which another woman might find interesting. Not this one.

For his part, he was staring at me with an intense curiosity.

"What?" I said.

"I'm just wondering if you'll come back alive."

"I definitely wish I hadn't asked now." I nodded at his chest. "Does it hurt?"

"Yes."

"Good."

He seemed to snap out of his trance, features darkening.

"Will you untie me for the trial?"

"No. A sickness runs in your blood, and I cannot trust you yet."

A sickness runs in your blood... I felt my heart constrict at those words.

"I don't know what you're talking about." My voice sounded hoarse and weary. "So the trial happens right here? With a woman tied up in your bedroom?"

He tilted his head, his eyes moving lower over my body, taking in the flimsy, enormous underwear from the Tesco value section. He frowned at the large white undies that barely stayed on my hips, and the thin tank top made for a man three times my size.

He didn't seem interested in me in a sexual way. Just curious at what exactly I was wearing, now that he was actually paying attention to me.

He reached out, touching one of the straps of my undershirt. "You were once so powerful."

"Are you judging my clothing? Because this is how modern people dress now." I did my best to lie convincingly. "In large white cotton underwear that elegantly hangs off the body. It's *fashionable.* You just have no idea because you're holed up in castle wearing armor like a medieval idiot." Well done, Aenor. Well done.

You were once so powerful. He was reminding me of the good old days when I lived in a tower, when the sea lulled me to sleep, when I could pull the waves to me like I was the moon.

I'd do anything to forget it. I needed peace. "Let's start, then."

He nodded, but he still seemed to be hesitating. "She's in the Unseelie realm. I'll open a portal. She'll tell me if your heart is true for this task."

He turned away from me, and golden light burst from his chest. He spoke a few words in Ancient Fae—in the particular dialect I recognized as Ysian. *"Egoriel glasgor beirianel gamrath, warre daras."*

A blast of cold sea air washed over me as a hole opened in the floor—a tidy portal ringed by silver. A chasm of dark water filled the hole, with chunks of ice floating on the surface. Shivers rippled through me, and I instinctively took a step closer to the Ankou—the only warm thing in the room. If he weren't such a jerk, I'd want to get even closer to him.

"Wait," I said. "Can you hold your horses for one second? How about I just swear an oath? I will give you an oath not to kill you again or whatever else you're worried about."

"Oaths can be manipulated. And the Beira has already given me a stark warning about you. A prophecy."

My forehead crinkled. "And what is the prophecy?"

"She'll tell you herself." He nodded at the water. I was supposed to jump in.

I stared at the dark ice water. A thin silver ring surrounded the portal—large enough for two people to fit in. I'd seen a portal before, but it still amazed me. Fae assassins —the knights—were the only ones who could open them. Traveling between worlds was the privilege of the elite.

The Ankou made a swift move for me and scooped me up, pulling me close against the warmth of his powerful chest for a moment. He looked into my eyes, and I had that sense again that he was hesitating. Maybe he wouldn't go through with it. Maybe—

Then, he simply let go. I sank under the icy surface, enveloped by the arctic sea. A little water dripped into my mouth—seawater, sadly, which I couldn't drink.

God of the deep, I hated the Ankou with a fiery passion right now.

I wished I'd killed him with a more painful method than bullets, even if he wouldn't stay dead.

CHAPTER 9

*C*lear, white light pierced the water's surface. The cold went right down to my bones. As a Morgen I could stay in seawater forever without breathing, but I still felt the chill.

Gina would say I should just float here until everyone gave up and went home for takeout and TV.

The only hitches were that I'd starve to death, and also lose my mind.

Whatever was about to happen, I couldn't actually avoid it forever. I just had to make sure to exude a sense of... *trueness of heart.* How hard could it be? Maybe I could charm her with my winning personality.

I kicked my legs fast, moving up and up until my head breached the surface. Silvery light hit me, and ice-cold air filled my lungs so fast they stopped working for a moment.

Still kicking my legs to tread water, hands bound behind my back, I looked around. I was trying to get my bearings. I seemed to be in an icy hole in the middle of a forest of silver trees. Slender boughs arched above me, spindly twigs jutting from their branches.

A strange bounty hung from the branches: jewelry, bones, a pair of jeans, a cell phone, a human skull, a chipped Victorian teapot, a silk scarf in flamingo pink... It was all strangely beautiful.

It also looked like the Queen of Misery might be some sort of demented witch hoarder.

My teeth chattered, and my breath clouded around my face. Moonlight gleamed off densely packed snow all around the icy hole. Now, I was shaking so violently I could hardly tread water—especially since my lungs were seizing up.

I wasn't entirely clear how I could get out of the portal with my arms bound.

My answer came in the form of a clawed hand gripping my hair by the roots, hoisting me from the watery portal.

Ah. There you are, Beira.

Beira, Ancient Witch of Winter, threw me down on the ice. Already, my cheap cotton underwear was freezing to my skin.

I looked up at her, my stomach sinking.

When my mother had told me stories about the Winter Witch, she hadn't mentioned that Beira was a giant, about ten feet tall.

Nor had she mentioned the pale frost that formed delicate webs over her blue skin, or the white hair that hung over her shoulders in long plaits.

Nearly as naked as I was, she wore only a tiny white sheath. And she stared at me from a single, bloodshot eye in her forehead. The pale eye blinked at me. She took another step closer, her bare feet crunching in the snow. Her toenails had the purplish hue of death.

A strange voice whispered in my mind. *Beira, Queen of Misery.* It wasn't just one voice, more like a hundred whispers, all at once, ringing in my skull.

"Hi." My teeth chattered so hard I could hardly form the word.

This was awkward. How *did* you charm someone, anyway? When I was busy scourging the wicked and harvesting their organs, I'd never mastered the art of flattery.

"You have a nice... eye."

Nope.

She pointed a long, bony finger at me.

I want what you have. I keep things. Give me what you have.

Her words kept whispering inside my skull. Her lips moved wildly, but the sounds didn't come from her mouth. They were in my head.

"I don't understand," I said. "What do I have that you want?"

A keepsake from you. A treasure. To keep me warm.

Even after she finished speaking, her lips kept moving soundlessly, twitching.

Once, I'd seen an execution—a decapitation of a traitor back in my drowned kingdom of Ys. The executioner held the woman's severed head up to the crowd. Her lips had twitched exactly like that for a few moments while he gripped her hair, blood dripping from her neck.

Clouds of frozen mist puffed from my mouth. My hair had begun to freeze, rivers of ice on my shoulders.

"What do you want from me?" I asked again.

She didn't answer this time.

Movement caught my eye, and I realized we weren't entirely alone. Women, with skin white as the snow, eyes blood-red, whirled between the trees. Dancing silently like snow squalls, they wore crowns of dark twigs. An oddly vacant look shone in their eyes. So much movement, so little noise.

Gods, get me out of here.

So far, this place was ranking somewhere below Ikea on the list of places where I most enjoyed spending time.

The Ankou had warned me about the cold. It was, in fact, the kind of cold where a tear rolls down your cheek and freezes part way, where atoms stop moving in the air around you and existence ceases. Where snowy owls develop the ability to speak just so they can beg the gods to send them into the relative warmth and comfort of outer space.

I looked up at Beira. "What do you need from me?" I asked through chattering teeth.

I need to feel warm. A hundred whispers crystallized in my mind into that one sentence.

"Something we have in common," I said.

Then, she spoke out loud—a strange, halting speech that I could barely discern. A word repeated, low in her throat. It took me a moment to realize she was saying, "Fear, fear, fear."

She threw back her head and howled—a keening sound, so shockingly lonely it cut into my chest.

Instinctively, I scooted away from her. I wasn't warm. I was godsdamn freezing. My veins were tiny glaciers of blood.

Fear. Fear. Fear.

What was she afraid of?

She shut her mouth, and a heavy silence fell over us. Nothing but the sound of my own heartbeat.

The witch fixed her eye intensely on me, then stooped lower, speaking out loud now. "Fear. Fear. Fear," her voice like iron scraping against ice. "She of the House of Meriadoc will bring a reign of death. She of the poisoned blood."

My stomach dropped. So *that* was the prophecy. The House of Meriadoc—my family name. I was the only one left. And apparently, I was supposed to bring a reign of death.

The dancing women swept closer, spinning maelstroms of snow. Flakes glinted in the air around them.

Beira reached for my chest, a clawed finger pointing at my heart. *Shit.* She was about to kill me, wasn't she?

I scuttled back a little more, my bare skin freezing to the icy ground beneath me. Wet skin on ice was like licking a pole in winter—you were just stuck there, skin melded. Her claw prodded at my sternum.

I ripped a little skin from the back of my thighs as I shifted away, but I kept my gaze trained directly on Beira's eye.

Something about the eagerness in her eye, her desperation—

She had a certain hunger in her expression. She reminded me of Karen, our phantom guardian. But why?

I thought it was the sense of loneliness.

Beira hunched over, her claw poking into my skin.

You have luck. Her breath misted around her head.

I couldn't say I felt lucky right now. Maybe luck meant something else to her. If the stories were true, she'd gone mad in the prisons. Her mind had become twisted from isolation.

Luck. She didn't seem to suffer from the physical cold, but maybe she just needed… love? Affection? Friends, maybe.

"We can be friends," I offered in desperation. A bitter wind whipped over me, stinging my skin.

Her breath sounded damp in her throat, a rough, rattling sound. Now, she was digging her claw into the flesh over my heart, the iron seeping into my blood. Red streaked down the front of my chest, and I tugged frantically at the magical ropes binding my wrists behind my back.

The dancers whirled closer, white hair whipping around them.

She was lonely. Of that much I was sure. And I had

someone in my life. I had Gina. That's what she meant by luck.

Gina had given me a ring for luck…

"Wait!" I said. "I have a present for you." An icy shudder rippled through me as her claw threaten to scrape my bone. "I have a present. A good luck charm. It's for you. Luck. For you."

Her claw stopped pressing in.

A present? Whispers fluttered around my mind. *Luck?*

With my stiff muscles, I slowly shifted my body enough to give her a view of my hands—of the ring. My underwear was pure ice now, and the blood on my chest had already frozen.

"A ring on my finger," I said. "It was a gift from a friend to me. For good luck. I'll give it to you for luck. To my new friend." I craned my head to look at her.

She blinked at me, her bloodshot eye close to my face. Then, she looked down at my hands. She reached out, claws scraping my fingers as she pulled the ring off. A girlish smile curled her lips, and she brought the ring to her face.

"Luck," she repeated, speaking the word out loud, her voice scraping at my eardrums. "Luuuuuck."

The snow-white dancers twirled closer to me, kicking up snow that shimmered in the moonlight. Their red eyes no longer looked quite as vacant. In fact, now they looked hungry, intent on me. Ravenous.

Then, Beira fixed me with her single eye once more.

You won't hurt the Ankou again.

The world had started to seem hazy at this point, the light dimming. I saw only white hands reaching for me, the dancers closing in.

I wanted to lie down on the ice. I just needed to fall into deep sleep.

"My heart is true." The words came out of my frozen lips from nowhere.

Without another word, Beira kicked me back into the portal. I sank into the salty seawater once more.

The cold had pierced right down to my marrow. As I fell under the water, memories of my old life flitted through my mind—the glittering fae of a drowned court. A ball, thrown by my mother, me wearing a crown of flowers. My mother had made it for me herself: buttercups, daisies, and a pale purple spring squill.

That night, she told me I was the most beautiful fae she'd ever seen. She told me I might rule the kingdom one day, and I didn't need a king to do it. I'd been so sure she was right.

The memory took root in my mind and grew more vivid, until I felt myself dancing and twirling along with the others, exhilarated by the music pounding through my blood, drops of dandelion wine on my lips. Lights floated above us, twinkling in the skies.

I hadn't needed a man, but it was nice to dance with them.

And among the guests, among the flurry of faces, I glimpsed a newly familiar one—a powerful fae with an angelic face and eyes the pure blue of a Mediterranean sky.

The cold sank through my muscles and bones until I was sure I was pure ice. Was I dying in here? The water would envelop me and pull me deeper.

In the dark water, I caught a glimpse of long, white limbs, hair pale as snow, fingers straining for me. The shock of it snapped me out of my memories.

One of the dancers had followed me into the portal. Her bony hand gripped tightly to my ankle, fingernails piercing my skin. A long tongue shot out of her mouth, lashing the skin on my thighs. Sharp pain followed, shooting up my leg.

CHAPTER 10

A pair of strong arms pulled me out of the seawater, and I looked up into the golden face of the Ankou. In some twisted way, it felt like a relief to see him.

When I looked down at the portal, I saw the snow-white hag climbing out of the water, a hungry look in her red eyes. The pale creature had followed me all the way through.

The Ankou dropped me on his bed, my back resting on his pillows. My underwear was still iced to my body, hair frozen to my shoulders. My limbs had gone numb—apart from the shooting pain in my legs where the wraith had licked me.

In a daze, I watched as the Ankou grabbed the snow wraith by her neck and pulled her from the portal.

Then, in a startlingly fast movement, he twisted her head sharply. The crack of bone echoed off the stone arches above us.

The creature's neck jutted out at an odd angle, and her red eyes dimmed to black. The Ankou dropped her limp body back into the portal. Once her corpse sank under the surface, the portal disappeared within the silver ring. The floor smoothed over into flat sandstone.

My breath puffed through my chattering teeth.

The Ankou turned and looked down at me, his prisoner.

"I h-h-h-hate you s-s-s-s-so much," I managed.

His attention was fixed on my thigh. Beneath my tan skin, it looked like my veins had been poisoned by a dark toxin. No wonder it hurt like the dickens.

The Ankou climbed onto the bed, staring at my legs, and then he climbed between them. He gripped the poisoned thigh. The dark blood was climbing higher up my body, moving to my hip. Fire shot through my veins, my nerve endings ignited.

"Don't touch me," I said through gritted teeth. The fury I managed to convey surprised even me. It was the wrath of a queen and not a frozen, half-naked wretch.

Apparently, it surprised him, too, because he pulled his hand away like I'd burned him.

His deep blue eyes met mine. "If I don't, the poison will kill you within thirty seconds."

This was where Giles Corey would say *more poison.*

Except—screw Giles Corey. I was pretty sure he'd beaten one of his servants to death. He made terrible decisions.

"Fine," I said at last. "Do your healing thing."

He gripped my poisoned thigh tightly. With his other hand, he began to trace a slow circle over my skin. One of his hands was a vise on my thigh, the other light as a dandelion puff.

I wasn't using my Morgen magic now, and yet I got a glimpse of how I looked to him. A quick flicker of how he saw me—breasts straining against the wet tank top, nipples hard, cheeks flushed, my legs spread a little, lips parted as I looked up at him. He was trying his best to resist his desire for me, trying to remind himself that my innocent appearance belied a dangerous spirit.

He swooped another circle over my thigh.

Slowly, the pain subsided, the fire simmering down. I sighed audibly as his magic danced over my body.

For a moment, his deep blue eyes were locked on mine, looking distinctly troubled. Then he focused on my thigh again. My pulse started to race as he leaned down. He pressed his warm mouth against my thigh, his tongue moving against my skin. My back arched a little at the sensation. He was going to *suck* the poison out.

As the pain subsided, a pleasurable warmth washed over me. No, not just warmth—an animal craving. Heat was moving up my thigh toward the apex of my legs as the toxins left my body. My breath hitched. All at once, I was acutely aware of the feel of the wet clothes against my skin, as if my breasts were growing heavy and swelling against the wet cotton.

Stop it, Aenor.

It felt like warm water was spilling over my cold skin. All the pain was disappearing, replaced by a new, more disturbing sensation: a burning need for him. My body was ripe with aching desire. His long hair brushing against my thighs was like a sexual torture, his lips moving against my thigh.

What was *wrong* with me?

I tried to ignore the raging desire. And yet my gaze lingered over his powerful warrior's shoulders. I felt my chest and my cheeks flushing, and molten lust spiraled out of control.

The entirety of my attention had narrowed to the feel of his mouth on my thigh. The ice was melting right off my body as my skin heated, curls of steam rising. *Gods, please tell me he won't see my flushed chest.* The only thing worse than enjoying this. If I lost control and let out a moan of desire, I could already imagine the smug smile he'd flash his little captive.

Another stroke of his tongue, and electric shivers rippled through me. I'm pretty sure my hips moved. Gods have *mercy*.

I hated men. I needed to remember that.

Crush your desire for him, Aenor.

I forced myself to think of Giles Corey—an old bloated man crushed by the weight of rocks, his swollen tongue sticking out. Total passion killer.

At that moment, the Ankou pulled his mouth away and spit the poison onto the floor.

Good. Okay. My breath was slowing, and we had spit and Giles Corey.

I tore my gaze away from his perfect face to look at my leg. The dark poison had started to disappear.

"It's done," I said through a clenched jaw. "You've done enough. Do not touch me anymore, and keep your hands and lips off me in the future, or I will cut them off."

Just as before, he pulled his hands away like he'd been stung. Still, he snarled, "You're welcome."

All at once, the ice returned to my body, and my muscles seized up.

"What was that?" I asked through chattering teeth.

"Leanhaum-shee. That's what that creature was. They have venomous tongues. Beira let you live, just about."

Shivering, I said, "I want you to know that I have not enjoyed my time here so far, and I despise you very much."

He pressed his hands on either side of my head, leaning down. His gaze slid over my bare skin like a caress. I knew that as much as he hated me, he liked how I looked. "You need to warm up."

"Well, well," I murmured. "You're as perceptive as you are

pretty. Was it my frozen hair that gave it away? Take the bindings off me," I rasped. "Or I will find a way to kill you with my mind."

"We've established that I can return from the dead."

"I will scourge you over and over," I seethed. "And I will make it hurt."

"I'm going to turn you over to get the bindings off."

Without his magic, my muscles were frozen stiff. "I can barely move."

He shifted me onto my side, facing away from him. I stared at the night sky outside. The setting sun had nearly slipped down past the horizon—a sliver of pumpkin under a blackberry sky.

My teeth wouldn't stop chattering.

I felt a strong tug as he ripped the bindings off my wrists, and I brought my hands in front of me to try to rub them, but my fingers weren't moving properly. Next thing I knew, he was wrapping me in a soft blanket and pulling me into his lap. He held me against his hot chest, and I felt his heart pounding against the blanket.

As much as I loathed him to his core, I found my head resting against his shoulder. His body was warmer than the bed. "Men are worthless."

I breathed in the scent of almonds.

"I'm trying to warm you." He pulled me in tight, close to his body.

My throat felt like sandpaper, and I glanced at a pitcher of water on the bedside table. And next to the water lay his arm sheath and dagger. I wasn't sure which I wanted more—the water or the weapon.

I ran my tongue over my lips, tasting salt. Then I nodded at the pitcher. "I need water."

He leaned over me, reaching for the pitcher of water, and

poured it into a cup. He handed it to me, and I clutched my stiff fingers around it.

I didn't think I'd ever been this close to a man for this long. I'd had precisely two sexual encounters in my long life, both quick and disappointing.

Now if I were the kind of person who got excited over hot guys, I'd be thinking about the Ankou's bulging muscles, or the strange tattoos that marked his skin. My pulse would race at the thought of his perfect mouth so close to me. I'd be picturing my legs wrapped around his body.

What on earth was happening to me?

I sipped the water. Had water ever tasted so amazing? My hands shook a little. When I had drained the cup, he pulled it away from me.

"Look at you," I said. "Showing kindness to a dirtling."

"I need to keep you alive. And you're still not warm enough."

He lifted me and carried me across the floor into a new room—one with arched sandstone windows that overlooked the sea, and ornate copper lanterns that hung from the ceiling. An enormous marble tub stood in the center of the room, and steam coiled from the water.

Heaven.

He lowered me to the ground, and I let the blanket drop. I climbed into the bath, letting out a sigh as warmth enveloped me. I leaned back against the smooth marble tub. At last, my muscles started to relax.

A thin stream of blood coiled from my chest where the Winter Witch had pierced me, and it turned the water around it pink.

I folded my arms around my legs. Had the Ankou really made good on his promise about Gina? "Tell me where Gina is," I said.

"At the Savoy Hotel. We established that."

In the bath, my white cotton underwear had become completely transparent. But the Ankou wasn't looking at me anyway.

Instead, he leaned against the wall in the shadows, staring out the window at the ocean, arms folded. The light from the lanterns danced over the beautiful planes of his face.

"Do you need to be in here?" I asked.

"I need to make sure you don't pass out and drown while you're in the bath."

I glanced at his blackened wound, just barely visible above his folded arms.

Now that I had a moment of quiet, I had to wonder exactly who I was dealing with here. The seneschals had said he was divine. I think they meant literally.

"You're a demigod, aren't you?" I asked.

"Was it the rising from the dead that gave it away?"

"What's your name?"

"Lyr."

Lyr. God of the sea. He'd been named for his father, the god I worshipped. No wonder I'd felt compelled to worship him when I first met him by the Thames.

Of all the people to kill...

CHAPTER 11

*F*or the briefest of moments, Lyr glanced at me, then his gaze quickly darted away like he'd been burned. He was trying very hard not to look at me nearly naked in the bath.

Like all gods, the sea god had many names, depending on the culture. Dagon, Lyr, Poseidan, Yamm, and so on.

In the warm bath, I hugged my legs closer to my body. "So you're half sea god, and half fae."

"Yes."

A breeze from the open arches rushed into the bathroom and lifted strands of his hair. A key around his neck glinted in the warm light. I wondered how much money I could fetch for a prize like that—whatever it was.

"And what exactly is an Ankou?" I asked.

His deep blue eyes shifted to me. For the briefest of moments, his face seemed to change, stoking a primal terror in the depths of my skull.

His eyes blazed with divine gold, his crown growing longer and spindly. The black tattoos on his body glowed with gold, shifting around his chest like living creatures. Shadows swirled around him, and his powerful body radiated light. He looked so terrifying and godlike that my heart stuttered to a stop.

This was how he'd appeared to me when he'd abducted me from my bedroom, but I hadn't been able to see him as clearly in the dark.

Then, the image was gone as quickly as it had appeared, and I loosed another breath.

"You don't know what the Ankou is?" he asked. "Do you remember so little from Ys?"

"The island drowned over a century and a half ago. It's been a long time. I remember some things. I remember the day it drowned most vividly. I remember how the land lurched, and the palace towers crumbled, the bells ringing and ringing and then falling silent, crushed under gold and cedar and marble. Along with many of our people. I remember the screams all around me as the island sank, and how it felt when my true magic was pulled from my chest. The things that happened before aren't quite as vivid. But I take it you lived in my kingdom?"

"In Ys I served your mother, the Queen, and I served the sea god as a high priest in the temple of the dead. I still do. I travel into the sea hell and help souls find peace. I grant solace to the worthy."

I tilted my head back, breathing in the heavy, steamy air. It smelled of sand and salt—and faintly of verbena. I never wanted to leave the bath, though I wished I could bathe alone. My eyes kept drifting to Lyr's chest, which irritated me.

"Do you ever wear a shirt?" I asked.

"I still have iron in my blood, courtesy of you. The sea air helps it to heal."

A sharp sting pierced my own chest, and I touched it. It

occurred to me that the Winter Witch had hurt me in the exact same spot where I'd shot Lyr.

"What happens next?" I asked.

"You seem to be recovering. Next, you get dressed. At dinner, we will explain your task to you." He turned and crossed out of the room, leaving me with a few unanswered questions.

Specifically—what was I supposed to wear? And would Melisande be there to make me bash my head against a rock?

I rose from the bath, my skin now pink from the warm water. Bathwater dripped off my undies onto the stone floor. A pile of neatly folded cream towels lay on a marble sink, and I grabbed one of them to dry off.

Through the open windows, the breeze smelled like the Mediterranean—balmy and tinged with lemons.

I glanced at the archway that led back to Lyr's room. Where did he expect me to change my clothes? I wasn't getting dressed in front of him. Not only did I not want him to see me totally naked, but I didn't want him seeing the scars under the tank top. Carved into my belly were the names of the demons who'd attacked me long ago, burned into my skin with iron.

What would the demigod think if he knew I'd been permanently defiled by demons?

I tucked the towel under my armpits, and I crossed back into the room with the bed. For the first time, I noticed all the bookshelves built into one of the walls across from the windows.

Lyr sat in a chair in the corner of the room, a book in his hand. He was still bare-chested, but he now wore a thin cloak over his shoulders.

He lifted his gaze from what he was reading. For one moment, his eyes burned with gold, and I could see his grip tightening on the book. "For the love of the gods, put some clothes on."

"What clothes?"

"Behind you."

I turned to find a gown on the bed—it was a deep blue, with tiny pearls inset into the delicate fabric. There wasn't much fabric, either—a bodice that plunged down, and a slit in the front that would expose one of my legs. Not the other, though. I could—maybe—make use of that discarded dagger and the sheath.

A pair of shoes lay by the dress—simple blue flats, not the heels I usually wore.

I turned and shot him a sharp look. "Will you close your eyes?"

"My eyes are on my book."

"Good."

I snatched the dress off the bed, then turned, glaring at him while I backed toward his bedside table. His eyes were, in fact, on his book.

Swiftly, I lifted the arm sheath—dagger included—off the table. I folded it into the dress.

"I'm going into the bathroom to change," I added. "Stay where you are."

With the weapon hidden, I slipped back into the bathroom. I dropped the towel, keeping my gaze trained on the door.

First, I slipped the dress on over my head. Where had it come from? Maybe it was Melisande's.

In any case, the smooth silk slid over my skin, and I let out a long breath at how good it felt against my body.

I'd once worn dresses this fine every day. I'd once sat on a throne—

I bit my lip, reminding myself I couldn't get used to luxury. I was only here for a short while, then it was back to life as a dirtling. I'd been a princess once, but I wasn't now. I'd spent the last hundred years carving away the vulnerable parts of myself, and I couldn't let myself go soft again. Attachment to luxury would make me weak again.

The important thing to remember here was that everyone in this beautiful palace wanted me dead or hurt. And that's why this dagger might come in handy.

I glanced at myself in the mirror. The difference between the dresses I'd worn long ago and *this* particular number is that this one showed off much more of my body. Apparently, aristocratic fae fashion had changed over the years.

The dress didn't leave me many options for concealing the arm sheath. I couldn't use my arms. The large dress slit would likely expose both calves when I walked. *One* thigh would stay hidden. Lyr's arms were huge, but would it really fit around my thigh? Not as it was.

I opened the sharp prong on the buckle, then jabbed it through the leather to create a new hole at the very end of the strap.

Then, I lifted the hem of the delicate dress and buckled the holster around my thigh. I could *just* barely get it around my thigh with the new hole—a bit uncomfortable, but it would have to do. I slipped into the plain blue flats.

As I crossed back into the bedroom, I tried to ignore the fact that I wasn't wearing any underwear—just his dagger under my dress.

Lyr closed his book, his blue gaze resting on me for a moment. "Better."

"You think?" I crossed to the window. "So where is this thing we're looking for? Nearby?"

"I believe so."

I leaned out as I looked down at the sandstone walls beneath us. As I did, my stomach curdled. Skulls dotted the walls—some horned like demons, but many were fae or human.

Worst of all, a fresh body hung from one wall in chains—a woman with pink hair and a white dress, the front of it stained brown with blood where her throat had been slit. Moonlight glinted off a collection of charm bracelets on one of her slender wrists. Blood stained her glittery tennis shoes.

I cleared my throat. "What happened to her?"

"I slit her throat." His tone was casual, almost bored.

Just in case I might have thought that the hot bath and fancy dress meant Lyr was a nice guy, the body dangling below me was a sharp reminder of the truth: I couldn't let my guard down around him.

CHAPTER 12

"And why did you slit her throat and hang her body from your walls?" I prompted.

"As a message to others who would break the fae laws. Every skull and corpse you see on the castle walls belonged to outlaws and dirtlings."

Dirtling, incidentally, was what he liked to call me.

I backed away from the window. I was no stranger to the macabre, but the sea fae had a very different notion of moral authority than I did. I didn't kill little girls just for breaking rules.

"What crime did she commit?" I asked.

He lifted the silver key from his neck. "She tried to steal this."

I knew the key had to be worth a ton of money. Worth risking your life over. "You slit her throat and hung her from a wall because she tried to steal your necklace?"

"Are you judging me for killing? You have slaughtered plenty, Aenor, Flayer of Skins."

"For very naughty things. Murder, disfiguring other people. Not, like, pinching jewelry, you know?"

His stare cut right through me, like every sentence I uttered was some kind of crushing disappointment to the entire fae race. "It's not *jewelry*. It's a tool that helps to open the worlds. It's called a World Key."

Good to know. Valuable.

The silver ring lay on the floor where the portal had appeared. Was that part of how the worlds opened? I knelt down to look at it. It wasn't attached to the stone, and I picked up. I dropped it around my waist, hula-hooping with it. "And this? Is this part of how you open portals?"

Lyr was watching my hips move rhythmically back and forth. Maybe the comb I'd used hadn't entranced him, but the hula-hoop seemed to do the job.

"That's not required, no. It just keeps the portal opening tidy." With what seemed like a lot of effort, he pulled his gaze away from my shifting hips, his blue eyes narrowing. "Do not even think of stealing the key from me. For one thing, you will find yourself on the receiving end of my justice, and for another, you probably wouldn't be able to use it. And if you did figure it out, it would sicken you to the point where you'd yearn for death."

"I wouldn't dream of stealing from you." I flashed him an innocent smile and kept hula-hooping, enjoying the fact that it seemed to throw him off guard.

He touched the key at his throat. "As Grand Master of the Institute, it is my duty to keep the magical realms shut." He lifted the key. "The woman you saw hanging outside didn't know she'd be unable to use the key, that it required *my* magical signature to open a world. She tried to seduce me and stop my heart so she could steal it."

Interesting. "And how far did she get with her seduction?"

Lyr's gaze had drifted to my hips again. "And why is that detail important?"

Why *was* that important? It wasn't—not to me. It's not

85

like I was thinking about what it would be like to seduce him. Only an idiot would be thinking about tying him down, straddling him, and running her tongue over him, a sexual interrogation until he gave up the answers. My body was growing hot in the humid Acre air.

I cleared my throat and let the silver hoop drop to the floor. It clanged over the stones. "It's not important. You said something about dinner?"

With the hoop on the ground, the sharp focus returned to his eyes.

He turned to the heavy wooden door and pulled it open. "Follow me."

I followed Lyr into a hall of dizzyingly high arches with torches on the walls. I kept thinking of the woman hanging outside. One misstep here, and I was sure I'd be joining her. Without my true power, I'd have a hard time defending myself against the knights.

As we walked further into the corridor, trees grew within the castle itself. Red-berried rowan trees arched over us, their boughs climbing the arches. Little white lights twinkled among the branches. These were sacred trees to the fae—native to our homelands. The sea fae must have imported them here from the British Isles.

On one side, rounded openings in the trees revealed a pool of turquoise water. Gosh, they had a nice place here.

Colored sea glass dappled the walls. Ages ago, I would have felt right at home in a place like this. Now, I'd be much more comfortable lounging on a sofa with Gina in a pair of stretchy shorts, watching reality TV. Eating Pop-Tarts.

I hadn't always been stuck underground. Humans didn't even know the fae existed till a few decades ago. But once they caught on? All supernaturals were under tight control, ruled by the knights.

Now, I'd come into their world, where the vaulted ceilings soared thirty feet high, and gold engravings glinted in the torchlight. Flags hung on the walls, decorated with family crests—eels, starfish, waves, the runic symbol for the sea god—

My blood raced at the sight of my own family crest—a mythical white horse emerging from frothy water. *My* family crest, from my mother's line. The House of Meriadoc. A long-buried power fluttered between my ribs like a dying moth, then sputtered out again, leaving me feeling empty.

"Your mother's herald." His voice held a sort of reverence.

"It's mine too." I waved at the flags. "Seems like a fire hazard. All the flags and the torches."

"Keep moving."

I straightened my back as the corridor opened into an enormous, dimly lit hall with a round table.

Only two of the knights sat at the table—the two males I'd seen before, Gwydion and Midir. Melisande wasn't there, luckily. I'm not sure I'd have been able to stop myself from trying to pull her wings off.

Gwydion rose abruptly, snatching his goblet of golden wine as he did. His boots clacked over the stones as he crossed to us, and a faint smile curled his lips. The torches bathed his brown skin in gold. "Ah. You recovered from your head injury." He frowned at Lyr. "You *healed* her?"

He shook his head. "The dirtling? I wouldn't touch her if I didn't have to. She healed herself."

That was a lie, which was weird.

At the table, Midir shuddered. "At least she has bathed."

"Maybe I should go back to the Winter Witch and hang out with her ice wraiths," I said. "Seems like a better time than this. More welcoming."

Midir leaned back in his chair. "I do wonder why Lyr didn't kill you a long time ago. If he'd wanted to, he could have ripped your head clean off your body. Just right off, like a child destroying a little doll." He seemed all too gleeful as he described this. "Did you know that Lyr slaughters with alarming efficiency? He can make a person's heart explode out of their chest, should the situation call for it. Though he's much more restrained than I would be."

"Relax, Midir," said Lyr. "The Winter Witch has sent her back to us. We do not need to kill her."

"It's lovely to see you both again," I said. "Are we going to move on to the details of the mission? Also, I heard there was dinner."

Lyr turned and nodded at the servants who lined the wall. "We're ready to eat." Then, he gestured to Midir, whose vibrant red hair was wreathed with a spiky crown. "You've met my seneschals already, I believe."

I nodded. "I learned all about their amazing torture hobbies."

Midir's eyes were dark as the bottom of the ocean. Everyone in this place was beautiful and terrifying. He twirled his wineglass, glaring at me. "You killed Irdion. He was useful. And he was my drinking buddy, if you must know."

Lyr crossed to the table, taking a seat. "And yet we *do* need Aenor, and you are never short of drinking buddies, Midir. In fact, you are much more pleasant to be around when you're drunk, so drain your glass." Lyr gestured at an empty chair. "Join us."

I pulled out a seat at the table. Lyr started to fill my glass with a golden liquid.

"What is this, exactly?" I asked.

"Dandelion wine," said Gwydion. "Sweetened with honey. Obviously."

It had been a hundred years since I'd tasted dandelion wine. No, a hundred-fifty. Gods, I remembered it being good.

A humid, salty breeze rushed in from the window, raising goosebumps on my bare skin. The wine tasted warm and summery, with just a hint of honey.

I took another sip, and it warmed me from the inside out. I'd forgotten how deliciously intoxicating fae wine was.

"Nice castle you have," I said.

Lyr was studying me. "If you weren't corrupted, you could have joined us here as one of the knights, long ago. You could have served the sea god."

"What would she do for us?" asked Midir. "She doesn't have power anymore. She's broken. She'd never survive the trials."

Truthfully, I knew probably just enough spells to compete in the trials to become a knight. I didn't know a cleaning spell, but I *did* know how to explode a few things, how to give myself speed in order to run and fight. I could survive underwater for long periods of time. I could enchant people, as long as I had water nearby. But, I wasn't going to bring any of this up. Let them think I was broken.

"Not to mention her disgrace," added Gwydion.

They'd subjected me to such an unrelenting barrage of insults that I hadn't had much time to wonder about the *disgrace* they kept talking about. I'd lost my kingdom and my power, but it's not as though that were my fault. Someone had invaded our kingdom of Ys and destroyed everything I had.

"What is this disgrace you all keep going on about?"

Gwydion's eyes went wide, a wicked smile curling his lips. "Oh dear. She really doesn't know, does she?"

CHAPTER 13

"Know what?" I asked, losing patience.

"That we all know the truth." Gwydion quite clearly found this hilarious. "We know your secrets. How you drowned your kingdom."

I stared at him. "You think I *what?*"

"The wanton princess who wrecked her kingdom and ran off to America in disgrace," Gwydion went on. "I *do* love a good tragedy, really. You drowned your own kingdom to appease a lover. The gods despaired of your recklessness and stole your powers. They left you with nothing but a ragged dress and a few spell books to your name as punishment."

"We all know," said Midir. "Everyone knows."

I was gripping the stem of my wineglass so hard, I thought I might break it. "Is *that* what you think happened? That I drowned my own kingdom?"

Midir's eyes were hard as flint. "Of course that's what happened. You took after your wicked father and flooded the island."

I could hardly form the words. "Y'all think I killed my mother, too?"

Gwydion shrugged. "I'm sure it wasn't on purpose, but a fae queen dies with her land, and you drowned the land. So, yes, really you did kill her."

Icy darkness slid through my bones. *This* is what everyone thought of me—all the fae who survived the drowning of Ys believed that *I'd* been the one who destroyed it.

But that wasn't what happened.

I clenched my jaw. "Start from the beginning. What's the story you all think that you know?"

Lyr's body had taken on a strange, animal stillness as he pinned me with his glare. "You had the power to control the sea and drown a kingdom. It was your birthright. Do you deny this?"

I stared back at him. "That part is true. But I didn't drown Ys. It was someone else. Did no one else see him?"

Gwydion sighed. "Look, you were young. We all know the story. You got drunk on wine, like you always were."

I bit my lip. "I was often drunk, yes. I did not destroy the kingdom because of it." Back then, I had so much power that it deafened me at times. The noise of it—the overwhelming rush of magic, the clanging cacophony and rushing waves—I needed the dandelion wine for a little peace in my mind.

"You had many lovers," Gwydion went on, "which I don't judge. In fact, I possibly admire it."

"I wouldn't judge that either," I said. "Except it's not true."

He rolled his eyes. "Oh come on. We *all* know. They've passed on the details. You had them wear black satin masks. Sometimes you strangled them *in flagrante,* and you forgot to stop before they died. Like I said, I admire that."

I could feel that my cheeks were bright red. "This isn't me."

"But then one of your lovers betrayed you with your cousin," Gwydion went on. "Whose beauty you always envied. In a drunken rage, your emotions got the better of you. You drowned the city." He shrugged. "It could have happened to anyone with that power, really. I once cursed an entire village to dance to death because my boyfriend got off with his tailor. In my opinion, it's perfectly understandable. But there's no reason to lie about it. Own it."

"What? Slow down." I stared at him. "I hardly had any lovers, let alone many lovers in masks." I'd had exactly two lovers in my long years. One a viscount's son who'd seduced me in an apple grove for all of four minutes, and the other a human in London who liked watching darts. Both forgettable.

"I don't get along with men, and I never have," I said. "I don't get jealous of other women's beauty. And I definitely didn't drown a kingdom because I was jealous. Was this story told to you by a man, by any chance? This sounds like a dude story. The girl who was sooo slutty she broke the whole world." I breathed in slowly through my nose. "And this all brings me back to my previous point. I don't get along with men."

Lyr stared at me with an extreme curiosity. I felt like a butterfly pinned under his gaze. Did he believe this whole *blindfolded and strangled* story?

"I wasn't finished with the story," Gwydion cut in. "We haven't got to the best part. After you drowned Ys, one of the knights of your kingdom tried to save you on his horse. But the gods called out, *throw the demon thou carriest into the sea, if thou dost not desire to perish.* That's when the gods took your power from you. You clung to the knight's body, promising him all sorts of sordid sexual favors if he would only carry you to shore."

My mouth dropped open. *Sordid sexual favors?* "This is not what happened."

"He kicked you off his horse anyway," Midir went on,

"and you washed up in your sea-torn dress on the shore, and lived out your days as a murderous prostitute."

"Frankly, it's all fascinating," said Gwydion. "It's honestly probably my favorite story."

My skin went hot. "You think I needed a man to save me from drowning? I can swim for hundreds of miles. I'm a Morgen, and no one stole that power. Is this story by any chance coming from the knight who says I promised him sordid sexual favors?"

"Yes," said Gwydion. "I mean, he was there."

"And you didn't think that maybe this is the kind of dumb crap men make up to impress each other?"

A silence fell over the hall for a moment, and Lyr scrubbed his chin. "That part about the swimming always perplexed me."

Midir licked his lips. "But you did sell your body to survive? You must have. What else would you have done? A broken princess with no skills."

I stole things, mostly. But I wasn't about to bring that up now, when it could get my throat slit.

"So what did it feel like when the gods stole your power?" asked Gwydion.

It wasn't the gods. It was a *fae* who stole my power.

A fae who burned like a star. One whose name I didn't know—so I called him the Nameless One.

Dark shadows sliced the air around Lyr. "I was the only one who believed the stories were wrong. I believed that as the daughter of Queen Malgven, you remained our true ruler. I didn't believe you would destroy your own kingdom. But in the end, when I saw you for what you really were, even I had to admit it was the truth."

I stared out the window, where the dark sea crashed against a rocky shore. Right now, I wanted to leap into it. It seemed impossible to clear my name.

This was the thing with men, as my mother—Queen Malgven herself—had warned me. It doesn't matter who you really are. They write their own stories about you. They cast you in one of several roles. The innocent girl who needed teaching. The lunatic who needed calming. The whore who'd break your heart. Or in my case—the demonic prostitute fueled by rage and jealousy. A fallen woman. That was my story, whether or not it was true. And as Gwydion had said— wasn't it a good story?

But why should I care what they thought? I knew the truth. Gina knew the truth.

This bunch of jerks was not worth my time.

"Interesting story," I said as calmly as I could. "It was all a long time ago."

"A long time ago," said Midir. "Yet it was only a few days ago that you killed one of our knights with iron. *Iron*," he repeated, as if it was the crucial bit. "So you haven't changed. You should be strung in front of our fortress, eviscerated, and doused with salt. Your head should decorate our front gate. The only reason it won't is that we need you."

Gwydion grimaced. "Bit garish, though, really, with the lurid blue hair. Probably best avoided if we can. It's bad enough with the pink."

I drummed my fingertips on the table, losing patience, and said, "Look, perhaps we're not that different. I kill people that I think are a threat to others, and so do you." I glanced at Lyr. "Those hearts you keep talking about? They came from demons who preyed on human women. That's who I killed."

He seemed to be considering this for a moment, his entire muscled body eerily still, pale eyes locked on me. The weight of his gaze felt somehow heavy on my shoulders. "You don't seem to be lying. Still, we can't allow vigilantes to rule the streets. Where's the proof of evil? Anyone could say the same. Without law and order, chaos reigns. We would drown in meaninglessness."

"Sometimes laws have to be broken," I argued. "It's not like I could call on the knights to help. Not when my entire existence is criminal. Anyway. You're breaking tons of laws. Torture is illegal. Improper disposal of bodies. I'm sure that's a law."

"What?" Midir looked genuinely perplexed. "Why would anyone care where the bodies went?"

"Humans care," I said.

"Human laws are subordinate to sea fae laws." Lyr shrugged. "Just as humans are subordinate to the superior sea fae."

Gwydion let out a dramatic sigh. "To be honest, we don't know what the human laws are. Humans are alive for like... twelve seconds, and then they rot and die."

"And what are the sea fae laws I need to know?" I asked.

Lyr leaned over the table. "Do you really not remember?"

"It was a long time ago," I said.

"Let me fill in the groundling." Gwydion held up a finger. "One, only the knights are qualified to conduct executions. Not vigilantes such as yourself. We determine who is a threat and who is not, using our skills and superior knowledge. Two, the souls of those we kill are committed to the sea god so that they serve a greater purpose."

"Three." Shadows seemed to stain the air around Lyr. His mood appeared to have shifted suddenly, from amused to furious. "No one is allowed to slaughter guests, or those invited to break bread."

It seemed oddly specific and pointed, but okay. "Guess I'm safe here then."

"Four." Midir's spine was stiff as a rod. "No using iron weapons, because it pollutes the body and the soul. They prevent a spirit from passing peacefully into the afterlife. *Princess.*"

"Before I came back to life," said Lyr, "I spent several hours in the sea hell, which felt like years, because my lungs were fucking exploding. So thank you for that."

"Just to clarify," Gwydion lifted his glass. "Irdion's ghost will now be trapped on earth forever, watching you when you shower and things like that. I do hope you're pleased with your choices."

Ahhhh.... so *that* was why they all got upset about the iron. It wasn't just the fact that it killed the fae, which I'd know. It was that it sent them to hell.

CHAPTER 14

"I mean…" I leaned back in my chair. "Does it make it better if I did not know what happened in the afterlife? Most fae don't. It's not like many people have experienced death, if they're not demigods."

"In any case," said Lyr, "I helped Irdion's soul to move on, but without me he'd be eternally tormented."

I drained my wineglass. It was like drinking liquid sunshine. "In that case, I will not shoot you with iron again, unless I really need to." I surveyed the room, desperate to change the subject. Where the heck was the food? "So where are the other knights?" I asked. "And Melisande?"

"The other knights eat after the Council of Three," said Lyr.

"So the men eat first," I said.

Gwydion crossed his legs. "We do have female knights here. They're just not seneschals, like we are."

Midir waved a dismissive hand. "Sometimes their contributions are worthwhile. But the gods designed men and women for different roles. Everyone knows that."

C.N. CRAWFORD

Lyr rolled his eyes. "The gods did no such thing. Midir, you really ought to pull yourself out of the twelfth century."

"Whatever." The smell of delicious seafood tickled my nostrils, and my mouth began watering. It was tempting enough that I could forget about my company for a few moments.

I eyed the human woman who was bringing a tray of food to our table, her rosy face dewy with sweat. She looked like she'd been laboring over the food. She also looked like probably the best person in the room.

I was once a great princess with great power. And now I lived among humans, with economy brand custard creams and cans of corn. Maybe the food was terrible, but it wasn't the worst thing, because I actually liked humans.

The servant lifted the lid off the dome, revealing salmon tinged gold with saffron. Nestled next to the fish were roasted, buttery morels and a salad of wildflowers: oxeye daisies, redbuds, violets, and clover.

This was the kind of fae cooking I'd once eaten every day. And right now, there was nothing else in the world but this meal.

Ohhh yes. I snatched my knife and fork off the table, measuring a perfect forkful of mushrooms and salmon together. As the fish seemed to melt in my mouth, I realized: a) that I was moaning out loud, and b) that Gwydion was still speaking to me. I swallowed my food.

"Sorry, what?"

"I said that I am fascinated by humans. I mean, sure, they're inferior, but... *fascinating.*" His eyes sparkled, and he picked at his food. "And you lived among them. Did you watch television shows? Have you ever worn a *flip-flop*? Have you eaten beans wrapped in bread that has the thickness of human skin?"

A stared at him. "A burrito?"

"That's it." He grinned. "Wonderful. And the butter that isn't real butter, but made of a tasteless oil and tinted yellow?"

Midir curled his lip at Gwydion. "Why are you being friendly to the dirtling?"

Gwydion shrugged. "I'm bored of insulting her now, and I don't really care what she did. So she screwed her way around Ys and killed Irdion. Let's move on. Someone was bound to kill that fuck pigeon at some point."

I swallowed another mouthful of food—the morels perfectly browned in butter. "Fuck pigeons are still not a thing."

Gwydion pointed his fork in the air. "And just like Lyr said, the fae are gracious-*ish* to our guests. Or at least we don't *slaughter* them at *dinner*." He arched a cautionary eyebrow at me.

There it was again. The "slaughtering at dinner" thing delivered in a strangely pointed way, as though I'd been spending the century murdering my guests over pizza.

I had the misfortune to catch Midir's eyes. He still looked furious and wasn't touching his food. "You may not care, Gwydion, but Irdion's parents are wailing with grief at the loss of their son. His mother tore out all her hair. And her scalp is weirdly bumpy, like a kneecap. She looks ridiculous."

I took a deep breath. "Look, I'm sorry I killed your friend. I thought he'd come to kill me. That was because he actually held up a sign threatening to kill me."

"Of course he did," Gwydion muttered under his breath. "Idiot."

Lyr shrugged. "He did give an option, Aenor. *Surrender or die a painful death*. You refused the option to surrender."

"Surrendering to someone who threatens a painful death

is not a viable option," I said. "If someone says 'come with me or I'll tear out your organs,' you are well within your rights to slit their throat."

Gwydion shrugged. "The way she phrases it, it sounds like she has a point."

When Lyr leaned forward, all eyes turned to him. The torches sculpted his muscles with gold and glinted off his crown. "None of that is important now. You're here for a reason."

"Which is?"

"We have received credible information that we might be targeted soon by an army of spirits, hells-bent on destroying us. That is why you're here."

"Interesting," I said. "Go on."

"You're here because I need your help to find an athame that will help us expel these particular spirits," said Lyr.

"An athame," I repeated. "You need me to find a magical blade for you? I don't get it. I'm just a Morgen. Tracking magic objects isn't in my skill set."

Lyr's powerful magic poured off him. "It's not your song that we need. It's the native magic in your blood. The athame we seek is the Athame of Meriadoc, used to conduct powerful sea magic by your family. Long ago, one of my ancestors made it, but it was crafted for your family. The last person to own it was your mother. Queen Malgven was a great leader. Her ancient athame is capable of killing these spirits, conducting sea magic in an attack against them."

"It's true, my mother *was* a great leader. She did have some males around to help her keep the place looking cheerful and help her with the business of raising children while she ruled the kingdom. Like you said. The gods designed men and women for different roles. Everyone knows that." I sipped my wine.

Midir's gaze could have curdled milk.

Lyr was tracing the rim of his glass with his fingertip. "A sorceress from my mother's line forged the athame eons ago with the blood and bones of your ancestors. You are linked to the athame. If you tune into it, you will be able to feel its pull. It's full of Meriadoc power, and you can hear its magic."

My heartbeat pounded in my ears. *Meriadoc power...*

I poured myself another glass of wine. "Surely it drowned with everything else in Ys. It's probably in my ruined kingdom. Which is nowhere near here, by the way." Ys was all the way off the coast of Cornwall.

Shadows seemed to breathe on Lyr's muscled body. "I have scoured the island's ruins beneath the sea. It isn't there."

"So let me make sure I have this right," I said. "This athame could be anywhere on earth, and I have to find it, just by listening for its magic, which only works if I happen to be near it. And if I fail to find it, you kill me."

Midir tapped his fingertips on the table. "That's an accurate summary."

"The good news," said Gwydion, "is that our Winter Witch Beira has promised us the athame is *somewhere* near the fortress. Though she didn't really define what 'near' meant, and she sort of grunted it in a guttural growl. She said 'near, near, near,' over and over."

I stared at him. "Fear. She was saying 'fear.' She says it repeatedly. Not *near.*"

Gwydion pointed at me. "You know what? You might be right about that. She is a little mental, to be honest."

"And what exactly are these spirits that are supposedly coming for you?"

Midir twirled a knife-tip against his index finger. "I don't think you need to know that, tunnel swine."

Lyr refilled Midir's glass. "She will figure it out very soon, and there's no reason to keep it from her. We have heard that the fuath are searching for us."

My stomach flipped. The fuath were mad spirits of vengeance—the ghosts of fae who lived on after death, propelled by fury. They could possess a person's body and force them to do terrible things—to kill their husbands or wives, or light buildings on fire.

I *knew* them from my curse books—the one I'd memorized.

"Who is controlling them?" I asked.

"We don't know," said Lyr.

I closed my eyes, trying to remember the pages of the curse book. "There's a way to protect against them, you know. The fuath. I read it in one of my spell books."

Gwydion steepled his fingers. "Do you care to share?"

I sighed. "If you'd simply come to me in my shop and asked for advice, I could have pulled out my rare and ancient reference book. You could protect yourselves from their spirits. But you drowned the book, so it's ruined."

Midir snorted. "That's convenient."

"It's really the opposite of convenient," I said. I remembered the charm, though right now I couldn't bring the image to mind exactly. "But it was a mark. You make it with your own blood over another person's heart, and then the fuath can't leap into your body. I just can't remember exactly what the mark looks like."

"That wouldn't entirely solve our problem," said Lyr, "unless we marked every person on earth. The fuath can possess anyone near us."

"Athame it is." I finished the last of the fish on my plate. "But now that I know what the stakes are, and that you're all certain to die without my help, maybe it's time to revisit the terms of our contract."

"Our contract," Lyr repeated it like a foreign word.

"If you help us," said Gwydion, "you can return to your

dirt hole in one piece, and we can keep your garish head from spoiling the look of our gate. Everyone wins."

"No. I need something better than what I have now. And Gina gets to stay in the Savoy forever."

Gwydion frowned. "Did you hear the part about how you get to keep your head attached to your body? That doesn't motivate you? What's *wrong* with you?"

"It doesn't motivate her," Lyr answered for me. "She doesn't care about her life sufficiently for death to be a threat."

"Well," said Midir, "That makes sense. She's lost her power and her crown, and she lives like a peasant. What does she have to live for?"

"She cares about the human girl," said Lyr.

Bile rose in my throat. Was that a threat? Maybe I'd miscalculated.

"If you successfully help me find the Athame of Meriadoc," said Lyr, "I will ensure that your human can stay in her current lodgings permanently. The Savoy Hotel. You'll live in an adjacent room. I will coordinate with the other Institutes. You will have total immunity, assuming you stop committing egregious crimes like torturing people to death in alleyways."

"That seems quite good." Gwydion pointed at me. "I'd take that one."

This *was* a good deal. "Fine. You have my oath."

Just like that, Lyr could make it happen. Imagine having all that power…

At one point, that power had been in my grasp. A snap of my fingers, and I could have had guards protecting anyone I wanted. From a throne of pearls, I'd commanded an army of servants. Maybe I'd abused my power a little. Once, when a visiting dignitary annoyed me by staring too long at my cleavage, I'd turned his ears long and hairy, like a horse's.

Terrible, I know, but what a thrill it had been.

I closed my eyes, breathing in the coastal air. In Ys, I'd wielded true power over the seas. I could flood a city with just a song, drown my enemy's kingdoms.

And what if the athame that Lyr wanted so desperately could give me some of that sea magic back?

CHAPTER 15

For just a moment, I hungered for that power so sharply I had to clutch my stomach and remind myself to breathe. Then, my eyes opened again, and I pulled myself back into the present.

My lust for power would eat me alive if I didn't control it.

"Fine. Life in the Savoy is worth fighting for, I suppose." Soft beds, meals on silver trays. At least, I assumed so. Could be a pigsty in there for all I knew. "I'll help you find your special magic blade. Or rather, *my* special magic blade that you'll be stealing from my family."

I twirled the stem of my wineglass between my fingers. "You know, you served during my mother's reign. Some called her the Queen of Bones. She didn't trust men at all, and I take after her. I don't trust a single one of you."

Lyr glanced down at his chest, which still had a black mark from the iron. "The feeling is mutual, Flayer of Skins."

"I know there are things you are hiding from me," I went on. "But here's what I really don't understand, Lyr. You hang my family's sigil in your fortress. The white horse rising from the waters. You said you were loyal to Queen Malgven."

"With all my soul."

"If you were loyal to her when she was alive, then why have you treated me like rubbish? Why did you believe this cock-and-bull story about the silk masks and drowning my own kingdom? You should know a daughter of Queen Malgven wouldn't be that dumb."

He leaned forward in his chair, elbows on the table, and golden light flecked his eyes. "You don't take after your mother. Your blood is poisoned. The fact that the gods stole your powers is a blessing to us all."

Before I could respond, the sound of a ringing alarm bell stopped me. And underneath that bell, the high, keening cry of the fuath, a sound that sent shivers over my body. The pungent scent of seaweed floated in on the breeze.

They'd arrived early.

Lyr shot to his feet, and a dark burst of magic rippled off him. He slashed his hand through the air. As he did, the windows sealed shut with a dark magic—a gleaming shield of black, enclosing us.

The two other seneschals drew their swords, and the rest of the knights came running into the hall, swords drawn. Melisande ran for Lyr, her dark hair streaming behind her. She stood in front of him protectively.

"They're already here." Lyr spoke quietly, but his voice carried through the hall. "We were too late."

Now, the air smelled of decay, like death was breathing all around us. I had the disturbing sense of being buried alive.

I closed my eyes, discreetly whispering a spell for protection. My magic crackled up my spine—my illegal, outlaw magic. But no one was watching me. Their eyes were all on the walls. It seemed no one knew what was going to happen next.

Forlorn screams of the fuath howled just on the other side of the sandstone walls, a rising wail that set my teeth on edge. So far, it didn't seem like they could get in, but their eerie cries rang in my mind.

"They won't be able to get in," said Gwydion, as if reassuring himself. "Not without knowing where to find the secret entrance."

I wasn't entirely sure why everyone had their swords drawn. The fuath were spirits that inhabited people. Who did they plan to stab? Each other?

And with that thought, I stepped back into the shadows. No one was watching me as I pulled the dagger from the holster on my thigh. I might need it for protection if the fuath possessed those around me.

A phantom wind rushed through the hall, snuffing out the torches, and darkness enveloped us. It felt like a heavy darkness, like wet soil on my chest. A human servant screamed, her terror echoing off the walls.

"Leus." Lyr's deep voice spoke the single word that called a sphere of light into existence. The pale-gold light gleamed off the drawn swords.

But even through the shield of my protection spell, I could feel the air dampening. I licked the salt off my lips.

"They got in," I whispered. "Around us." Seemed like someone had told them about the secret passage, because that did not take long.

Now, it felt like a wave was washing over the room—heavy, ice-cold. On the other side of the hall, a knight arched his back, his eyes going wide.

I held my breath. It was happening. The fuath were starting to possess people.

Right now seemed like a good time to get out of Dodge. I stepped further back into the shadows, slowly moving toward the corridor—

But before I could make a break for it, a powerful arm grabbed me around the waist, one hand clamped over my mouth. I stabbed my attacker in the hip, but he didn't seem to feel the pain. He kept my mouth sealed as he pulled me behind one of the heraldic flags.

I heard the faint click of a door opening, then my captor shoved me hard into a dank tunnel. Within the next heartbeat, the door was shut behind me.

In here, the golden sphere of light illuminated Lyr's beautiful face. He leaned against the narrow tunnel walls, boxing me in, searching my face. And while he did that, I was scrutinizing his.

It was nearly impossible to tell if someone had been possessed by the fuath. A fuath possession didn't change a person's appearance.

"Did you avoid—" I spoke in a whisper, but he still lifted a finger to my lips, silencing me.

I stared into his deep blue eyes long enough that I was reasonably certain it was still him. Same cocky arch of his eyebrow and strangely penetrating gaze.

Blood streaked down his hip.

I was still gripping his knife, my hand now slick with his blood.

I mouthed the word "Sorry." It was a good thing demigods healed fast.

I felt a moment of relief till I glanced at his neck. The fuath had stolen the key from his throat.

The key that could open worlds.

What did they have planned for that? Lyr had said it required his magical signature, so I wasn't sure they could use it. Still…

Lyr nodded at the tunnel. Built of golden sandstone, it looked like the rest of the fortress, but much smaller. Shadows enveloped most of it, so I had no idea where it led.

As we walked, Lyr had to bow his head, and we were cramped side by side. His arm brushed against mine as we walked. We were moving fast, practically running. A few alcoves interrupted the stone walls, and some tunnels branched off from the main one.

I glanced behind us. Even in the dim light, I could tell none of the possessed knights were coming for us.

I whispered, "Were they after the key on your neck?"

"It would seem that way. Not that it will do them much good. I'll probably get it back before they figure out how to reverse the spell I've put on it." He shot me a sharp look. "I was wondering what you'd end up doing with my knife. I'm regretting my decision to wait and see how it all played out."

"You knew I had your knife?"

"Your dress doesn't conceal much."

"It's also not really ideal for the sudden combat and fugitive situation we've found ourselves in. I could have used the black armored stuff you're all wearing."

"At least I gave you practical shoes."

"Back to the key. Is that the whole reason the fuath attacked?"

"Perhaps, but they won't be able to use it easily. They will need to know the right spell."

The sound of a door creaking behind us made my heart race, then Lyr snuffed out the light. With one hand around my waist, he pulled me into a cramped alcove. I was pressed in close to his powerful body.

"*Dorcha.*" I whispered the spell for concealment in shadows.

Packed into the small space, my head rested on Lyr's chest, which rose and fell slowly.

"Oh, Grand Master!" a voice trilled, and it took me a moment to recognize it as Midir's. Before, he'd spoken in a flat monotone. But now? He sounded almost like he was singing. "Grand Master! They're all gone. You can come out now. Allll safe. It's your knight brother friend!"

The good news was that the fuath didn't seem to know much about their hosts, and they weren't good at impersonating them.

I closed my eyes, tuning into what I could hear. Footsteps —faint, but multiple.

It wasn't just Midir in here. In fact, I thought at least five knights were coming for us—all of them possessed by the fuath. If the spirits were after the World Key—why were they still coming for us?

We couldn't stay here in the alcove. Soon, they'd be able to hear our breathing if they got close enough. A bunch of possessed knights with swords, all coming to kill us. If I had a comb on me now, maybe I could do some damage, but Lyr hadn't let me bring it along.

A burst of gold light in the hall sent my pulse racing faster, but when Lyr tugged my waist, I saw something new. We weren't simply in an alcove, but a long, curving passage. We started running, quietly.

We rushed down the curving hall, until the light disappeared. In the dark, Lyr grabbed my hand. My heart leapt as the floor disappeared, and I fell.

Stairs. Okay.

I'd fallen into Lyr's strong back like an idiot, but I now understood that the floor hadn't disappeared, and that we were in a stairwell.

I traced one hand against the damp wall to steady myself as we walked down.

In the stairwell, the ceiling was hardly five feet tall, and the top of my head rubbed against it.

Did dwarves build this place? I couldn't see him, but I imagined Lyr was bent in half to get down the stairs.

After what seemed like ages, my foot plunged into cold water. It smelled of the ocean down here. When I took another step, it came up to about my knees. We were at sea level now, apparently. I didn't hear any of the knights coming for us, so we might have escaped their notice.

In the damp air, a chill rippled up my spine.

Lyr turned abruptly, and I slammed into his brick wall of a chest in the darkness. "Ouch."

He leaned down, then whispered, "We've lost them for now. But when we come out of the tunnel, we'll need to move swiftly and silently. The fuath in bodies can hunt by scent. Now, we no longer have the World Key to make a fast getaway."

He turned, moving fast through the water. I followed close behind.

"Where does this open up?" I asked in a whisper.

"Not far from the shore. If we can get to the water, they won't be able to scent us out. We can swim a few miles, and then you can find the athame. As soon as you can get it, this is all over."

"And you believe this blade is nearby because a witch grunted something. *Near*, but it might have been *fear*."

"We are low on options for survival. Or rather, you are. I can return from the dead."

"Why would the fuath want me dead? I have nothing to do with this. Perhaps I could bargain with them. I could give you over to the fuath in exchange for my freedom. They could torture the answers out of you," I suggested.

"Mmmm," his deep, rich voice thrummed over my skin. "But you wouldn't do that."

"Because you know I'm a good person?"

"Because I don't die, and you would not get far from me. And moreover, if you were seriously considering it, you wouldn't have told me."

"Fine. But everything has become a lot more complicated since we last negotiated our contract. We now have a whole fortress full of possessed knights after us, wanting me dead. We need to renegotiate our terms."

"I don't know why you think we have a contract. You'll just do what I tell you to do. That's our contract."

"Of course. I don't know why I expected someone who brutally kidnapped me to be reasonable."

"I believe the brutal part was when you shot me."

Whatever. I'd just keep my mouth shut and the dagger ready. We were temporarily working together, but this man was my enemy just as much as the rest.

CHAPTER 16

*H*is arm brushed mine again, and a ripple of his magic shivered over my skin.

"Why are these tunnels so small?" I asked.

"Because they were built by human crusaders a thousand years ago when they invaded."

Rays of silver light glimmered at the end of the tunnel. They shone over worn, stone stairs that led upwards.

I glanced at Lyr. A few rays of light just highlighted the perfect planes of his face. The word *sublime* rang in my head. Beauty and death linked in one man. He was like the underworld itself—unknowable, concealed. He kept secrets about himself. Like death, Lyr was a mystery.

I could hear him whispering a spell under his breath, and his magic washed over me.

When we reached the stairs, he turned to me and whispered, "I've chanted a spell that will protect us from the spirits, but it won't last forever. A few minutes, maybe? In the next moments, when we exit the tunnel, we run across the street. We leap over the wall's edge into the ocean."

His body looked completely tense as he stepped up the stairs. I reached for the dagger holstered at my thigh.

I whispered another protection spell, and I heard Lyr call on shadows to conceal us again. With the shadows around us, I could hardly see him. He was a silhouette now, like the light wasn't quite touching him. When I looked down at my own body, I saw that shadows cloaked me too.

We reached the top of the stairs, and he paused in the entrance. The coast *looked* clear. Across the street, a stone wall overlooked the ocean. All we had to do was cross the street. Then, the ocean was our protection.

I whispered another spell—quietly—for speed.

From here, I could hear the waves crashing against the rock. We were so close to the sea.

Please tell me it's not shallow enough to break my legs when I hit the rocks.

Lyr turned to me, his blue eyes piercing the shadows.

He nodded once—the signal to go. Then, he moved like the wind across the cobblestones.

I hiked up my dress to my knees and broke into a run behind him, darting across the street, propelled by my spell for speed. The sea wind whipped over me.

Lyr reached the wall first, then turned to look for me. When his blue eyes went wide, my heart lurched.

That's when I felt someone gripping my hair from behind, pulling me back.

In the next moment, they were all surrounding me—all the possessed fae knights, swords drawn.

Midir stood before me, a sinister grin on his features. He pointed his sword at me. "You'll be staying with us, Daughter of Malgven."

How did the fuath know who I was?

By the stone wall, Gwydion pointed his sword at Lyr's neck.

God of the deep, I hadn't been fast enough.

"What do you want, exactly?" I asked.

Midir—or the fuath possessing him—stared down at me, his red hair bright against the night sky.

"We're after your kingdom," he said in a singsong voice.

My heart thundered against my ribs. *That's* what they wanted? It didn't exist anymore. What the hells was wrong with them?

The Nameless One—our unseen attacker—destroyed it. The dark fae who slaughtered my mother, who stole my true power, and sank the whole thing.

"It's underwater," I snarled. "Off the coast of Cornwall. Feel free to take what's left. It's all yours."

"Is that what you think? You don't—" A blur of movement cut him short. Lyr had knocked Gwydion to the ground and snatched his sword, so fast it had looked like one swift movement. He pointed it at Gwydion's neck.

"Aenor," Lyr said in a calm voice. "Get into the ocean."

The fuath began to surround Lyr. None of them really cared if he slit Gwydion's throat. After all, the knight was just a host.

I stepped back to the wall, but I wasn't going to leave without Lyr. How would he make it out of here? I needed him to make sure Gina was okay. Plus—I needed to know why the fuath were talking about *my* kingdom.

Melisande lunged for Lyr, piercing his shoulder with her sword.

I threw my dagger at her, catching her in the neck. Blood spurted from her throat, and she dropped to the ground.

Sadly, I was fresh out of weapons.

Lyr stumbled, blood pouring from his shoulder, just below his collarbone.

He'd shifted again—crown glowing gold, tattoos sliding over his skin like living creatures. He snarled like a wild beast, then picked up Gwydion by his throat. Blood poured from the wound in Lyr's chest.

I lunged for Melisande's body, pulling the weapon from her throat. Her blood slid off the blade onto the pavement.

We were wildly outnumbered—completely surrounded now.

Midir pointed his sword at Lyr's neck. "We will torture the truth out of you. Even if you can't die. Walk back to the fortress the way you came."

Now might be the time to unleash the attack spells I'd been keeping under wraps.

Low and under my breath, I chanted a fae spell. *Lotherus neachan angou.*

Green sea magic crackled down my arm, then shot out of the end of the dagger. I whirled, using the blade to conduct the magic with precision. I hit the knights in a wide arc of sparkling magic.

It wouldn't kill them, but it would certainly knock them on their butts for a while. When I'd flattened them all, I met Lyr's gaze.

We both turned fast for the wall. As I scrambled over the ledge, I gripped tightly to the blood-slicked blade. Just as I started to leap, a sword caught me from behind, ripping though the dress and my skin.

I tumbled forward, the wind rushing over me as I fell toward the sea. I plummeted toward the water, sinking under its surface.

I dove deeper into the cold, dark sea, clinging to the dagger with every fiber of my being. The saltwater stung my back where someone had cut me. I blocked that out, focusing on the sea. Through low vibrations in the water, I could sense the direction of Lyr's swimming. I followed after him.

I was at home in here, in the cold and the gloom. A few rays of moonlight pierced the water.

Every magical creature had its own distinct sound if you tuned in enough, and Lyr had a deep and forlorn dirge. As I moved closer to him, I saw a faint glow of gold in the dark water. We were moving fast. I doubted the other knights could keep up.

But the longer we swam, the more I started to feel Lyr losing strength. It was like his song was growing dimmer, the golden glow around him fading. Blood poured from his wound, swirling in crimson eddies around his body.

We'd stuck fairly close to the shore. Through the water, I could hear the waves crashing against the beach. As Lyr's strength began to fade, I decided to bring him onto the sand.

I swam up to Lyr until I was close enough to meet his gaze through the murky seawater. Blood coiled around him. He didn't seem to be healing very well.

Once his blue eyes were on me, I pointed at the shore. He nodded, turning to swim for the beach.

As soon as we got the chance, I wanted him to tell me *exactly* what he knew. Why they were talking about *my* kingdom? Because it had kind of seemed like he'd shut the spirits up so that I couldn't find out the truth. He'd used a sword to cut them off.

When my feet touched the rough sand, I turned to look at Lyr. He seemed to be standing okay on his own, though his eyes were unfocused as he trudged out of the water in the moonlight.

His *Ankou* state had faded, his tattoos no longer moving around him. When I glanced at the wound on his shoulder, I saw that the blade had cut clean through muscle and bone.

Injured, he was less threatening to me. But we also had to get away from the fuath. It didn't look like he'd be getting far in this state.

"I can help you." I pointed at a palm tree. "Sit down. But I want you to tell me what's going on."

He arched an eyebrow at me, then slumped down next to the palm tree.

I knelt next to him and pulled the dagger from the thigh sheath. Fast as lightning, I pressed the blade against his jugular. "You're weak now. It seems like a good time to get answers."

Glistening in the moonlight, droplets of water dappled his golden skin. "Aren't you enterprising. Please be aware that I'm only temporarily injured."

"Tell me truthfully. Is Gina safe, as far as you know? Is she in the hotel like you said?"

He held my gaze, his head pressed against the trunk of the palm. "Yes. She's safe. We made the arrangements like I promised, and only the other knights know where she is."

His steady gaze and even tone told me this was the truth.

"And why were your knights talking about *my* kingdom?"

"You have a tendency to become imperious, do you know that? It's almost enchanting." Even bleeding as he was, his voice had taken on a sensual edge.

I clenched my jaw and pressed the blade a little harder against his skin. He didn't move—not a twitch of a muscle.

"I'm imperious because I am Aenor, House of Meriadoc, Flayer of Skins, and heir to the kingdom of Ys. And more importantly, I have a knife to your throat."

CHAPTER 17

*H*e took a deep breath. "I don't know why the spirits were talking about your kingdom. We all know Ys drowned, though apparently we have different views about how it drowned. The spirits must be confused." The way he hesitated gave him away.

"You're lying." Of course he was. I hadn't known him long, but I already understood that Lyr kept the truth close to his chest.

He glanced at the dagger. "I didn't know that you could throw a knife with such skill until you hit Melisande. Your blade went right into her neck."

"Did I kill her?"

"No. You hit the back of her neck. She might be paralyzed temporarily, but she'll recover. Eventually."

"You don't seem very worried about her," I pointed out.

"She probably deserved it."

"What do you mean? I thought she was your girlfriend?"

His expression changed, now perplexed. "*Girlfriend?* What is that?"

"Your lover, I guess."

Pure confusion. "Yes. What's that got to do with anything?"

I blinked. "I don't know. What do you mean she deserved it?"

He fell quiet. "Is any of this actually important?"

A heavy sigh, and I pressed the side of the blade a little closer to his skin. "Actually, no, it isn't. I got sidetracked. Why do the fuath think I have a kingdom?"

"I also did not know you had learned any real magic or that you were capable of attack spells. I assumed that you used iron weapons because you were too dimwitted to learn the ancient fae arts of fighting and magic. You have surprised me a number of times so far."

"Speaking of being dimwitted, you are insulting someone who could make you feel a lot of pain at any second."

"Ah, but then I might never tell you about *your* kingdom, as you call it. Flayer of Skins." His velvety voice swept over my damp body. "Heal me. If I ever trust you enough, I might tell you the truth."

"Okay, at least tell me this truthfully. Do you know what the fuath are talking about, and did it make sense to you?" I demanded, losing patience.

"Yes. But that's all I'll tell you, and I don't really care if you slit my throat, because I'll return and punish you tenfold."

My mind reeled. What the hell was going on?

It was becoming clear that physical threats did not work very well on immortals. No wonder the pink-haired lady had tried seduction instead.

Slowly, I pulled the knife away, and my gaze landed on his bleeding shoulder. It looked terrible. "Why aren't you healing faster? You're a demigod."

His pale eyes bored into me. "Someone shot iron into my body and stabbed me in the hip. I still haven't recovered fully from death, and it's drained my magical powers. I can't heal all the injuries you've given me at once."

"I didn't know it was you when I stabbed you." I pulled the dagger from his throat and slid it back into the sheath on my thigh.

Lyr carefully watched the movement with a keen interest, then dragged his gaze back up to my eyes.

He breathed slowly. "We can't stay here long. The other knights will track us down. We're too close to Acre."

"I know." I touched his shoulder just above where he'd been stabbed, then whispered a spell for healing. Magic snaked down my arm and blazed over his body. I kept chanting, channeling the power of the sea god.

A smile ghosted his lips. "Good. As long as you know I have valuable information, you'll stay close to me, and help me stay clear of the fuath. Now that I know how useful you are, I think I'll really like having you close to me."

I watched as the wound in his shoulder began to close up as my magic coiled around it. "What if instead of healing you, I just tortured you with iron?"

"You wouldn't do that."

"Because you know I'm a good person?"

Another flicker of a smile. "Because you're starting to like me."

I glared at him. "Yeah, I love people who kidnap me and throw me in prison. Are all demigods as arrogant as you?"

He shrugged. "Midir and Gwydion certainly are."

"They're demigods too?"

"They're my half-brothers."

"Oh. No wonder you have to tolerate them."

The wound closed up a bit, but not as much as I would have expected. A deep, angry gash still cut across his shoulder, swollen in a way that looked like it was about to open up at any moment.

"It's not working that well."

"It's the iron in my blood. But it's good enough. We need to get back into the ocean."

I shook my head. "No, that's just going to burst open again."

I stood and searched our surroundings—a fancy hotel stood just to our right, windows blazing with gold light. Gods, it would be amazing to have a night in there right now.

I mean, not with Lyr.

Just in general.

In any case, we had no money, and the hotel porters weren't about to admit two bleeding fae for free.

Son of a gun.

Lyr rose, and the wind whipped the cloak around his shoulders. "We will need to move around like humans. I will take one of their vehicles and drive it."

My eyes flicked to the parking lot. It wasn't the worst idea. If we had a car, we'd be able to get out of here much faster...

"I guess you don't think stealing is that illegal."

He shrugged. "Depends what it is."

"I have an idea."

"Explain."

"Just trust me," I said.

"I actually don't trust you at all. I thought that had been established."

"Right." I started walking. "You ever wanted to learn how to hotwire a car?"

"No." The sea breeze sent droplets of water rolling over his golden skin.

I winced at the sharp pain in my back where the sword had caught me. Lyr's eyes slid to me, catching my grimace. "Turn around. You're hurt."

"Don't we have to go fast?"

"It will only take a second."

I turned my back to him, and he brushed his hand lightly over my back. Warmth rippled through me, sensual and electric at the same time. Goosebumps rose over my sea-damp skin.

I closed my eyes, giving in to the pleasure of his healing magic that slipped over my wet body like silk. My pulse sped up, and my nipples tightened under the thin fabric of my dress.

Abruptly, I stepped forward. "That's probably enough."

I glanced at him, and his blue eyes looked keen enough to see into my soul...

"We can head to the hotel parking lot." I glanced behind us. I didn't see any possessed knights crawling from the ocean, ready to slaughter us for the secrets to my kingdom.

I just had no idea what that meant. Nothing had survived of Ys. I'd been back there myself. In the first few years after Ys sank, I visited it often. The towers had crumbled. The gold lay under marble. Our famous bells had cracked open. Enterprising thieves could have found a way to pry the jewels from the temple walls, deep under the ocean.

I'd stolen many things in my life, but I could never bring myself to steal from Ys. It felt like grave-robbing.

All I knew was that the kingdom was gone. So what the fuath meant about looking for my kingdom—I had no idea.

We crossed into a dark parking lot, where a streetlight lit up the cars. I picked one that had no car seats in it. I also chose the oldest-looking car in the lot, hoping it wouldn't be fitted with any kind of security systems and that the hotwiring would work roughly as it had decades ago. It was a small, beat-up piece of crap.

"Humans track cars by the license plates, so disguising it is step one," I said.

"Can you do that?"

Luckily, I knew a spell to scramble things up. I closed my eyes, trying to remember the words I'd spoken when I'd turned all my books into gibberish. Then, I stared at the license plate and whispered a spell to rearrange the numbers. I slid the two behind the seven, the seven after the four. And *voila*, no one would recognize this car as stolen.

Assuming I managed to steal it. I hadn't actually tried to hotwire a car since the nineteen-seventies, and I believed cars had changed a bit since then.

I crossed to the driver's seat. "Now we just have to unlock it." I rubbed a knot in my forehead. "I vaguely remember an unlocking spell, but it's a bit rusty, and even on a good day it takes a few hours."

"We don't have a few hours. How do the locking mechanisms work?" he asked.

"You use a key. But without that… I think there's something with like, a coat hanger you can slip in to get the door open…" We didn't have a coat hanger. "Or a wedge."

Lyr stood next to me, edging me out of the way. Without another word, he slammed his fist through the window, shattering the glass.

Immediately, an alarm blared, deafening me. *Son of a gun.*

Lyr frowned at the car, then crossed to the front to lift up the hood. "What's that noise coming from?"

"The alarm," I shouted.

He managed to find the alarm speaker with surprising efficiency, stopping the noise by ripping it out. He dropped it on the pavement. The car still made a sort of buzzing sound, but it wasn't loud.

"How do I drive it?" he asked.

"You don't." I pointed at the passenger seat. "You sit there. I'll drive."

"Are you giving me orders?"

"Yes." I slid into the driver's seat and stared at the steering wheel. "I'm just going to need you to use that raw physical strength again to rip off the bottom of the steering wheel, because I don't have a screwdriver."

He narrowed his eyes at me, then leaned over and punched the plastic cover of the steering column so that it split. Then, he worked his fingers into the crack and pulled off the broken plastic.

"Perfect." I reached in, pulling out three bundles of wires.

I chewed my lip, trying to remember what was what. One set of these led to the battery…

Lyr inhaled deeply, which I was certain was impatience.

Then, he added, "They're coming."

Shit. "I don't suppose any of them have a car, do they?"

"No, none of the knights know how to drive."

"Right, the World Key. Opening portals. Good. They won't be able to catch us."

"The speed at which we're moving suggests otherwise."

"Stop talking." If I could remember which one was the ignition…

Brown, I thought. *Usually* brown, though you really needed the manual, and without it, I could potentially electrocute myself.

"They are within half a kilometer," said Lyr. "And we are sitting still in a vehicle with a broken window."

"Shhhhh…"

I twisted together what I *thought* were the battery wires. Then, I connected the brown to the yellow, and—

The headlights turned on, and the radio began playing an old Nirvana song. "Yes!" Air conditioning blasted out of the vents.

"You've got the music on," said Lyr. "But we're not moving."

No gratitude. "I need to get the engine on." I breathed in

and out slowly, stripping the tip of the wires. "And this part could kill me."

"Let me do it then."

"Shhh."

"They're on the beach, just behind us now."

When I'd carefully exposed the tips of the wires, I touched the battery wire to the starter wire.

The engine ignited. "Yes!" I revved it a few times. "Get your seatbelt on."

CHAPTER 18

"Seat-belt?"

An irritating beeping noise in the car set my teeth on edge.

"I barely know how to drive," I said. "You're going to wear the seatbelt."

I hit the gas, and we lurched onto a road lined by palm trees. There weren't too many cars on the road, and I stared at the lines, trying to stay between them.

"What's that beeping?" asked Lyr.

I glanced at the dashboard, where a red light glowed— showing a figure with a seatbelt. "That's the car telling you to put your seatbelt on."

He reached for the belt, fumbling as he figured out how to connect it. When he clicked it, the beeping went quiet.

Cold air blasted my wet body, and my teeth chattered. Not only was the AC blasting, but the wind whipped at me through the shattered window. My hair flew into my eyes, and I shook my head to get it out.

"Can you turn down the air conditioner? The cold air?"

Lyr jabbed at the dashboard, but the cold air kept blasting.

The headlights of another car were coming at us faster than I would have liked, and I veered to the right, panicking a bit. The side of our stolen car scraped against a concrete barrier, and adrenaline shot through my nerves. This was possibly scarier than facing the possessed fuath.

"These streets are not big enough," I muttered. "It's ridiculous."

"Why is it that you know how to steal a car, but not to drive one?" he asked.

"I had a brief stint in the seventies as a car thief. But I didn't have to drive them far. I just dropped them off at an empty lot near an abandoned railroad, and someone would strip them for parts, or... I have no idea, actually. All I know is I got a few hundred bucks for each car."

"I understand. You've spent a hundred years breaking laws."

"I don't see you objecting to this lawbreaking right now. We're in a stolen car."

At that moment, I felt an unwelcome sting around my thighs and rear, like my skin had been lacerated. I sucked in a sharp breath at the pain. "I just realized I'm sitting on broken glass." With all the adrenaline flowing, I hadn't felt it till then.

"I'll heal you when we stop."

An image flashed in my mind of his hands on my thighs again, and my legs clenched. "I can do it myself." It came out sounding a little angry.

"You're very tense sometimes."

I glanced at the dashboard. A packet of bubblegum lay on the top of it. *That's* what I needed. "Lyr. I need a favor."

"Oh really?"

I gripped the wheel with white knuckles. "I need you to

pick up that pink packet, unwrap a piece of gum, and pop it in my mouth. Please."

He did as I asked, and I opened my mouth. He popped in a stick of gum, and I started chewing. Finally, I began to relax. "Thanks."

When the song on the radio changed, I felt like the gods were blessing me. *Can't Help Falling in Love* began playing.

"Can you turn this up?"

"This music is terrible."

I popped a bubble. "You shut your godsdamn mouth, or so help me Elvis, I will shoot you again with iron bullets."

"You like this?"

"Elvis is the god of music."

"El-vis." He said the name like he'd never heard it before. "I haven't heard of this god."

"I touched his shirt once." I giggled, then focused on the road again. "You should probably stop distracting me while I'm driving."

I glanced at him quickly out of the corner of my eye and saw a smile curling the corner of his lips. "I thought you hated men."

"Not *all* men. There are exceptions. Elvis being one of them. And the Horseman of Death is nicer than you'd imagine, given his title."

"Is that right?"

I was beginning to relax a little, although my eyes were still locked on the road. I wondered how long I could go without blinking before I'd go blind.

It didn't look like there was much around here. Palm trees. A road. Some shrubs. "Do you know where we are? Or where we're going?"

"We're just south of Acre, and we need to find a place to hide while I can heal myself properly. My spirit needs to go into the death realm. We need to find an empty human habitation where we will be safe while I do it. And you'll likely need sleep."

"Likely at some point." My hands were sweating on the steering wheel. "Speaking of healing... Why did you tell your brothers that I healed my own head in the prison? I didn't."

He closed his eyes and settled back into his seat. Wind rushed in the car, whipping his long hair around him. "If I'd shown any softness toward you, they would have found ways to torment you more harshly. In the days after Ys fell, I was the only one who defended you before I changed my mind. They still think my mind was warped."

So the lie had been... protective of me. That was a surprise, and yet he'd also thrown me into a freezing pit with my arms tied behind my back, so I wouldn't be warming to him too much.

Another car came toward us on the opposite side of the road, and my stomach tensed.

I couldn't look at the signs, because I was concentrating too hard on trying to stay on the road without hitting the concrete barrier.

I breathed in deeply, trying to think clearly as the air conditioner blasted over my wet dress.

As my mind quieted for a few moments, the words of the fuath returned to me. *Your kingdom...*

I stared at the headlights on the dark road. Lyr had defended me at one point, and now he no longer trusted me. "So what changed your opinion of me, Lyr? At one point you thought no daughter of Queen Malgven would ruin her kingdom."

"I saw you in London once. After Ys fell. At that moment, I was sure that truly your father's blood ran in your veins. It was clear you had to indulge every base and cruel pleasure that excited you."

I popped a bubble. "You think I'm like my father? I could kill you for that comment."

"Of course you could. You're driven by bloodlust, just like he was."

Oh boy. I had some bad days after the fall of Ys. The loss of my sea powers felt like my soul had been cut right out of my chest. I felt strangely empty, like I'd already died but my body kept stubbornly living on. I was a shell of a person. And if I'd been unfit to rule Ys at twenty-five, I was far worse after it sank. I went through a gin phase and slept in hovels. I spent time around the worst sort of humans. And when I avenged crimes against other women, it wasn't always pretty.

The tension returned to my body, and I gripped the steering wheel hard. "What exactly did you see me doing that was so terrible?"

"I saw you standing over a body, bathed in blood, and pulling out someone's heart. A human heart. Not even a demon worthy of fighting."

"That's, that's..." *Entirely possible.* "I'm sure I had a good reason."

In the early days, when I'd first arrived in Victorian London, there were some *bad* men around. Men who killed prostitutes and poor children. I'd been there to clean them up.

But I could see how it looked bad. I had to wonder why he'd let me live at all. A rogue fae, covered in human blood.

"Until that point," he added, "I was sure you were as noble and strong as your mother."

I felt my heart squeeze. "Why were you so devoted to my mother? You're a demigod—why defer to a fae queen?"

"Your mother killed someone I loathed."

"Who?"

"Your father." His blue eyes opened a crack, and he looked at me.

"Ah, yes. Lots of people hated him. That was her favorite bedtime story for me. It was how she put me to sleep every night. A lullaby, then the story about the time she murdered my dad."

"I want to hear it."

I sighed. I knew it by heart, so it wouldn't even distract me from my death grip on the steering wheel. "On her wedding day, she dressed in beautiful gossamer, with a crown of pearls and cockleshells on her head. Just before the ceremony, my father showed up to find her."

Sometimes, when I talked about the old days, my accent shifted back. I lost the American twang, started to sound a little Cornish again.

"She was madly in love with my father: Gradlon, the King of Ys," I went on. "So she was happy to see him, even though it was bad luck before the wedding. She was pregnant with me, already showing. Except he wasn't there for love. He'd already found a new lover—a younger and prettier one. A richer one. And he didn't want a child anyway. What if I took his throne one day? What if I was a boy? So he put his hands around my mother's throat, and he tried to take off her head with his bare hands."

Silence filled the car for a moment.

"But my mother killed him instead. She cut his heart out with a dagger, and left it on the banquet table, where it dried out. She left his bones there, as well. She took his crown, his armies, and ruled Ys. She presided over the golden age of Ys —the best art, the most prosperity. And she never took off her wedding dress, stained with his blood. She raised me with one lesson burned into my mind. Don't trust anyone— but especially don't trust men. At the time, I thought she was mistaken. But when I got to London in the 1800s, I saw things that would make even your blood curdle."

Lyr was listening attentively.

"And that's how I knew my mother was right. There are wolves all around us. Wolves who'd kill you as soon as they got the chance." And that's why I'd be keeping the dagger as close to me as possible. Because sometimes, the wolves were very beautiful indeed. "And why did you hate my dad so deeply? Besides the fact that he was a psycho?"

But Lyr didn't answer. Instead, he closed his eyes, seeming to retreat into himself. Pretending to sleep, perhaps.

I stared at the dark road ahead of me. The more we talked about the old days of Ys, the more I longed for my former powers. That long-buried hunger was stirring again, the lust for power.

Yesterday, I hadn't known the Athame of Meriadoc existed. Now, I wanted nothing more than to possess it, to feel its power charging my body.

* * *

I PASSED about ten gas stations, a few factories, but I wasn't going to find a human habitation as long as I stayed on the main road. So after a half hour of driving, I turned off the main road.

The buildings in this town all looked alike—square and concrete apartment buildings. Balconies jutted beneath small windows, and laundry hung from them in the open air.

I drove slowly along the road. Some of the windows had metal grates over them to keep out burglars. Humans cared about security, but they were often careless. If I was patient enough, I'd find someone who'd left a door or a window open.

I rolled along the street slowly, scanning the balcony doors for open just a crack.

A car pulled up behind me, honking frantically. *Apparently* I was driving too slowly.

I cursed under my breath and took a left, hoping that I'd suddenly turn onto a street with a dark, comfortable home and an open door.

Instead, I found the next best thing.

On the right side of the road, construction had stopped for the night on a tall apartment building. Now that was as perfect as we were going to get. No doors to stop us.

I rolled over the rubble outside, pulling up next to some rows of concrete blocks. There wasn't much light here. In a ground-floor apartment across the street, a TV glowed blue through one of the windows, and a streetlight flickered above us.

A woman stood outside the apartment, smoking. But her eyes were on the ground, and she wasn't paying any attention to us. She flicked her cigarette, and a tear rolled down her cheek.

I touched Lyr's leg to wake him. It took a moment for his eyes to open, then he stared at my hand on his thigh.

I yanked it away. "Good. You're still alive. I found us a spot to rest and heal."

He frowned at the empty building. "It will suffice."

"Great, because we don't have tons of options."

The car door creaked when I opened it, and I winced as the glass in my rear tore at my skin. I tugged up my damp dress as I stepped out of the car so I wouldn't trip on it, ragged as it was. I looked over my shoulder at my backside, and I saw blood streaking down my thighs where the glass had ripped my skin, staining the blue fabric. The blood-stained gown reminded me of Mama.

I grimaced as I started hobbling into the building. How *was* I going to deal with the shattered-glass-in-my-bum situation? I could heal myself reasonably well, but not until I got the glass shards out.

When I glanced at Lyr, I saw that he was in much worse

shape than I was, and the gash across his shoulder had split open a bit. The black bullet hole still marked the center of his chest, just over his heart. I felt an unwelcome sense of guilt for shooting him.

Before we crossed through the empty doorway, I glanced back across the street. The smoking woman still wasn't paying us any attention. A bruise darkened the skin beneath her eye.

Wolves...

I turned away from her, crossing into the chilly building. I didn't see a man around, but if I had to guess, someone she loved had hit her. Or someone she used to love.

In over a century, I'd met so many human women on the streets. So many like Gina, trapped in terrible lives. I tried to make my shop a refuge for them. Sometimes they moved on to another guy. Sometimes they stayed with me. But human lives didn't last long.

I hugged myself as we crossed toward a stairwell in the darkened building. *Never let your guard down, Aenor. Don't believe the beautiful lies that spill from the lips of beautiful men.*

Talking about Ys had stirred up memories of my mother. It was like she'd come alive again, and she was whispering in my mind.

We climbed a few floors of the concrete building. Lyr was practically dragging himself up the stairs, trailing blood at an alarming rate, but he didn't complain.

After a few flights, we found an empty room tucked inside, no windows to let the wind in.

It felt lonely in here, and I missed Gina.

As soon as I could get my hands on a reflective surface, I'd see if I could get a glimpse of her.

Time to find out if this beautiful and terrifying man was telling the truth at all.

CHAPTER 19

*I*n the empty apartment, Lyr sat cross-legged in the center of the room. "I'll need to heal myself before I can heal you. I'll need to transform into my Ankou form. You might not want to watch."

"Why?"

"I've been told it's terrifying in its purest form."

"So when I saw you transform before—that wasn't your purest form?"

"No."

Well *that* sparked my curiosity. I wanted to get to a mirror to check on Gina, but first, I wanted to get a glimpse of the true Ankou.

Lyr rested his hands on his knees and straightened his back. His body started to glow like a dying sun, tingeing the air around him with gold. His pale hair wafted around his head like he was underwater.

As his crown grew longer and sharper, dark claws grew from his fingertips. Golden tattoos began snaking around his body, and I caught my breath. His magic reverberated over my skin like a dark warning.

My stomach swooped. Instinct alone had me turning away from him.

I crossed into the next room, eager to get a glimpse of Gina. This room had holes where windows would go.

Scanning the floor, I searched for something shiny I could use as a scrying mirror. After a moment, I found a broken metal rod lying in the corner. It looked like part of a towel rack or something—reflective enough that I could see my own face clearly in it. In just a few moments, I'd know if Lyr was lying to me about Gina.

I picked up the bar from the floor. I winced. Every time I moved or shifted too much, I could feel the glass digging in a little deeper.

Ignoring the pain, I held up the metal bar to the moonlight, and I whispered the spell for scrying. My heartbeat sped up, and I thought of Gina—her dark eyes, her wild curls. Her habit of sitting on the floor to do her homework. When I opened my eyes again—I saw her there, reflected in the metal.

She sat slumped against a stack of large white pillows in a room with gold walls and lights. She was watching TV, eating something. It was hard to see in this tiny bit of metal, but I thought it was an omelet maybe. She licked her fingers.

So *that's* what the Savoy looked like. White and gold. Better than I'd imagined, even.

Gods, I wanted to be there.

I let the spell ripple away, relief washing over me. Gina was safe. Lyr had been telling the truth. Things were not as dire as they could be.

Outside, thunder rumbled over the horizon. The hair on the back of my arms stood on end, and I didn't know if it was the charge of an oncoming storm, or Lyr's magic.

When I crossed back into the windowless room, my heart

skipped a beat. The Ankou in his true form left me breathless with awe.

Sublime.

It was the closest word in English to convey a concept unique to the fae: the terrifying beauty of the gods. Horror and perfection mingling together, demanding devotion.

The sight of him stoked a primal fear in my mind, part of me desperate to run from him. *Monsters lurk among men,* my mother's voice whispered in my memories. *He will destroy you. Kill him before he kills you.*

Another part of me just felt compelled to worship him. My knees felt weak, like they were pulling me down to the concrete floor. The gold around him grew brighter, and I could see his scars healing before my eyes.

I knew I was watching something not meant for the eyes of ordinary fae like me. It was dizzying, really. Watching him felt like a violation. I was trespassing on the true face of a god.

Lightning cracked the sky outside, then a loud boom of thunder that shook the walls. Rain started hammering the building.

Shadows snaked around Lyr, ensconcing his golden glow, and his white-gold hair wafted around his head. But his body remained still as the concrete beneath him.

I wasn't going to kneel, even if I wanted to. If he opened his eyes to find me kneeling before him, I'd have to throw myself out of the building to save myself from the embarrassment.

Think of not-divine things, Aenor.

Baking shows. Spanx. Dogs eating old Cheerios out of a baby stroller. Old men shuffling along boardwalks licking ice cream cones.

And yet the beautiful vision blazed before me like a holy fire.

I ripped my gaze away from him, and crossed back into the next room. With each step I took, I winced at the tiny bits of shattered glass in my backside and thighs.

Cold rain started slanting into the room, and I stared down at the apartments across from us. The smoking woman had gone inside, but a car had pulled up out front. Rain now soaked the clothing she'd hung out on clotheslines.

Something about the way the car was parked bothered me—completely crooked, half on the sidewalk. The person who'd parked it was either drunk or in a serious rush.

Then, the distant sound of shouting tightened my chest. It was a man's voice, bellowing in another language—Hebrew, I supposed. The woman shouted back at him from inside her apartment.

I took a step closer to the window, watching as the woman flung open the door and rushed out onto the rainy sidewalk. She was young. Twenty, maybe?

Then—her *friend* followed after her. He wasn't tall, but he was muscular. He wore a black T-shirt with dollar signs all over it, and a Yankees cap pulled down low. He looked like he was about to start something nasty.

I hiked up my dress and pulled the knife out of the holster.

Halfway down the sidewalk, the man grabbed her by the ponytail and pulled her down to the ground. She screamed as he started dragging her back to the house by her hair. Caveman style.

For a split second, I considered just killing him. I could do it from here—toss the knife, aim it for his heart. But then I'd be leaving behind one very traumatized woman with a murder charge on her hands.

I turned from the window, hiking up my dress to run through the empty apartment—past the glowing death god himself. My wet flats slapped against the concrete stairs as I rushed down, bounding to the lowest floor. The woman's panicked screams filled the air as I rushed outside.

Fury blazed in me as I watched the man force his victim inside the apartment. He slammed the door shut behind them. My fingers twitched, but I slid the dagger away in its holster. I didn't think I'd need it.

Their shouting penetrated the door. I crossed to it and lifted the hem of my dress. I kicked the door, again and again, hitting it near the doorknob until the wood splintered and broke. One more kick, and the door was open.

Both of the humans stared at me, stunned.

The man had pinned the woman to the wall. Her lip was swollen and bleeding, tears streaking her face. Her hair and clothes were wet. The man looked like he'd been trying to pull down her jeans, but hadn't gotten far with her belt on. He gripped her by the back of her neck, like she was a wild animal. I took a step closer.

Mom was always right. Monsters lurk among men.

I lunged forward. "Hi, friend." I pulled him off the woman, then gripped him by the throat, slamming him against the wall. He started to kick me in a rage, but the enchantment took hold within moments.

Without a comb and water, enchantment was a difficult task for me. Melisande had been brilliant at it. The more sophisticated and intelligent your victim was, the harder it was for me.

Without my Morgen tools, I was not particularly good at it. I could enchant only the very dumbest of humans.

My Yankees fan here was perfect.

"Do you understand English?" I asked.

He nodded.

"Good. I need you to go out into your car, and drive away, and never return here. And what's more, you will never touch another woman again."

His eyes were bulging now, but he nodded. I dropped him, and he stumbled toward the ruined door, pushing past the broken wood. When the man had fled, I was surprised to see Lyr out there—standing on the pavement in the rain.

How long had Lyr been watching me?

I glanced back at the woman. Beer soaked her clothes and hair, and her body was shaking. She looked me up and down —taking in my wet dress, streaked with blood. I probably looked worse than she did, but at least no one had dumped beer on me.

She was simply staring at me, her hands shaking.

I crossed to the door. I closed my eyes and whispered a spell for mending wooden objects—piecing it together, one broken shard at a time. When I'd finished, I walked out of the apartment, turned the doorknob to close the door, and crossed into the street.

Lyr's golden eyes were on me, and his body tinged the air around him with amber. He'd taken off his cloak altogether and now stood in the rain, shirtless. He looked more like himself again—less godlike.

"You didn't have to come out," I said.

"I started to sense that we were being watched, but I couldn't find anything."

I looked down the darkened street, but I couldn't see anything amiss.

"Why did you come out here?" he asked.

We started crossing the road, heading for the empty apartment again. "Because that woman's boyfriend was beating her up, and I wanted it to stop."

He frowned at me, his expression curious. "You're not what I—"

Then, he froze, his entire body taking on the stillness of a wild animal. He held out a hand, motioning for me to stop. He sniffed the air. A chill skittered over my skin.

I couldn't see anything in the darkness. But I could hear raspy breathing coming from somewhere around us. I sniffed the air, too, breathing in the scent of marsh air, moss, and rotten ferns.

Gwyllion.

Gwyllion were fae that I knew from Ys, and they definitely weren't native to Israel. They were creatures of the night, scared off by the sun. But in darkness, they were vicious beasts.

I reached down and pulled the dagger from its holster. This would be a perfect time for an *iron* weapon, but I supposed I didn't want to be responsible for any more souls trapped in hell eternally.

The rotten scent of the gwyllion grew stronger, and dread cut through my bones. These ancient monsters were the stalkers of the fae realm. They often camped out behind rocks, just watching. But they could move *startlingly* fast when they needed to, tearing out throats with their teeth. They could gnaw a person down to bony twigs faster than one heartbeat.

I turned, and my gaze landed on a set of gray eyes, and tangled gray hair falling in front of a bony face. My heart slammed against my ribs.

I whispered an attack spell, and magic sparked down my arm, charging the blade. The gwyllion leapt for me, but a blast of magic knocked her back. Still, the spell didn't kill her, and she snarled from the pavement.

A gwyllion shot from the shadows, latching onto Lyr's neck. But just as I started to charge the dagger with magic again, one of them snatched my arm, claws digging into my flesh. I sliced her wizened throat with the blade, and dark blood poured out.

From the darkness, a large, male gwyllion knocked me to the ground. He pinned down my wrists, claws cutting into my skin. The glass still in my backside tore at my flesh. The gwyllion squeezed my wrist so hard I thought he might be breaking the bones. The knife clattered out of my hand, and I gasped.

The gwyllion's wide gray eyes hovered just inches above my face, and his wiry beard tickled my skin.

"Beautiful one... just like her." His breath could kill flowers.

"Who are you working for?" I asked.

"We need to know how get to Nova Ys." He started to thrust his hips back and forth over mine, which made me want to vomit. "Beautiful…"

Nova Ys?

Well, well, well. *This* was the interesting secret that Lyr had been keeping from me.

CHAPTER 20

The gwyllion grabbed my breast hard, claws digging in, and I snarled.

Lyr ripped him off me, his features furious as a wrathful god. His eyes burned with gold, canines bared.

I scrambled back, scanning the darkness. I didn't see any other signs of movement.

I looked up at Lyr, who was speaking quietly in Ancient Fae. Using his magic, he'd suspended the ancient gwyllion in the air. I gaped as the gwyllion's chest exploded, blood and bits of bone spraying from his gaping ribs. The corpse dropped to the ground, and I choked down my nausea.

I rolled onto my hands and knees, shifting off the shattered glass. I wanted to be sick. I retched for a moment, then looked up at Lyr from the ground.

He stared down at me, his pale hair wafting around him, body glowing with gold. The bodies of six gwyllion lay around him, most with their chests exploded. *Unsettling.* I hadn't even seen some of them creep out of the shadows before Lyr had killed them. Catching my breath, I crawled a few inches to reach for the knife that I'd dropped.

"They're all gone," he said. "I don't smell any living gwyllion."

"You could have let that last one live long enough for us to question him."

"He angered me." His voice sounded distant, and he crossed to the clothesline outside the woman's apartment, the clothes now soaked with rain. He yanked a large, red soccer T-shirt off the line, and pulled it over his head.

Slowly, I rose to my feet, still holding tight to the hilt of the knife.

I let the rain wash the gwyllion blood off. "Are you sure they're all gone?"

"Yes."

I hobbled a little as I walked, the glass in my body now deeply uncomfortable. "What's *Nova Ys*? The gwyllion said he was looking for Nova Ys."

"It's not your concern."

"Are you kidding? Not my concern?" I slid the dagger into the sheath on my thigh. Lyr was watching the move very closely, body glowing with gold. "Is that my arm sheath that you have wrapped around your thigh?"

"Yep. So?"

"It's practically cutting off your circulation."

"It's fine." It actually bothered me that he'd never asked for it back. He just let me steal his weapon from him. *That's* how much he did not see me as a threat.

I started marching back to the empty apartment.

Was there a new kingdom—a Nova Ys? Lyr wore a crown. Had he crowned himself? King of my freaking kingdom?

He might be a demigod, but he was not the heir to the crown of Ys. *I* was.

As we climbed the dark stairwell, the golden glow from his body lit the way.

When we crossed into the room, he sniffed the air. He said, "You're still bleeding. Worse now."

Now that the adrenaline was wearing off, the pain from all the glass cuts was coming roaring back. I needed healing. Then, I needed to sleep for, like, eight days. And *after* I slept, I needed to punch Lyr in the face until he told me the truth.

"Yeah, I'm bleeding. I still have a whole bunch of glass in me from when you smashed the window and I sat on it."

"Take off your clothes and lie down. I need to get the glass out."

As if I'd just strip off in front of this usurper. *More glass,* as Giles Corey would say.

I narrowed my eyes at him, crossing my arms. "You have another kingdom, don't you? You stole my crown. King of Nova Ys."

"It's not your kingdom, considering you drowned the last one. Take off your clothes. I need to heal you."

"So there *is* a new kingdom. And no, I'm not taking off anything in front of you—*usurper.* Are you the one who made up that story about me drowning the kingdom, so you could take what was mine?"

"No. I already told you. I didn't even believe it at first. Take off your clothes—the smell of your blood sickens and infuriates me."

"You have a wonderful bedside manner for a healer."

He *did* look angry. "Lie down on the floor on your front."

I took a step back from him, my shoulders resting against the wall. Then, I pulled out the dagger again.

I shook my head, my fingers tight on the hilt of the knife. "You gave up on me for no reason at all. Because of some rumors and an… unfortunate situation where I removed a human's heart. Give me specifics about that particular scene."

"The fact that you require specifics suggests to me that this is something you did many times."

I pointed the dagger at him. "You just made five hearts explode in a storm of blood and bone. So we both have a violent side. The question is whether or not it's justified. That's why I'm asking for specifics."

"It was over a hundred years ago." His crown—the *stolen* crown—blazed with gold. "I don't remember specifics. Just that I found you in an alleyway, ripping a man's organs out from between his ribs."

I didn't normally eviscerate people when I killed them, but I *had* done it at least once. I remembered this one vividly because he'd been one of the first.

Everyone remembered that man. They still talked about him, trying to figure out who he was. Was he a prince? A freemason? A butcher? They didn't know his name. To humans, he was a Nameless One, just like mine.

"Was he wearing a deerstalker cap?" I asked.

"I don't remember," said Lyr. "Frankly, I was more focused on the organs you were removing than his sartorial choices."

"Near Fashion Street in Spitalfields. Just before the sun rose."

"It's possible. Yes, it was just before the sun rose. Near Spitalfields."

"Right. He was the first recipient of my vigilante justice. A guy named Sam. He'd just finished slaughtering the fifth and final woman he'd ever kill. Mary was a friend of mine. And you should have seen the state she was in when he was finished with her. I assure you, it was much messier than what I did to him. And the police were never going to find him. They didn't have a damn clue. So I killed him, and I moved to Tennessee. He never killed another woman."

This seemed to silence Lyr. He cocked his head as he stared at me, evaluating if I was telling the truth.

"They always talked about how he killed prostitutes," I

went on. "But it's not the real story. I mean, they were prostitutes, yes, but that's not all they were. They were just people who'd done what they needed to do to survive. Mary was ridiculously funny. She used to do a wicked imitation of a naughty vicar on a seaside vacation. And I was teaching her to read. And then one of her customers, a psychopath named Sam, tore out her insides for no reason at all. So I had to put an end to his little hobby. Humans still talk about him, in fact. That's how terrifying he was. They call him Jack the Ripper, although his name wasn't Jack."

"So you had a reason to kill him," he said at last. "Assuming you're telling the truth." The way he said this last part suggested to me that he wasn't assuming that at all.

Then, he glanced at the open window. "But you're not exactly as I expected. You seem to care about protecting weak people. You don't seem like the sort to drown your own kingdom out of spite."

"I'm not. And I didn't know the rule about spirits."

"Your *father* knew the rule."

"I never even met him, Lyr. Apart from the constant lessons from my mother, I was sheltered. All the courtiers kept me sheltered. I just thought my mother was nuts till I got out into the real world. I never saw death, or poverty, or sickness. And I definitely didn't know about a dark, evil fae who would drown a kingdom, but apparently no one else knew about him either. But that is what happened to Ys. I remember him. He killed my mother. I was there."

Lyr took a step closer, pressing his hands against the wall as he stared down at me. "You are telling me the truth? Another fae drowned the kingdom?"

"Yes." I smacked one of his arms away. "I remember him that day. I just don't know what he looks like."

"Who is he? Why haven't you been hunting him if he stole your power?"

"Two reasons. One, I don't know who he was. He appeared just like a bluish white light. He smelled like fae, but he looked like—like a star. I heard his voice. He spoke in the fae language, though his accent sounded ancient. He told my mother he was there to kill her, and then her head came off, like it had been sliced with an invisible sword. *Then* the island started to sink."

Lyr's jaw tightened. "And what's the other reason you haven't hunted him down?"

"He stole my power, so I have no capacity for revenge, even if I knew who he was. What am I going to do? Stab him with a stupid dagger? His power was immense."

Like yours...

"And you have no idea what he looked like?" asked Lyr.

I shook my head. "No idea. He just looked like light. And as the island was sinking..."

I trailed off as the memory blazed in my mind, so vivid it was like a movie replaying. I stood before him, and the Nameless One burned with blue light like a star. His magic seeped into my mouth like seawater, filling my lungs. When he ripped his magic out again, he took mine with it. I thought I was dead.

"It felt like he'd stolen my soul," I said at last. "The ground was rumbling, the floor cracking. The palace breaking apart. My mother's head rolled on the ground. The water was rising through the cracks in the floor. The marble columns tipped over, smashing her head open, but she was already dead. And then—the sea swallowed us whole. I sank beneath the sea's surface, and I just let myself sink because my chest was so empty I was certain I no longer existed. I'd become a hollow shell, completely alone in the dark."

I realized I was shaking—and gripping the knife so hard my hand hurt.

I wiped a tear off my cheek. "I just remember that he was there like a star. And then my heart broke."

I felt the old emptiness welling inside me.

"I can see that you're telling the truth."

I glared at him. "And I can see that you're hiding things. So tell me about Nova Ys."

"After I heal you. Your blood is a distraction."

"You sound like a vampire."

He shook his head. "I don't want to drink it. It bothers me. Without your powers you seem breakable."

Breakable. My chest ached to have my old powers back.

Chilly wind rushed in through the windows, bringing the rain with it. I still didn't want to pull off my dress in front of him. He couldn't see me naked. And it wasn't just modesty. I *really* didn't want him to see the demon names carved into my stomach. "There's got to be another way to do this."

He quirked an eyebrow. "Your modesty borders on neurosis."

"I just need to keep my guard up around you. You seem like you could be unhinged."

"*I* seem unhinged?"

"Your whole death god thing. The moving tattoos. The exploding hearts. The claws."

Shadows danced around him, like darkness was trying to claim him. "In the Ankou state, my primitive side takes over a little. But I can keep it under control."

I pointed at him. "I knew it. Unhinged."

I felt a magnetic pull between us that bothered me.

For a moment, I wondered what his *primitive* side would do when he had a woman lying naked before him, and my thoughts filled with base desires that were foreign to me.

Then, I pushed the thought away again, keeping a death grip on the hilt of my knife. *Wolves, Aenor.*

CHAPTER 21

My pulse started to race as I tried to resist the strange pull between us. "Before you heal me, we should protect ourselves against the fuath. At any moment, spirits could come flying in here, and there's nothing to guard us from them. There's a protection against the curse."

"And you know it?" he asked.

"I might be able to remember it." With my shoulders against the concrete wall, I closed my eyes, trying to remember how it looked in the ancient curse book. It was a fae rune... I tried to imagine the shop vividly—how it smelled of dried herbs, the sound of Elvis on the crackling record player, Gina sitting on the countertop eating Pop-Tarts. I'd sit by the bookshelves and pore over the curse book, looking for something good...

On the page about the fuath, someone had drawn an image of a human eating another person to illustrate possession. Blood dripped down the man's chin. It was one of those weird medieval drawings where people had really calm, bored facial expressions while something horrific was happening.

On the opposite page, there were instructions about protecting your loved ones with your blood. The picture—now I could see it so vividly in my mind's eye. It looked like a sort of sharp flower with triangular petals.

I opened my eyes. "I've got it," I said. "Once we do this, the fuath won't be able to possess our bodies. But this is about to get a little weird. And you need to take off your shirt."

He did as he was told, dropping his T-shirt on the floor. My gaze swept over his muscled, warrior's body, glistening from the rainwater.

Now, that tug between us felt even stronger.

"We need blood from each of us." I pricked my fingertip with the tip of the dagger, then handed the blade to him. Droplets of blood pooled on my finger.

Then, I painted on his chest. His skin was silky smooth, with steel underneath. I stroked the symbol over his chest—around the blackened bullet hole—the dark heart of the sun.

When I'd finished, he looked down at it.

Was this perhaps a sign of trust? He'd just let me mark him with my blood, using a magical symbol that could be anything.

I pulled the neckline of my dress open. "Now you need to do the same thing with your blood. See? I told you it was weird."

Lyr jabbed himself with the dagger—probably harder than he needed to, his body beaming with gold for a moment. He painted me with his blood, and it dripped down my chest. He copied the symbol, and as he did, magic shivered over my skin.

I wasn't entirely clear about the logistics beyond this. If the blood washed off, did we have to reapply, or did this last forever? The ancient texts often left out helpful details like that.

Lyr finished with a precise swoop of red, then his eyes met mine. "What other curses do you know about?"

I shrugged. "I memorized a whole book of them. So, you'll have to be more specific. Some of them had to do with blighting crops, drying up cow's milk, causing venereal diseases. Exactly what kind of curse are you dealing with?"

"I can't always control the Ankou state as well as I once could. It comes and goes when I don't want it to."

"Because someone put a curse on you?"

The wind whistled through the open windows down the hall, toying with his hair. "I did something I should not have done, and now the Ankou appears when it should not."

Curiosity roared. "What did you do?"

His gaze shuttered. "It doesn't matter right now." He nodded at my blood-soaked dress. "Let me get the glass out of your skin. Take off your clothes."

"Can you turn around while I get undressed?"

He turned in the other direction, crossing his arms.

I pulled up the hem, and I unhooked the sheath around my thigh. Tight as it was, it had left deep, red marks in my skin, and an imprint where the buckle was. It was a relief to have it off.

Then, I pulled off the gown, which was disgusting at this point. I had no underwear on, since Lyr had never given me any.

Cold and naked, I felt acutely aware of every inch of my exposed skin.

With a twinge of shame, I looked down at the names carved into my body with iron long ago. The writing was so messy I could hardly read the demon names, but I still remembered them. Abrax, Morloch, Bilial...

Whatever else Lyr saw, I didn't need him seeing where demons had branded me. It occurred to me at this point that I could simply keep the dress on and pull it up to my waist. So I pulled it on again, then lay flat on the chilly floor. I pulled the dress up past my bottom, which frankly probably looked more obscene than just being totally naked, because my backside was out there for all the world to see.

Not a big deal, I told myself. I was covered in blood and glass, and it was just healing. Like a medical situation.

We were both just trying to find a magic knife. And if finding the athame meant sticking my rear out in the air while Death Man plucked glass from it, then I guess this was the story fate had written for me.

"I'm lying down," I said from the floor. The concrete chilled my body, and goosebumps had risen all over my exposed skin.

I closed my eyes, turning my head away from Lyr.

Then, I felt the sharp pricks in my thighs as he started to pull the glass out.

"Do you have tweezers?" I asked.

"I'm using my fingertips," he said. "When we were still in Acre, you could have escaped, you know. Without your help, they likely would have torn me down and thrown me into prison in iron chains."

"Maybe I just wanted some answers." I grimaced as he pulled a large chunk out of my upper thigh.

"Hold on." A ripple of his healing magic washed over my body, and a tendril of heat snaked through my core. Reflexively, my hips shifted forward, thighs clenching together.

"Stop moving."

"I wasn't moving." My nipples had gone hard against the cold concrete, and my breath started coming faster. "Stop it," I rasped, my voice breathy. "What's that magic you're using?"

"What do you mean? It's just taking the pain away."

Well, I wasn't about to explain to him how amazing his magic felt on my body. I wasn't going to tell him that I never felt desire for men, and now my body felt too hot. His magic skimmed over my skin, and I remembered how he'd looked at me when we'd first met—his eyes lingering over my legs, my breasts, my tiny shorts.

An uncontrolled ache built between my thighs. My hips shifted again as lewd thoughts started to spin in my mind.

What was *wrong* with me? Any moment now, I'd be writhing and moaning naked on the floor in front of him.

I still held the knife. "What is Nova Ys?" I asked, my voice sharp.

"I'm done getting the glass out. I just need to close up the cuts—"

I didn't even hear the rest of his sentence, because his magic rushed through my body in sensual waves, heating my core. My blood pounded in my belly, nipples tightening against the cold concrete. Since when did lying against a cold concrete floor feel so amazing? I pressed my palms hard against the floor, fighting the urge to climb into his lap and wrap my naked thighs around him.

"Are you almost done?" I asked through gritted teeth.

I tried to think clearly through the haze of pleasure still rocking my body. I had basically no clothes to wear, nothing that wasn't shredded, wet, and covered in blood.

"Your skin is healed perfectly. I need to clean you off a bit." He dragged a cold, wet cloth over my thighs, and I shivered. His warm thumb brushed over my skin, and my breath hitched. My nipples were rock-hard against the cold concrete.

He swept the cloth higher over my backside, and I felt as if my legs were opening of their own accord. Oh gods, I just wanted his hand to feel me...

I bit my tongue so hard I drew blood. "What are you using to clean me, anyway?"

"The T-shirt I stole." His voice held a deep growl. "I'm done. You can cover yourself again." He sounded tense.

Relieved, I pulled the dress down, then sat up against the wall. I was still clinging to the hilt of the dagger, my fingers tense.

I was sure my eyes gleamed with wild lust. Did he realize? Did he see the way my chest moved up and down, my pupils dilated?

His gold eyes had returned to their blue color, and something looked different in his expression, too. His gaze lingered on me longer than it needed to. For just a moment, I saw myself through his eyes, as though I were enchanting him. I got that little bubble into his soul.

I saw my heart-shaped face, my big green eyes. I looked beautiful to him, with my long sweeps of dark eyelashes. The dress was hanging off me in ragged threads, but he was more focused on the curves, on the bare skin. He thought I was delicate, which was a bit of a miscalculation. The way I was sitting, he could just barely see up my thighs...

I felt what he was thinking, too. He was thinking about how I'd looked after he'd cleaned me off. He thought my ass had looked perfect, that he could almost see everything, if I'd just opened my legs a bit more... His desire had made him frustrated. He didn't want to lust after me.

The bubble popped, and I was back to my own thoughts. But it was like I'd become tainted somehow, and the thoughts in my mind were growing dirtier. That ache pulsed hot between my legs, turning me into an animal. I wanted to slip my fingers between my thighs.

I gritted my teeth. The effort to stay in control had me practically vibrating with tension.

Before me, Lyr started to shift into his primal state once more—eyes blazing with gold, tattoos moving over his skin.

He moved closer, but stopped an inch from me, hands on either side of my hips. His mouth hovered over my neck, breath warm on my throat, making me shiver with excitement. I felt wet and hot, slick with desire.

My breasts strained against the silky dress, the lightest of touches like slow, sensual torture over my nipples. A feather light tease driving me crazy until I could think of nothing but stripping the dress off and fucking Lyr right here on the floor. *Oh gods, I want to fuck him.*

His hands were either side of my hips, just barely brushing against them—another sexual torture that made my core swell with need.

"I hear your heartbeat racing when I use my magic. I see your skin flush." His silky voice was like a hand stroking my thighs, making me shudder.

My legs fell open, and he moved in closer between them. Gently, he grazed my throat with his teeth.

A ragged strap on the gown fell down, exposing one of my breasts, my nipple hard as a breeze chilled it. I didn't move to cover myself. Lyr kissed my neck, and I moaned, closing my eyes.

Wild heat swooped through my belly. The words erupting in my mind were almost foreign to me... *thrust... fuck... lick... cock...* I wanted him deeper between my legs. I needed him to fill me, to fuck me hard now. I started to pull him closer, when I realized I was still gripping the dagger.

My eyes snapped open.

What was happening to me? I needed to stay on guard.

Stay in control, Aenor. Think of what he's done to your life.

Never trust the wolves. Never let them get too close. I pulled my neck away from him and pulled up the strap of the gown.

"No," I said with an iron will. "You don't get to kidnap people and then seduce them. Lesson learned."

He pulled away fast, like I'd seared his skin. He looked shocked. Then, he looked away from me.

I wanted him so bad it hurt.

CHAPTER 22

*S*itting on the floor, he met my gaze, his golden eyes gleaming with desire. Then, his angular jaw tightened, and he stared at the ground.

He narrowed his eyes at me. "You need clothing to cover yourself. You can't sit around in wisps of fabric all day and expect me to ignore it."

"Oh really? Twenty minutes ago, I was neurotically modest."

"I'll find some clothes for you."

He started to stand, but I held up my hand to stop him.

"Wait. What about Nova Ys? Stay where you are."

He stared at me for a long time, his golden eyes turning to blue, before he answered again. "The physical kingdom of Ys drowned. And the queen died. But many survived. Do we have to have this conversation now?"

"I know all the citizens of Ys scattered around the earth," I pressed on. "Humans call that... They have a word for it. A *diaspora.* But what is Nova Ys?"

He shook his head. "But the citizens of Ys did not all scatter. Many lived in the same neighborhoods in Cornwall. No one told you, because—"

"Because they all believed I was the one who drowned the island." My ribs felt hollow. They'd made a new kingdom without me.

"We found an empty island off the coast of Cornwall. An empty one that's shrouded in mists. We rebuilt there, and cloaked it in glamour so no one could find it. I move between Nova Ys and the fortress in Acre."

A sharp hunger cut into my gut, a desire to have what was mine—the crown of Ys, and the ancient power of the Meriadoc.

I leaned back against the wall. "Has it occurred to you that the person looking to get into Nova Ys might be the same person who destroyed the old one?"

He narrowed his eyes as he looked at me, assessing me. "This is all new information to me. Everyone was certain Aenor Dahut drowned Ys. I was certain of it, until recently."

"Tell me about Nova Ys," I said.

"When we first built it, we flew the sigil of Meriadoc to honor your mother—the white horse rising from the water. Those flags remain. Its location is secret."

"And you don't think the fuath can get there with the World Key?" I asked.

"Not even my half-brothers know how to find Nova Ys. Their mothers didn't live in the real Ys. So no, they won't be able to find it, and I don't think they'll be able to use the World Key, either."

I glanced at his crown, eyes narrowing. "Are you the king of Nova Ys?"

"I refused the title of king. I am their protector. My job is to make sure no one finds it."

"And you really have no idea who would want to get to Nova Ys? Who might be controlling the fuath?"

He shook his head.

Wind rushed through the open windows, making me shiver. "You still haven't told me why you hated my father so much."

"My mother lived in Nova Ys. She was a lady of the court, and very well loved. She'd been blessed by the god of the sea, after all. The sea god had given her a son. That worried your father. What if they wanted me to rule in his place? I'm a demigod. I was a threat to him."

My heart thumped in my chest. When I'd first met Lyr, I'd had no idea our worlds were so entwined.

Lyr continued. "King Gradlon invited my mother to dinner. He said he wanted to discuss marriage. How could she refuse such an invitation? The people of Ys loved her. They wanted this match—a great lady blessed by the sea, married to the king. But your father had no intention of marrying her."

"What did he do?"

"He served her roasted quail laced with a sleeping ointment. When she fell asleep on the dining table, he stripped her naked. He impaled her on an oak tree with iron nails through her limbs, which tore her flesh and poisoned her body. He broke every fae law. He let the citizens of Ys know what happened when they loved someone too much."

I stared at him, dread spreading through my veins. That was my dad. No wonder people thought I was *poisoned* with evil.

Lyr's back was straight as a rod. "King Gradlon did not do terrible things to protect his own people. He served only his own interests."

I could hardly breathe. "I never knew. No one ever mentioned it."

"Her name and image were carved off every building. Her

sigils were destroyed. The king took her home as well, and carved his own name into her stone walls."

For a moment, silence reigned.

"It took her seventeen days to die," he added. "The iron in her body stopped her from passing on peacefully, so her soul lingered in the sea hell. She stayed there until I became the Ankou to help her soul move on. And then, I did the same for others. And your mother," he went on. "Queen Malgven—was the one who killed him. She ushered in the golden age of Ys. She was the greatest ruler the kingdom ever had."

I wanted to be sick. I ran a finger over my lower lip, thinking about what he'd just told me. *Seventeen days to die...*

"I'm not really anything like my dad, you know," I said. "Spoiled, yes. A long time ago. But I was never ruthless."

He glanced at the dagger I was still clutching. "Do you plan to use that on me again?"

"If I have to."

"You look cold. I'll get you something else to wear. Then, you can see if you can sense the athame from here."

"What will it sound like?" I asked. "I don't know what I'm listening for."

"It sounds like the music of your family—the House of Meriadoc. I'm not a Morgen. I can't hear the music of magic like you can. But I know it was forged with Meriadoc blood and bones, and will sound like the Meriadoc song."

He stood and crossed out of the room into the dark stair-well, leaving me alone to listen to the sound of the rain hammering the concrete walls. A chilly gust of wind rushed inside the room.

When Lyr left me in the dark, the silence felt oppressive. I wasn't sure I'd felt this alone since the Nameless One had stolen my power.

I let out a long breath, still stunned by the revelation that Nova Ys existed. I wondered if they'd rebuilt the palace there.

I'd spent a century and a half trying not to think about that palace, but all this time—the kingdom had gone on without me. Memories of the old court flitted through my mind—the walls hung with gleaming cockle shells, black pearls, and gemstones from the sea. Cedar trees grew high in marble halls, gold dangling from their boughs. The strange bell song of the Ys spires filled the air. In those days, we threw parties in gardens that overlooked the sea, dressed in the finest silks.

And my true-born power bonded me to the sea.

I could control the waves. The sea was once part of my soul. I could part the waters to walk between the waves if I wanted, which I'd done once to impress a courtier. I could slip into the ocean and travel through it, fast as the speed of sound.

If I'd wanted, I could have drowned a city. A kingdom.

I *hadn't,* mind you.

But the power of the sea once hummed beneath my skin, an electrifying magic that made me feel alive. Exhilarated.

Since the Nameless One had stolen my true power, I'd tried it, again and again. Every time the results had me cracking into a kind of hysterical laugh-cry. I'd call the ocean to me, luring it closer with the power I should command. And what did I get? Droplets. Mist. A fisherman irritably complaining about *pea soup fog.* No waves or storms. No parting of the seas.

At some point, I had to give up. I'd buried the memory. But now, my longing for it had awakened. It felt like a gaping cavern had ripped open in my chest.

My teeth chattered, and I looked at the empty stairwell. I'd been so shocked by what Lyr had just told me that I hadn't really thought about where he'd be getting the clothes. A half-naked fae, strutting around a residential neighborhood in the night, looking for a shop.

I felt his power before I saw him cross into the room.

He wore a black sweatshirt that didn't quite fit across his enormous chest, and it was partially unzipped, straining against him.

"They were clean, and dry. Under the cover of balconies." He handed me a pair of tiny black shorts and a long-sleeved T-shirt. "Options were limited."

He hadn't given me any underwear again. I wasn't sure if that was because he didn't know about underwear, or if he'd correctly figured out that I'd be totally weirded out by wearing another person's undercrackers. He turned away, giving me the chance to dress myself. I pulled on the T-shirt, which said *Hot Skateboard Fun* in silver letters. It wasn't bad. If I'd had a pair of high heels, it wouldn't look too far off what I normally wore.

I wasn't sure if I was relieved or dismayed that he hadn't picked out a bra for me as well. In any case, being in dry clothes felt good.

"You can turn around again," I said.

Tiredness sapped my muscles. "You want me to try to just... hear the athame?" I heaved a sigh. If it were near, I was pretty sure I'd be able to hear its music already, but I'd humor him. "Let me give it a try."

He crossed his arms, watching me expectantly.

I sat down against the cold concrete wall, and I closed my eyes. I rested my hands on my knees.

I could attune to magical objects through sound if they were powerful enough—and especially if they were linked to me. The song of the House of Meriadoc was powerful. It had a deep, dolorous melody that boomed around it. It was an intense and undulating sound, like a funeral choir. I listened out for it, trying to feel the vibrations of my family's dark song.

All I heard was Lyr, his song like a melodious battle drum

that rumbled over my skin. I couldn't hear the athame from here.

My eyes opened again. "I don't hear it. We might not be anywhere near it. I have to be within a few miles of it to hear it, and we don't really know where it is. It might be back near Acre."

He ran a hand over his chin. "I'll need to find a way to get more information out of the Winter Witch."

"Oh, you think? More than just her gibbering something that rhymes with 'fear'?" The sarcasm was maybe a little harsh.

"You're cranky. You need sleep." He nodded at the inviting hard floor. "I'll keep watch."

I yawned and curled up against the wall, the concrete cool against my bare legs. I slid the dagger back into its leather sheath, then pulled it in to my chest. For a few moments as I tried to sleep, my mind filled with the image of the dead girl hanging from the walls of the castle in Acre, her pink hair draped over her delicate shoulders, neck bent at an odd angle. Blood stained her body and her dress where Lyr had slit her throat.

I pulled the sheath in tighter to me, like a little girl held a doll.

I'd never sleep if I was thinking of her, so I thought of Gina instead, sitting on the fluffy stack of pillows, shoving forkfuls of omelet into her mouth. Sleep washed over me like a wave.

And when I slept, I dreamt of wrapping my legs around a beautiful, golden-haired man who smelled like almonds and the sea. In my dreams, he kissed my neck, and my body shuddered with pleasure.

CHAPTER 23

My dreams shifted, growing darker. The humid sky turned to icy rain. A beautiful fae woman hung nailed to a tree, naked and screaming for her son. Coldness pierced me to the bone, a teeth-shattering chill.

I dreamt of the ice that filled my chest when the Nameless One ripped my power from me. Ice slid through my veins, and my lips turned blue. Lyr ran a knife across my throat, then hung me from his castle wall in chains. My teeth couldn't stop chattering.

Until at last, warmth covered my skin.

I woke in the dark, covered in something soft. With a start, I realized Lyr had put a blanket over me. Even on a bed of concrete, the softness of the blanket felt amazing. I hugged it around myself. Then, I breathed in Lyr's scent—oddly comforting. Almonds and the ocean.

I sat up to inspect the blanket. Once my eyes adjusted in the dark, I could just about make out a symbol stitched into the material—a triangle with a shell shape embroidered in the center. It was the same one I'd seen in the prison cell. Lyr's cloak.

I surveyed the room, but I didn't see Lyr. Where had he gone?

Holding the cloak around me, I stood up and listened for him, his deep melody. After a moment, I felt his vibrations skimming over my skin, and I crossed out into a hallway. After a few minutes of searching, I found him in another room, standing in an empty window. The wind whipped at his hair as he stared out onto the dark landscape.

He turned to look at me. "Why are you awake? Go back to sleep."

"What are you doing?" I blinked the sleep out of my eyes.

"Making sure no one finds us."

"Thanks for your cloak."

He frowned. "Your teeth were chattering too loudly."

"What's the symbol on the cloak?" I asked.

"It was the symbol of my mother's house." He turned away from me, looking outside again.

So that had definitely been Lyr's cloak in the prison cell. He'd come into my prison cell, put me to sleep, then put a cloak under my head as a pillow. None of which he wanted to admit.

I pulled his cloak tighter around me, watching him.

Why had he let me run free all these years, if he thought I was a psychopath? I was breaking every rule he held dear.

"You left your cloak for me in the prison cell, too," I ventured.

He looked like I'd caught him off-guard for a moment, turning to me with surprise. Then he looked back to watch the storm outside. "Go back to sleep, Aenor. Tomorrow, we try again for the athame. I'm looking out for the fuath. They might be able to find us through a scrying mirror, but I'll see them before they arrive."

Sleep called to me again. I crossed back into the empty room, and I curled up with Lyr's cloak around me for warmth. I shot a quick glance at the dagger on the floor, then pulled it close to me.

Never let down your guard, Aenor.

* * *

POWERFUL ARMS SCOOPED ME UP, and I woke with a jolt.

"What's happening?" I asked.

I still clutched the sheathed dagger to my chest like a sleeping child clutches a doll.

"The fuath are coming," said Lyr.

I was about to protest that I could get down the stairs myself, but he was moving like a storm wind over the ocean. Swift as a squall, even with me in his arms.

Once we reached the ground floor, he let go of me, and I sprinted for the car.

This time, the hotwiring went faster. I had it going within a minute. I turned on the ignition, and we sped off.

It was still dark, and I wasn't sure where we were going. At this time of night, there were almost no other cars on the road. Except the headlights behind us, which seemed to be closing in on us.

"Is that them?" I asked. "I thought you said they don't know how to drive."

"They're in the car. I can smell them. But they're not driving. They have a human driving them, perhaps someone who they've bribed with money."

"A cab driver. We call that a cab driver." I hit the gas a little harder, ramping up the speed, and the wind whipped at my hair through the window. It took me a moment to realize that at some point while I'd been sleeping, Lyr had cleared off all the glass from the driver's seat.

Thank the gods. He really was a good protector.

"How did they find us?" I asked.

"Scrying, probably. I felt it not that long ago." He looked behind him. "Can you go faster?"

I wasn't a skilled enough driver to outrun them.

We were zooming through a town center now, the road-sides lined with some shops and crowded with concrete apartment buildings.

"I'm bad at driving. We need to just... confuse them," I said.

I veered around a corner—the turn was absurdly wide, taking me onto the wrong side of the road. Lucky for me, there was no one on the other side to hit, though I clipped a street sign. Adrenaline surged as I fought to regain control of the car.

"*Dorcha.*" Lyr uttered the spell that would partially cloak our car in shadows.

This was not the *safest* way to drive, especially considering it cloaked most of our headlights, and no other cars could see us.

I took a sharp left, leaning heavily on the gas on a wider boulevard. One side of the road was lined by gas stations and construction, and the other by a rocky hill covered with shrubs.

It was too flat and open here, and there was no chance of losing them. I veered back, careening wildly over the rubble divider to head back toward the town center.

Lyr cursed under his breath.

I took a sharp right, wheels screeching as we veered back into the town center. From here, I took a series of sharp turns that sent my stomach lurching, then sped through a gas station parking lot.

Lyr launched into another spell—a powerful spell for protection—as I swung wildly around a tiny rotary.

God of the deep, I was not great at this.

Lyr's magic rippled over the car, shielding us. I let out a slow breath.

I took a sharp lap around the traffic circle, then veered off wildly in the direction we'd come from. Ha! That should confuse them. I was driving like a maniac.

I leaned on the gas again, then banged a hard right down a residential street.

"We've lost them," Lyr said at last.

I let out a long breath. "Can you take the shadows off now? I can't see a thing."

Lyr's magic skimmed over me as he pulled the shadows from the car. "Get back on the highway. We need to drive south."

"South? You're issuing these directions like I have some sense of where the sun rises and sets or an internalized compass."

"We will have to lose the car," he said. "The fuath know what it looks like. And we will need to get to a large city. The fuath can hunt by smell, and a large population will confuse them."

"Fine. Just tell me where to go."

But he went silent.

I took my eyes off the road for just a moment to glance at him, and I saw that he'd shifted again. His hair wafted around his head like he was underwater, and his body glowed with the otherworldly gold light. His dark claws had extended.

A shiver snaked up my spine. Something about the way he looked in this state just made my heart stop. I couldn't help but feel like there was something *wrong* with it.

Is that how he'd looked when he'd slit the pink-haired girl's throat? Like a demonic god?

I wondered if he'd felt the slightest bit of guilt when her blood stained her white gown.

I drove around blindly until I found the highway, and then I followed the signs to Tel Aviv.

* * *

WE DROVE for another forty-five minutes, the morning star rising in the sky above us—a cold blue glow in the violet sky.

Then, the sun began to rise, staining the sky with amber and hot coral. Lyr stayed in his Ankou state until rosy morning light pulled him out of it.

My stomach started to rumble as we pulled into Tel Aviv, the streets crowded with restaurants and offices. A few people were on the sidewalks with steaming coffee cups.

Outside a closed restaurant, I found a parking lot that was mostly empty, which was the only situation I could actually park in without damaging all cars involved.

I pulled up diagonally over two spaces, then stole another glance at Lyr. My chest unclenched as I saw that the claws were gone, and his eyes had returned to a serene blue.

I wanted to know what he'd done to bring that curse on himself.

What was worse than killing people?

"What are you talking about?" he barked.

"I didn't say anything."

"You said *what's worse than killing people?* And then your stomach growled, again."

"I didn't know I said that out loud."

"You need to eat again."

I rubbed my eyes. "Hang on. I'm going to try for the athame again first." I gripped the wheel, closing my eyes to tune into the sweet music of the Meriadoc. I wanted to feel it thrumming up my spine...

Instead, I just felt Lyr's vibrations, and the hunger rippling through my stomach.

I opened my eyes again. Then, I strapped the sheath around my thigh once more. It looked ridiculous with the short shorts, and I wasn't sure if this was at all legal in Israel, but I wanted to keep the knife on me. "You definitely need better intel from the Winter Witch, because this blows."

"Getting to her will be a bit of a problem." He swung open the car door and stood, sniffing the air. "Let's get you food, first. Maybe your tracking skills will work better when you're not hungry. We'll find a quiet place for you to sit and concentrate until you can hear it."

"I don't think my tracking skills are the problem." I stretched my arms over my head. "Also, we don't have any money for food."

He ignored me and strode into the street, his hair gleaming pale gold in the morning light. He was crossing the road, heading for a wide, pedestrianized boulevard. Tree-shaded streets lined either side of the walkway.

"We can take food if we need it," he said.

"I am intrigued by how eager you are to break human laws, given your rigidness with fae laws."

"Fae laws are superior. I already explained that."

I hurried to keep up with him as he crossed the road. My dreams from the night before were still flickering in my mind. "That's convenient. Because you can basically do whatever you want. It's fine to slit a girl's throat and hang her body from your castle, as long as you don't use iron when you do it."

Just as he got the walkway, he whirled abruptly, staring down at me.

It seemed I'd struck a nerve.

CHAPTER 24

*J*cocked a hip, staring back at him. "I was just thinking about the girl with pink hair. And how you killed her. And how she could have been me."

"Are you referring to the body you saw outside our fortress?"

"*Yes*. The girl who tried to steal your necklace."

"At four hundred and seventy-two years old, she could hardly be called a girl. Her body has been there for over a year, but does not decompose. And do you know what would happen if she'd taken the World Key from me and figured out how to reverse the spell?"

"Is that possible?"

"All spells can be reversed with enough time and skill." He folded his arms, staring down at me. "And what do you imagine a nefarious person might do with that power?"

"Sell the key, make lots of money, and buy a nice house with lots of guards to protect them from assassins like you. Live in luxury, above ground, where no one calls you a dirtling."

"That's what *you* would do with it. What Lady Leianna

intended was to open a shadow demon realm, demand fealty from a legion of monsters in exchange for their release. She wanted to use the key to raise armies of demons to take over the world. She was a twisted lake maiden, and she fed off human misery the way a succubus feeds off lust. She has killed countless people, children among them. For fuck's sake, Aenor, don't sentimentalize her as a helpless *girl* just because you think she looked like you."

With my arms folded, I tapped my fingertips against my elbow. Maybe he had a point. "I can see why the key might be a problem, in the wrong hands, and why you'd need to make sure you sent a message."

A cool morning wind rushed over us, and Lyr stared down at me, gold glinting in his eyes. "I have sometimes had to do terrible things to protect the people of Ys. And I've sometimes had to do terrible things to keep humans safe from the supernaturals."

"It sounds like you understand me, then. We're the same in that way."

He arched an eyebrow, and he didn't look like he was willing to concede this point. "I'm not sure that we are, entirely."

"What?" I said. "Why?"

"The Winter Witch has prophesied your future. She says your blood is poisoned."

"She said the same to me. It could mean anything. Do you have any idea how many value-brand cookies I eat per day?"

"That wasn't all of it. I'll show you."

He leaned down and cupped my forehead, his hands warm and gentle on my skin. I closed my eyes.

For a moment, my mind went blank. Just totally empty. Then, a winter storm whipped up around me with whirling eddies of sparkling snow. The Winter Witch trudged closer, her eye blinking.

Hair whipped into my eyes—the same blond color as Lyr's. It took me a moment to understand that this was one of *his* memories. He was channeling his memory directly into my skull.

The Winter Witch was upon him now.

"Tell me," Lyr's deep voice boomed over the white landscape. "What will become of Nova Ys?"

The witch's mouth opened. "She of the House of Meriadoc seeks to bring a reign of death. She of the poisoned blood seeks to rule a realm of bones."

She let out an ear-curdling shriek. Then, "The daughter of the House of Meriadoc. Her beauty hides her true nature. Her heart turns to ash, her soul infected by evil. She seeks to sever your head from your body, to fertilize Nova Ys with your blood. Death spills from her."

Another ear-piercing scream, one that sounded harvested from the depths of hells.

Then, Lyr pulled his hands away, and the vision vanished from my mind. "The Winter Witch is never wrong."

I tried to catch my breath, and I stared at him, my heart slamming hard against my ribs. And as prophecies went, that one did not sound great.

It didn't sound like me, though. I didn't want to cut off his head and fertilize Ys with his blood. And why would I want a kingdom of bones?

I felt a sharp chasm open up in my chest, a wild desire to prove to him that he was wrong. "You can't really think that's me."

His deep blue eyes drank me in. "It's you. The Daughter of Meriadoc." He brushed a strand of my blue hair out of my face. "The Winter Witch has never been wrong before."

"So if you think I'm going to cut off your head, why are you letting me hang around you? Why are we working together?"

"She said that you'll *seek* to do it. Not that you'll succeed. I intend to stop you."

Electric energy crackled between us. "And how do you intend to stop me?"

"By whatever means necessary."

I was grateful for the sheath cutting off circulation to my leg right now, because it had a weapon in it. At any moment, Lyr could decide that I was about to cut off his head, and he'd feel compelled to try to stop me.

"I don't believe it." I didn't want a kingdom of bones.

Unless something changed me… The athame, perhaps? When I touched it, would something change me?

"I have no desire to fertilize a city in your blood. I'd cut off your head, maybe, if you deserve it, but the dang thing would probably grow back." My stomach rumbled, and I was getting so hungry that maybe I was a *little* at risk of trying to drown a city in Lyr's blood. I needed toast or something before I actually did try to decapitate him.

"But mostly, I don't care a lick what the Winter Witch says. She's wrong," I said with much more conviction than I felt. "Put it out of your head, and let's get breakfast."

"Wait here a minute. I'll get you something to eat."

He crossed to a coffee stand in the center of the pathway, striding up confidently in his cloak and crown, as if he didn't look bizarre. What was he going to do? Terrify them into giving him some croissants?

The barista slid a tray with a coffee cup and two brown paper sacks onto the counter and called out the name "Shira!"

Lyr shot out and snatched the tray, moving in such a fast blur I wasn't sure anyone else saw him.

I wasn't even sure if he understood that you usually paid for food. For most of his time in the human realm, he probably just had servants handing him things.

He'd crossed the road and joined my side again within moments, and he shoved the tray at me. "Fill your belly. Then try again to find the athame."

Fill your belly. Weirdo.

By my side, he was striding along the wide sidewalk like he knew exactly where we were going.

"Do you know of a space around here we can use?" I asked. "For my athame tracking?"

We crossed the road again, heading for what looked like an apartment building. "I'll find one."

Hungry as I was, the coffee smelled amazing. I grabbed Shira's latte from the tray. It burned my tongue just a bit, but once the taste of caffeinated drink hit my tongue, I couldn't stop myself. Ahhhh, glorious stimulants mixed with milk... "I love coffee. I love Shira right now. I even love you, Lyr, you brooding, coffee-providing monster."

He shot me a confused look, and I took another long sip.

As we walked, I peered into the paper bags. Shira had amazing taste, too, because she'd selected a *pain au chocolate* and an egg sandwich on French bread. My mouth watered.

"Do you want any of this?" I asked, hoping for a no.

"I'll eat later."

Brilliant.

Lyr stopped walking in front of a short concrete building. Above us, narrow balconies overlooked the sidewalk.

Lyr stopped at the door, then pushed all six of the apartment building's buzzers. After a moment, someone spoke in what I *thought* was Hebrew. Lyr replied fluently. No idea what he said, but the buzzer sounded a moment later.

Apparently, Lyr knew more about the human world than I'd given him credit for.

He pulled open the door, and I followed him into the cool hallway, and the door shut behind me.

He turned to me. "Just give me a moment. I'm going to discreetly find an empty apartment."

By the look of him, Lyr wasn't the best choice for discreetly scoping out a building. Nothing about an enormous blond fae was particularly discreet. Except that Lyr had a certain way of moving fluidly though the shadows that I couldn't mimic. It was how he'd been able to steal Shira's breakfast out from under her nose. A breakfast I now desperately wanted to devour.

I leaned against a door. Then, I balanced the tray on one knee, taking a bite of the *pain au chocolate.*

Our plan was starting to feel increasingly ridiculous. I was supposed to sit in an apartment and just listen out for the sounds of an athame. Lyr seemed sure I could find it if I simply *focused* enough, but that wasn't how it worked.

I took a huge bite of the pastry, and I felt the hair raising on the back of my neck. Someone was using a scrying mirror to watch me. I started to run for Lyr, but I had only taken a few steps when the world fell out from under me—the floor rumbling, cracking open.

I plunged into an icy portal, and a hand clamped around my ankle. Tragically, the chocolate pastry fell into the water with me.

Underwater, I fought to swim to the surface. Swimming I could do, even in the most powerful of currents. And yet now, magic was dragging me under like light pulled into a black hole. It happened fast—the break through to the other side, the rush of air as rough hands yanked me from the portal.

The ground closed up immediately behind me, and I found myself back in Acre, surrounded by the possessed knights.

CHAPTER 25

*J*lay flat on the stone ground, and Midir pointed the tip of a sword at my neck. Morning sunlight washed into the hall, lighting his red hair ablaze.

It would seem the possessed seneschals had figured out how to reverse the spell on the key.

Midir stared at the floor. "Did the bloody portal close?" he asked in his singsong voice. "We don't have Lyr. He was the important one. Why did you grab her first? This is a fucking disaster."

"She was right there." Gwydion came up behind him. "Just open it again."

"It took me an hour to open this, and I was vomiting the whole time. We didn't reverse the spell on it properly. I feel that my host's body could be falling apart." The fuath-Midir was whining now.

He looked sick—his eyes bloodshot, skin sallow. His cheeks looked sunken. "I don't speak the Ys dialect, and I need that to reverse the spell properly." He covered his mouth like he was about to vomit.

The World Key gleamed from his throat. Deep, booming voices echoed off the stone walls.

"Where is Lyr?" It seemed everyone was asking the same question at once.

"We need to open the portal again!" possessed Gwydion shouted. He pulled out a gun and pointed it at me, then flashed a wide grin. "Tell us how to open it."

"I have no idea," I said. "Who are you working for? Who is looking for Nova Ys?"

Gwydion kept the gun trained on me. "Things being as they are, little one, I don't believe you're in a position to interrogate me."

Fair point.

By Gwydion's side, Midir was chanting the spell to open the portal. But the fuath possessing him couldn't get the accent right. It was in the language of Ys, and he was screwing up the words. I listened in, trying to remember the words to the spell. If I was going to make it away from them, I'd need to somehow get the key from Midir, and open a portal myself.

"I need to make sure you can't escape," Gwydion went on. "You attacked us with magic before."

Uh-oh.

I had to think fast. I had a few spells at my fingert—

The bullet ripped through my shoulder so hot and sharp I didn't even hear myself screaming. I only felt mind-bending pain spreading through my body. The way the pain rippled through my veins, I was sure it was iron.

Gods, is that what Lyr had felt when I'd shot him?

When the haze of agony cleared a little from my mind, I stared up at Gwydion.

"Tell us how to get to Nova Ys," he said. "You're the heir. You must know how to find it."

"I genuinely have no idea."

"You know." Midir flashed me a brilliant smile. "As soon as you begin to chant one of your attack spells, I will shoot another part of your body. And you should know that I've been slowly starting to learn from some of my host's memories. And my host is *very* skilled at torture, as it happens. First I think he'd cut off your nipples. Then, he'd slowly carve away at the rest of your breasts—"

I tuned out the fuath's macabre listing of all the parts of me he wanted to cut off. They were going to try to torture me into giving them information that I simply didn't have.

If I still had my true power, everyone in the fortress would drown. From here, I could hear the ocean, the waves pounding against the rock. I tasted the salt on my lips. The sea called to me, and I wanted to draw it down over the fortress like a tsunami.

A searing pain in my side snapped my attention back to the room. Gwydion had cut me, and blood dripped from his sword. "I felt we were losing your attention."

"So tell us." Midir pointed the gun at my kneecap. "How do we get there?"

The pain was so blinding I wasn't entirely sure I could form a sentence. My body felt uncomfortably hot, and sweat beaded on my forehead.

"I don't know," I managed.

Once, I would have drowned them all.

Now? I could make fog. I broke into a wild, hysterical laughter that made tears run down my cheeks, then I instantly regretted it because it felt like my side was splitting open where they'd cut me.

"I don't know," I said again, this time through real tears.

Stop crying, you idiot.

"Well then," said Midir. "What good are you? We will have to cut you up into tiny little pieces of princess."

I let out a slow breath, blocking out all the torture threats and trying to focus on the hall around me.

That wild laughter was threatening to bubble up again. *Fog.* Maybe I could just confuse them all with fog, like the baffled fishermen—

You know? It wasn't the worst idea in the world.

"Then," Midir went on. "I'll cut off your thumb."

"Tell her," said Gwydion. "Tell her who we have captured."

"What? Captured who?" I snapped.

I needed him to stop interrupting my thoughts.

I closed my eyes, tuning into the sound of the ocean, the waves crashing against the fortress. I hummed a low tune in my throat, calling the sea to me. The air thickened, and a faint ocean spray cooled my heated face.

A chilly mist pooled in the hall, and I hummed a little louder. The fog roiled in around us, a soothing balm on my body. Salt stuck to my skin.

"What the hell is this?" Midir trilled. "Stop it."

I shifted on the stone floor, agony shooting through my shoulder as I did. But the fog was so thick now, I couldn't even see a foot in front of me.

When the fuath shot his gun again, the bullet only grazed me.

Clenching my teeth, I rose as swiftly as I could.

I had a plan. I needed just a *little* more chaos in this cloud of sea spray.

I blocked out the pain as I rushed to the side of the room where the flags hung. Then, I pulled one of the torches from the wall. In the heavy dampness of the air, it was hard to light the fabric, but once I let a little oil drip off the torch, a corner of a flag went ablaze.

I pulled the dagger from its sheath.

Just a little more pandemonium.

"The room is on fire!" Someone shouted.

The scent of burning fabric and smoke curled through the air. Screams and commands filled the room. Luckily, I could find people based on sound.

"I need to open the portal again!" Midir shouted in his high-pitched voice. "I can't even think clearly. I want to be sick."

He probably didn't realize that his voice told me exactly where he was. He hadn't moved.

Through the fog, I crept up behind him.

I jammed my dagger into his neck—into his trachea, so he couldn't make a sound. Since he was a demigod, it would hurt like the devil, but it wouldn't kill him.

Then, I ripped the necklace from his throat. It isn't *easy* to break a silver chain, and it bit into my fingers as I yanked it off. Sticky red blood coated the key.

Midir fell to his knees, not making a sound except the gurgling from his throat.

I rushed for the window, and I crouched on the foggy ledge, sea air whipping up mist into my face. Smoke from the burning flags billowed from the room.

I stared down at the shore, thinking of how shallow the water might be where it crashed over the rocks, and how it would feel to smash my legs on impact. I'd be stuck there with shattered bones, waiting for the fuath to torture me to death while I failed to give them the answers I didn't have.

Time for a new plan.

Better to run through the secret tunnel again—the one that Lyr had showed me. I could find a clear space, and try to remember the spell for the World Key.

With the heraldic flags burning around me, I found the door to the secret passage. I slipped into the narrow hall without any of the other knights noticing, a plume of smoke wafting in as I opened the door.

The shouts of the fuath echoed around until the door clicked shut behind me.

Once again, the pain from my shoulder ripped through my mind, pulsing like poison in my bones.

Now—what *were* the words to that spell?

CHAPTER 26

I couldn't think straight. I felt like my mind had been infected.

Iron was poison to the fae. Was this what the witch's prophecy meant about poisoned blood? Maybe.

I slowly walked through the tunnel. Wincing, I reached around my back, feeling for an exit wound. I grunted with pain. I did feel a ragged hole in my shoulder, which meant the bullet had gone through to the stone floor behind me. Even without the actual bullet in me, it still hurt like the dickens and made it hard to think.

Now, to figure out how to open a portal again...

A bit of light cracked into the dark passage as someone opened the door behind me. Rays of orange beamed through the smoke and the tendrils of fog.

Oh, gods.

I forced myself to start running, and I called the sea mist closer to me. I cloaked myself in a cool fog as I ran, my breath ragged.

I whispered a healing spell, and it started to work slowly

over my skin, taking some of the pain away. I picked up the pace, and the fog cloaked me in the dark tunnel.

Injured and bleeding, I felt my thoughts start to wander back to my old life as I ran, down the dark stairwell, into the flooded tunnel at sea level. A hundred years ago, I'd gone to a party in grove of blackthorn trees. I'd danced and danced until my feet ached and sweat ran down my gossamer dress. I'd gorged on blackberries until my lips and fingertips turned purple.

Then a darker memory flickered in my mind: my dagger, plunging into a demon's heart, and the strange exaltation I'd felt when ending his life.

Heart turns to ash, soul infected by evil.

It seemed like ages till I reached the tunnel's exit into the sunlight. This time, the fog protected me. All of Acre was a cloud of thick, salty mist.

Midir's blood dripped down my hands from when I'd slit his throat. *Death spills from her.*

My pace had slowed, and when I looked down at myself, I saw that I was bleeding not only from my shoulder, but from the cut in my side. I'd forgotten about that one, and now the blood loss was dizzying me. I stumbled, careening into a wall.

It was hard to remember the words to the spell when I couldn't think straight. I gripped my side, trying to keep moving. Gods, I wanted to lie down.

A man shouted something at me in Hebrew, but I ignored him.

I needed to hide, just long enough that I could clear my thoughts. I'd find my way back to Lyr, and we'd find this godsforsaken magic blade to stop this nightmare.

In the thick fog, I didn't have a *great* idea where I was going. All I knew was that I needed to lose the knights. I turned off the road into a narrow alley that smelled of fish.

Another turn took me into a covered market. Here, market stalls lined a cobbled passageway—bakeries, fruit stands, almond pastries.

The mist thinned once inside, but when I turned around, I didn't see anyone coming after me. Just the baffled vendors wondering why a bleeding, blue-haired woman was stumbling through the market, veering into their halva and pistachios.

When I reached an empty alleyway off the market, I slowed.

I leaned against the stone wall, catching my breath, and I closed my eyes. I touched the key around my neck. What had Midir been saying when he was trying to open the portal again? It had been in the Ys dialect. Luckily, I spoke it fluently.

Something about a door, a kingdom…

A gunshot rang out, and a bullet cracked the stone wall just to my right.

I whirled to find Gwydion, a dark smile curling his lips. "I'm glad I got your attention, Aenor." He pointed the gun at me.

My heart slammed against my ribs. "I can't help you. I simply don't know how to get to Nova Ys."

"I believe you. But that doesn't mean you can't help us. You know, the bodies we inhabit slowly start to give us some of their memories, if we take the time to sift through them. And what we learned from Gwydion is that you don't care so much about your own life. You care about the human."

Oh, *no*.

A second knight came up behind him—one with golden hair. He flashed me a smile that didn't reach his eyes, and he drew his sword. "We had a hard time finding Lyr, you know. And he slipped away from us so fast."

I touched the World Key at my neck, swallowing hard. I

didn't have enough energy to fight these two. "What did you do with Gina?"

Gwydion shrugged. "It was easy to find Gina. Our hosts knew exactly where she was. Melisande remembered." A thin smile. "The Savoy Hotel. This was discussed."

The other pulled something from his pocket—a necklace I recognized as Gina's. It had an octopus pendant and googly eyes. "I wanted to take her finger, but I was told to wait."

I started shaking, and a bit of magic started crackling between my ribs. "Where is she?" I looked toward the fortress. Flames rose from some of the windows, and dark smoke curled into the air. I could hear my own breath coming fast. "Is she in there?"

"Don't be an idiot," said Gwydion. "We're not hiding her in an obvious place like the fortress."

"Then where the devil is she?" I knew they wouldn't answer, but pure frustration had me screaming at them anyway.

Gwydion wagged his finger and prowled closer. "Ah, well. When you give us what we want, you can have your human back, and we'll do our best not to cut anything off her."

The world had gone quiet except a ringing in my ears. I summoned my magic. Despite my weakness, power was rising higher inside me, charging my body. Anger gave me fire. "And what do you want me to give you?"

"Lyr," said Gwydion. "You can keep the World Key. Use it to get to Lyr. Shoot him with iron, like you did before. Open the portal. Dump his body in it for us."

"What will you do to him?"

Gwydion didn't answer, but I already knew. They'd torture him until he went demented with the pain.

I gripped the dagger. I could use it to conduct another attack spell.

I whispered a spell and unleashed a blast of attack magic at the two knights.

The blond knight lunged for me. I had one last blast of magic in my reserves, and it electrified my arm, then exploded from my fingertips. I managed to catch him right in his chest, and he fell back.

Elvis bless my soul.

What was the spell to open the portal? With all the blood I was losing, it was no wonder the knights had found me so fast.

I tried to run again, desperately wanting to rest. I was moving at a snail's pace. Why wasn't Gwydion catching up to me?

My heart was pounding hard in my chest, loud as a drum. Or *was* that the sound of a drum echoing off the walls? No, it was footfalls—someone chasing me.

A seductive scent curled around me—the sweet, wine-ripe scent of pomegranates tinged with dark smoke. I froze, and stole a glance behind me.

Seemed someone new had entered the fray. A fae I hadn't seen before.

Behind him, the bodies of Gwydion and the blond fae lay broken—ripped apart. Only Gwydion would return from the dead.

I stared at the stranger, who moved toward me with an elegant grace. His beauty felt like glass shattering in my heart.

Dark hair swept over his forehead, and the morning light blazed over his face. His eyes were dusky hues—purple streaked with gold, and his cheekbones were blade-sharp. *Possibly* the most beautiful man I'd ever seen. I realized I'd simply stopped walking.

"I believe those two fae were bothering you," he said. "I had to kill them."

"Thanks," I said. I still clutched tight to the bloodied knife.

His eyes gleamed, and he arched a dark eyebrow. "You look like your mother."

My stomach swooped. He knew way too much about me.

"Who are you?"

As I stared at him, the sound of a low drum pulsed in time with my heart. It seemed to me that it was a sacrificial drum, a sound echoing off rock. I don't know why that word popped into my mind—*sacrifice*. I felt dreadfully hot, and phantom flames seemed to rise and burn around me. *Boom, boom, boom...* A drumbeat to drown out screams.

However gorgeous the man standing before me was, the drum was telling me to *run.*

CHAPTER 27

Shadows cascaded behind his back like wings. He smelled fae, and he seemed ancient.

The world seemed blurred around him, as if no one existed but us. That low, rhythmic beat pounded in my body.

I stood, immobilized, while the man with the bright eyes took another slow step forward. Peering down at me, he stroked a fingertip along the side of my face. His touch was hot. I had the strangest, strongest urge to kiss his hand.

"The Daughter of Malgven," he said. "I might need your help someday." His voice was like a lover's touch that skimmed under the fabric of my clothes, sending hot shivers rippling over my body.

My heart pounded harder.

The man pulled something out of his pocket—a ripe, red piece of fruit. My mouth watered as he held it out to me, hunger and desire mingling in my belly.

"You look hungry," he murmured.

My gaze locked on his sensual mouth.

Whoever he was, eating from his hand was a terrible idea.

The fae believed that food could be used to control others, to poison their minds, to enslave.

Still, I was desperate to taste it. I wanted to bite through the skin into the fruit, to feel its sweet tang on my tongue. I wanted to lick the juice off the beautiful man's fingertips just like he wanted me to. I closed my eyes, and I could almost savor the sweet sting on my tongue.

"Taste it," he said. "And tell me where she is."

"Who?" I asked. "I don't imagine you're talking about Gina."

He arched an eyebrow. "No, I have no idea who Gina is. Are you playing coy with me?"

He wasn't after the World Key, which seemed strange. Nor did he want to know about Nova Ys, or the athame. Who was *she?*

He took another step closer, holding the ripe fruit to my lips. The hunger overwhelmed me. I stared into his dusky eyes—like a twilight sky over a burning city.

Gina. We were talking about Gina. Now, at least, my mind was clear.

Surprise flickered in his eyes when I took a step back—then another. I'd ripped my mind free of his allure. Clarity scrubbed my thoughts clean of all the confusion and panic, and the words of the portal spell rang in my brain.

"Egoriel Lyr, warre daras."

I spoke the words that would bring me to Lyr.

I took another step back, and the stone ground opened up beneath me. I sank into the glorious embrace of the cold portal water. My arms floated over my head as I drifted in deeper, heading for Lyr.

When I looked up, I saw that I'd come into the portal alone. The bright-eyed man—the one who smelled of pomegranates and smoke—hadn't followed.

Blood from my shoulder and my side pooled around me

in crimson swirls. My mind was dimming, flickering with old memories—blood and blades, a pearl-studded goblet.

She of the poisoned blood. Death spills from her...

I could hand Lyr over to the fuath, and maybe they'd give me Gina back.

It's just... I really didn't want to hand him over to get tortured. There had to be another way to get Gina back.

The toxins from the iron bullet soaked into my muscles, making them freeze up as I drifted through the portal. My thoughts were slipping by, like blood spilling through water.

As the water pulled me under, I realized I could have gone anywhere in the world with the key around my neck. Anywhere in *any* world. The spell on it had been unlocked, and the power was in my control.

And out of all the places in the world I could go, I chose to join him.

The absurdity of this hit me only after I'd plunged into the portal, and then my whole world went dark.

* * *

MY EYES OPENED a bit as Lyr pulled me from the portal. The iron had worked its way through my system, making my muscles cramp.

I glanced over at a tile floor, where the portal closed up behind me. To my relief, no one else came through.

Violent nausea roiled in my stomach. I rolled over onto my hands and knees, and heaved up a little bit of Shira's latte.

I felt the sharp sting of the chain pulling against my neck as Lyr ripped the World Key off.

That was what he was interested in?

I turned to him, anger rising along with another dry heave. "I came back to you half dead, and you just want the necklace?"

"Aenor." Lyr's voice was soft as he cut me off, holding up the key. "This is what was making you feel sick. It's part of the spell. The fuath managed to weaken the spell, but it's still there, poisoning anyone who uses the key. Only I can use it without consequences."

"Oh." My whole body was shaking. Everything about me felt completely *wrong* right now.

My teeth were chattering wildly.

I felt Lyr pull me close to him, and I rested my head on his chest. I let myself lean against him.

"What happened?" he asked.

Let's see... "Shot once, iron bullet. Stabbed. They have Gina." I thought that just about covered it.

But the warmth of his body radiated around me, and I could hear my heart beat. I closed my eyes, and Lyr lifted me, carrying me to another room.

I looked up into his determined face, and at the stark line between his eyebrows. His eyelashes were so shockingly black against the blue of his eyes.

A sound like the rushing of water filled the room. Whatever instinct had propelled me back to him had been the right one, because Lyr was the only one who'd know how to fix this spell situation.

My thoughts were drifting back again to Ys, and my mother combing through my long hair as we sat at a mirror. She wore her bloodstained wedding gown, her mark of pride.

My teeth chattered again, and I curled into Lyr's warm body. But he wasn't letting me rest. In fact, he started to pull off my shirt.

"What are you doing?" I asked through chattering teeth.

"Helping you."

I tugged it down again, making sure to keep my scars covered. "No."

"Saltwater will help you heal," he said.

"Saltwater can go through the fabric."

He scooped me up and lifted me again. My vision was fuzzy, but with all the tile around us, I knew we were in a bathroom.

When he lowered me into warm water, fatigue wrapped around my mind, warm and soft. Steam kissed my bare skin. I kept my eyes closed.

"This will sting a bit," he said. "I'm adding salt to the bath."

"I have things to do," I muttered.

"Not right now."

I winced a bit as the salt stung my wounds.

Lyr's warm hands gripped my shoulders, and I heard him murmur a low spell. Immediately, it started to soothe my pain.

Within moments, I could already feel the saltwater healing me, cleaning my open gashes. Then, Lyr's magic whispered around me.

Should I tell him what the fuath wanted? I could hand him over in exchange for Gina. After all, he'd live. Gina was only a human, and she might not.

I forced my eyes open for a moment, looking at his golden skin, his cheeks a little pink in the warm steam of the bath. A few strands of his pale hair stuck to his face.

He met my gaze. "Close your eyes." A warm, soothing voice that hummed over my skin.

I couldn't give him up to be tortured, even if it made logical sense. If I handed over Lyr, I'd be condemning the entire kingdom of Nova Ys to an invading army.

Blast it.

I had no options.

CHAPTER 28

"Getting shot with iron really hurts," I mumbled.

"Getting shot with anything hurts."

"Iron especially."

"Yes, I recently experienced that. Is that an apology for our first meeting, by the way?"

I sighed. "I suppose it is."

"Be thankful you're alive," he said. "And didn't have to spend any time in the hell world."

I was trying to work out some sort of plan, but my body felt completely *wrong,* and my thoughts flitted by like autumn leaves in the wind. My mind danced with images of Ys, and the sun streaming through oaks and palm trees onto a soft, mossy ground. Bonfires burned in the orchards under a canopy of stars.

"The only thing consistent about you, Aenor, is your ability to surprise me," said Lyr. "Why did you come back here to me instead of escaping to England with your key?"

Steam curled around me in the bath.

Sweat rolled down my temple. How hot was this bath? "Because I've learned about Nova Ys, and I feel responsible for it, even if they all hate me. And also, the fuath have Gina. They are threatening to hurt her unless we tell them how to get to Nova Ys. I need to get her back."

When I glanced at him, I saw a flicker of the Ankou—his tattoos. "Clearly, we are not going to sacrifice a kingdom for one human. We need to stay focused on the athame."

My eyes snapped open. "We can't let her die."

He splashed the warm, salty water over my body. "Finding the athame is the fastest way to stop them."

"We could get Gina first before they cut her fingers off."

"Why would they cut her fingers off?"

"Hang on. I can use the bath to get a glimpse of her. It will work as a scrying mirror." I leaned forward, trying to get a good look at the bathwater.

Then, I blinked as sparkled flecks danced before my eyes, and my vision went dark. "Hang on."

"Relax, Aenor."

"Gina's allergic to nuts. She needs an EpiPen, and she can't eat anything unless she has one."

"She needs a *what*?"

My pulse raced. "It's medicine to keep her alive if she eats nuts. When I ran through the market in Acre, there were pistachios and almonds everywhere. Particles in the air. She won't do well here."

He looked baffled. "Humans can die from eating nuts?"

"Some can."

Lyr pressed his hand on my chest. "Your heart is still beating unnaturally fast. It's like a hummingbird. Stop thinking about the human for two minutes." He pressed on my chest. "Do you want to see Nova Ys?"

My kingdom? "Yes."

A charge pulsed through his fingertips, and my mind spun with images of a sun-dappled orchard and a stone palace with spires that pierced the clouds. Ships with glittering masts bobbed in a nearby bay, and colored wild-flowers spread out over a rolling hill. Singing filled the air—a little girl with a haunting, melodic voice. It was a song about a mermaid with a broken heart.

I could see her now. She was making a wreath of dande-lions, and her strawberry-red hair shone in the sun. Then, smiled, handing me the wreath. "A crown."

I glanced out at the bay and breathed in the fresh, salty air.

Lyr pulled his hand away, and the vision disappeared, popping like a bubble.

"How did you do that?"

"I just gave you one of my memories. Now you know what I'm trying to protect. Do you remember that song from Ys? It was an old children's song."

I shook my head. "No. I don't remember singing."

"Ah. My mother used to sing to me when I was little."

Steam rose around me, and Lyr brushed his fingertips over the cut on my side, and an electric thrill skimmed my skin. Gods help me, I *liked* being tended to by him.

"Let me see where they stabbed you." He lifted up my shirt just a little on the side, his fingertips radiating heat. Warmth poured through me.

Then, Lyr stopped abruptly, fingers freezing in place.

With a shock of horror, I realized what he was looking at. He'd moved closer, staring at the scars on my belly, and I tugged down the hem of my shirt. His face was close to mine as he leaned over the tub. He let me tug down the hem of his shirt, but he kept his hand on my waist, his palm warming me through my shirt, like he was covering the marks protectively.

Lyr kept his eyes locked on mine. "How did you get those scars?"

"It was a long time ago."

"But how did you get them?"

I sat up straighter in the bath. "It was in London, not that long before you saw me ripping out Sam's heart. I was walking, when someone slammed a glass bottle over my head from behind. Another demon bit my neck. They said they hated fae, and women. They beat me unconscious and left me for dead. I woke up with the scars. Demons can be jerks, you know?"

"How do I find them?" Lyr barked.

I blinked at him. Was he... was he offering to avenge me? How gentlemanly and old fashioned.

"No, deathling," I said. "I'm not waiting for you to avenge me. I already killed them a long time ago."

"I hope you ripped out their ribs from their backs."

"No, I used a revolver like a normal Victorian person. Then I killed Sam. Then I moved to Tennessee."

"How did you end up living with a human?"

"I've lived with lots of them. Many in Tennessee, some in London. I help keep them safe. I met Gina when I killed the ancient demon who was preying on her. And now, I need to keep her safe from the fuath who have her captive."

I rose to my knees in the bath, and I brushed my fingertips over the water's surface. I chanted the scrying spell, and a tingle rippled up my neck as the magic started to take effect.

I stared, holding my breath, as an image took hold in the water. The image looked murky, but soon Gina's dark curls and copper skin came into view. She was lying on a pale stone floor with her hands tied behind her back. They hadn't gagged her, at least. Her clothes were soaked though, probably from portal water.

"Do you know where that is?" I asked. "Is that the fortress in Acre?"

"It's not our fortress." He frowned. "It looks like Jerusalem stone."

"So she's in Jerusalem?" I asked hopefully.

"It's possible, but it exists elsewhere too. So I couldn't say for sure."

I gripped the tub's edge, staring at her. "She's only a kid."

She must have been terrified. Was there something I could do to let her know I would come for her?

"I'm going to sing to her," I said. "Brace yourself."

I swirled the water in the bath, and I started singing— Miley Cyrus's *Wrecking Ball*. I changed the lyrics, letting her know I was on my way to find her. The music wended its way through the water, vibrating through the scrying reflection.

I saw Gina's eyes fly open. Then, she wiggled her body, swinging her legs around so she was sitting up. She'd heard me.

I touched the skin under my shirt where I'd been shot, and I found it totally healed over. Then, I brushed my fingertips over my side where the fuath had stabbed me. Smooth as silk.

"I'm healed," I said. Relief and surprise bloomed in my chest. "But we need a new plan. I can't just sit around random places trying to listen for an athame. We need something a little more substantial to go on. I want to end this all now."

He scrubbed a hand over his jaw. "You're right. And I think I have an idea." He quirked an eyebrow. "You rest for a bit. I'm going to get you more information from Beira."

"The woman who thinks I'm destined to slaughter everyone."

"She's never been wrong before."

"Mmm-hmmmm."

I wasn't going to try to cut off his head and fertilize Nova

Ys with his blood, but it seemed I couldn't convince him of that.

* * *

I woke to the scent of coffee, and already my mouth was watering. I sat up straight, and for the first time looked around the apartment. It was tiny—one room combined with a kitchen. And it had obviously been decorated by someone with feminine tastes. Right now, Lyr was sitting on a white sofa surrounded by pink sequined throw cushions. A knitted unicorn blanket hung over the sofa behind him.

Elvis was playing from a laptop. It kind of felt like heaven.

Something seemed off about Lyr, though. Different. Maybe it was the fact that he'd set two plates of Froot Loops on the coffee table before him. Not bowls, plates—along with a knife and spoon lined up on a neatly folded napkin.

Maybe it was the fact that his entire body was dripping water onto a pastel unicorn blanket.

"I was just about to wake you," he said.

I rubbed my eyes. "The smell of coffee woke me. You're wet. Did you get to Beira?"

"Yes."

"Did she reiterate that I'm evil?"

"I made you coffee." He pointed to a mug on the bed next to me. "You seemed keen on it earlier."

I raised my eyebrows. "You know how to make coffee?"

He glared at me with the offense of someone who was just asked if he knew how to read. "Coffee is a Ysian delicacy. Its ancient traditions were passed down to me by the finest coffee makers. Also, I found Nescafé."

I picked up the mug, breathing in the scent, and I took a long sip. He'd added milk, and it tasted amazing. "How is Elvis playing?"

He nodded at the laptop. "God of music."

"Please tell me the Witch gave you some useful information," I said.

He shook his head. "I asked her how to find your human."

I sat up straight. "And what did she say?"

"She said that Gina is in the city of the evening star."

"What is that?"

Lyr lifted a hand, and a bright, bluish light shone above it, like a star. It transfixed me. "The evening star, deity of the dusk, was also known as Shalim. Or Salem. He gave his name to Jerusalem. And moreover, she said that the athame is there, too."

I smiled. *Finally,* we had some direction. "Brilliant."

He nodded. "We just have to get there first."

"Well good thing we have the—" It was at this point that I realized what was different about him, and what exactly was missing. "Where is the World Key?"

"Beira doesn't give out valuable information without a sacrifice. She asked for either you, or the World Key."

My mouth opened and closed. "But—won't she be able to rip open worlds and harvest demon armies now?"

Lyr shook his head. "It's only a temporary loan, and I strengthened the protective spell on it. She doesn't want to use it, anyway. She just wants adoration. Giving her the key I protect has fed her need for love."

"It doesn't seem like quite a fair deal," I said.

"It wasn't just a bit of information." Lyr reached into his pocket, and he pulled out a small, glowing, sea-green gem.

I stared at it in his palm, entranced. I wanted to snatch it up in my hands. "What is it?"

"A gem that once belonged to my mum's family. Beira said it would stop you when you try to take my head off."

I arched my eyebrow. "If I'm such an evil threat, then why

are you telling me how I can be stopped? I could just steal that from you and I'd be unstoppable."

He shrugged. "Two reasons. One, I can overpower you easily even without a magic gem, and two, maybe I like the thought of you crawling all over me and frantically trying to get into my trousers."

I rolled my eyes, but my cheeks heated too.

Lyr stared at his breakfast again, and he scooped up a spoonful of Froot Loops. He took a bite and grimaced. "Is this food? I was under the impression that it was food, but I see now perhaps I was mistaken."

"It is food. And if you're not going to eat it, I will."

I rose from the bed and crossed to the coffee table. Starving, I shoved a handful of Froot Loops into my mouth. Had a frosted breakfast cereal ever tasted so delicious? "Why did the Winter Witch want a world key that she can't even use?"

"A sacrifice isn't about utility. It's about offering up something the supplicant cares for."

The Winter Witch had asked for the key—or me. Did that mean Lyr cared for me?

I watched him as he pulled an entire roast chicken from the fridge. He pulled off a leg and started eating it.

"Take it with you," I said. "We can drive. We have to get to the athame before the fuath do."

The city of the evening star...

With a jolt, I realized I hadn't even told Lyr about the fae I'd met in Acre. The one whose eyes looked like twilight. "Wait. There's something you should know. Someone came after me in Acre. A fae male I'd never seen before. He knew who I was. He called me the daughter of Malgven. He said he might need my help someday, and he wanted to know where *she* was. He was very intent on that point. He wanted me to eat some enchanted fruit and tell me where *she* was. But I don't know who he meant."

"You really have no idea who he was talking about?"

I shook my head. "No. I was hoping you'd know."

He narrowed his eyes, considering this. For a moment, I thought he looked unnerved, but then he schooled his features again. "Tell me more about the fae."

"He was beautiful."

Lyr arched an eyebrow.

"Large, a powerful warrior like you. He had dark hair, skin tinged a little with gold. His eyes looked like dusky indigo and amber. He gave the impression of having wings, but he didn't have them, if that makes sense."

"It definitely does not."

I sighed. "And his magic sounded like... like low drums echoing off rocks. I felt heat around him."

Lyr stared at me. "Did he wear any symbols of any kind? An insignia?"

"No."

"Do you know what court he belonged to?"

"No idea. Shadows? He didn't smell like the sea. He smelled... like smoke and fruit."

Lyr shook his head. "I have no idea. All we can do for now is look for the athame." He tucked the chicken under his arm.

I moved for the door, then paused for a second and grabbed a glittery purple pen and a rainbow notepad, and I wrote a quick note—

Sorry we took some food and used your apartment.

I considered writing, "If you ever come to London I'll give you free demon hearts," but decided that would probably terrify her more than anything else.

CHAPTER 29

*a*s I drove, Lyr stared at the road signs with the intensity of a cat watching a rabbit. He had a better sense of Israel than I did, but neither of us was used to driving.

The afternoon sun blazed hot into the car, making it hard for me to see where we were going. I understood now what the air conditioner was all about. It was glorious.

As we drove out of Tel Aviv, past the airport, the vegetation on either side of us began to thin. Lyr thought it was less than a hundred miles from Tel Aviv to Jerusalem, which meant it might not be long till we found the athame.

And then? All I had to do was tune into the sound the of the Meriadoc magic, find it, and destroy the fuath.

Assuming that the Winter Witch wasn't just plumb crazy.

"Are we going the right way?" I asked. "I can't take my eyes off the road to look at the signs, or we will die in a fiery explosion."

"I think so, yes."

We'd been driving for over a day with a broken window,

and I was surprised that the police hadn't pulled me over yet. "What's your situation with human police?" I asked.

Out of the corner of my eye, I saw him shrug. "We operate with impunity. We keep the demons and goblins in check, so they're fine with whatever we do. The World Key proves who I am, and the other knights have golden cuffs. Now, I don't have the World Key, and if humans find a stray fae with no identification, they will probably alert the Court of Sea Fae of Acre. Who are now possessed by the fuath." He frowned thoughtfully. "I suppose I could kill the police officer to end the problem."

"Humans definitely frown on that."

"Even if he inconveniences me?"

"Let's just try to not attract the notice of the police."

There wasn't much traffic at the moment, which was a blessing, but every time a car passed us, my whole body went tense. And it was happening a lot, because it seemed like I was driving half the speed of everyone else. Did humans really not realize that they could burn to death at any moment if they made a wrong move in one of these things? That they could end up with permanent physical deformities and pain because of a momentary lapse of judgment?

How immensely human to be scared of bumblebees and ghosts while speeding around in flaming death machines all day like it was nothing.

"You seem tense," said Lyr.

"No more talking."

"Right. We could die at any moment. You have mentioned this several times."

"*I* could die. You're fine." A tingle ran up my spine as I clutched the wheel. "Are you doing something with your magic?"

"No, but I felt that too."

It was that sense of being watched.

Lyr leaned forward in his seat. "Someone is scrying. They've found us."

"Bollocks. So they know we're heading for Jerusalem, and that we don't have the World Key."

I bit my lip, eyes focused on the white lines, the few inches of paint that kept me from breaking my neck.

I could feel the tension rolling off Lyr.

"I know what you're thinking," I said. "If they can keep seeing us in the scrying mirror, we're screwed. What we need is basil."

"Basil protects against scrying?"

"Yep, little-known fact. It's as simple as that I had some in my apartment, though somehow you found me anyway." I scowled. "You can put it in your pockets, and no one will see you. Except the shorts I'm wearing have no pockets."

"The other knights are skilled in magic, but I don't believe they know that."

"Well, maybe you should have found me to become one of your knights. I could have taught you things."

Lyr leaned forward, staring out the window. "Pull over here. There's a gas station. They have a shop."

I didn't love the thought of crossing over a lane, but there didn't seem to be anyone coming, so I slowed the car even more and rolled into the parking lot. I parked the car crookedly across two spots, and Lyr hopped out. A bell rang when he pulled open the door.

Maybe I was starting to get the hang of this driving thing, I thought.

I watched Lyr searching the shop, filling up a basket with a bunch of stuff—container of herbs, some household items, food, water...

He still had no money whatsoever. I didn't want to attract any police attention—not when they'd alert the fuath.

But when he crossed to the counter, I caught the smile of

the woman working at the register. Lyr leaned closer to her, whispering something. He tucked one of her curls behind her ear. I had no idea what he was saying—but the woman handed him a plastic bag full of his goods. She blushed and wrote something on a piece of paper, then motioned to the door.

Seriously?

Even without the World Key, he really could just get whatever he wanted.

He pulled open the car door. "Let's go. I'll make us basil charms."

"Oh really?"

I pulled out of the parking lot and rolled onto the road again. I could hear the crinkling of the plastic bag next to me. I wasn't entirely sure what Lyr was involved in, but it seemed to be some kind of arts and crafts.

We had been on the highway for another four minutes or so when something unfortunate happened. Our trusty car that was rightfully ours by virtue of theft sputtered out and died, slowing to a roll. We came to a complete standstill on the highway, the afternoon sun beaming hot into our car.

And to my utter shock—all the cars around us had slowed down, too. All the traffic just—stopped. The car started to bake in the heat.

"What the heck just happened?" I asked.

Lyr looked perplexed. "Melisande knows a demechanization spell. It shuts down all the machinery around her for days. Maybe the fuath got it from her somehow? Maybe they hurt her."

I was still gripping the wheel. "The fuath said they could sift through memories and learn things. They're starting to take the knights' memories. They saw us driving through the scrying spell, and they acted."

A graveyard of stalled vehicles spread out over the highway. No one was getting out of their cars yet. They were all probably as baffled as we were, although within an hour they'd be baking to death.

"And it lasts for days? Gina's tied up in a basement right now." I snatched the gum off the dashboard and pulled out another piece. "We can do this. Let's think rationally. Are you sure you can't get the key back from the Winter Witch?"

"I'm sure, yes. But we can walk. We're already a third of the way there."

I glanced at the blazing sun. "How far is it, exactly?"

"If you walk fast, we can maybe make it in nine hours."

Wonderful.

Clutching the pack of gum, I opened my door, stepped out, and shielded my eyes in the sun. Nothing to do but walk in the heat, I guess.

"Come here." Lyr was holding the plastic bag from the gas station. He was holding something else, too: thick string threaded through baggies full of basil. "Our scrying protection."

"Aren't you crafty?"

I stepped closer to him, and he tied a charm around my waist. He wore his as a sort of bizarre necklace. "They won't be able to see us now."

"We just need to get off the highway, fast, because they know we're here. We don't want to be standing around here when they send minions."

Before we took off, I turned back to the car and ripped off one of the side mirrors. I now had my own personal scrying tool to take with me.

And so we began our journey on foot, running fast over rocky, forested terrain, our bodies slicked with sweat.

CHAPTER 30

*A*fter running fast from the highway, we'd spent the day walking for about five hours in the heat. The path took us over rocky, tree-lined hills. I gripped my little scrying mirror the whole time, and Lyr carried the bag of food and water.

I wasn't complaining about our death march through the burning heat, but nor did I particularly feel like chatting as we walked. Neither did Lyr, it seemed. The only noise we heard was the wind whistling through the branches above us.

Along the way, we shared a single bottle of water and a bag of chips. Every hour or so, I stopped to scry into the car mirror, making sure Gina was still okay. She seemed to be sleeping for most of the time.

I swear steam was rising from my chest, the moisture on me evaporating. Sweat had dripped down my temples and between my breasts as we walked, and I imagined myself showering in cool water. I tried not to imagine Lyr showering with me, or washing my most sensitive parts. Just showering alone, the ice-cold water running over my body.

At last, the sun slipped down behind the trees, and the sky darkened to the color of plums.

Lyr turned to look at me and handed me the bottle of water. To be honest, he'd hardly drank any of it all day.

"Don't you need some?" I asked.

He shook his head.

As we walked through the darkening trees, the hair on the back of my arms stood on end. The temperature was dropping fast, and clouds were rolling in above us.

"A storm is coming in," said Lyr.

No sooner had he said the words than a light rain started to fall. Within moments, it had turned into a torrent, slicking my hair to my head, plastering my clothes to my body. Looked like I'd be getting my cold shower after all.

After walking all day in the heat, dehydrated, the rain was glorious.

At least it was, until the wind picked up, whipping dirt and leaves into our faces.

Lyr turned to look at me, his brow furrowed. "This doesn't seem quite natural."

"No, it's picked up too fast. I don't suppose any of your knights know a spell for storms?" I asked.

"They can access books."

Everything seemed so dark with the moon and stars hidden.

A high-pitched keening floated on the wind, then the rumbling of thunder. Lightning touched down, hitting a tree just below us on the hill we were climbing.

When we reached the summit, I peered out between the trunks at the hilly terrain around us. When lightning cracked the sky, I could see that the storm stretched out for miles around us.

The fuath didn't know where we were exactly, but they'd

spread out the storm for miles, covering lots of area. The air smelled like ozone and burning junipers.

The rain picked up even more, hammering my skin so hard it hurt. Another flash of light touched down, striking a tree only a hundred feet from us.

"We have to find shelter," he said. "I think there are caves nearby."

He started walking fast, and I hustled to keep up.

Lighting struck again, igniting the branches on a juniper tree even closer to us. The needles ignited like little torches, some of them smoking as the rain extinguished the flames.

With another strike of lighting, I saw a flicker of movement between the trunks. Maybe the night had shielded us from the burning sun, but it also gave cover to the gwyllion. I sniffed the air, confirming their presence with the stench of rotting plants and their high, keening call. My stomach turned.

"Do you smell that?" I said.

Lyr nodded. "Yes."

The gwyllion hunted by scent.

I pulled the dagger from the sheath. When a twig cracked behind me, I whirled. A gwyllion lunged for me, claws out. My blade was in his eye within the next heartbeat.

Lightning cracked the dark skies, and I caught a glimpse of gray gwyllion eyes in the distance. Many, many eyes, moving for us. Any army of claw-fingered hags.

"Did you see that?"

There were too many of them to fight, crawling toward us up the rocky hill. We were surrounded.

Lyr turned to me, eyes tinged with a gold that told me the Ankou was flickering in his consciousness.

"We'll go faster if I carry you."

"Seriously?"

He pulled me to his back and hoisted me up by my rear. "Legs around me."

I gripped the scrying mirror as I held onto his neck, and I wrapped my legs around his waist.

He took off at a shockingly fast run, like the wind rushing through the trees. I nestled my head into Lyr's neck. I could feel his pulse throbbing under his skin. As he ran, his heart was beating against mine.

I had no idea where we were heading, but I was sure we were moving faster than the gwyllion could.

He hadn't been running for more than five minutes when he took a sharp turn, veering off the rocky path into a cave. I unwrapped my legs from him, and he let me go.

Lyr—the Ankou—turned and flicked his wrist, sealing up the cave. Dark, glittery magic blocked the cave entrance.

Lyr caught his breath, then called up a spell for a glowing, golden light.

I slumped against a cave wall, my legs burning after the day of hiking. "We can wait here till the sun rises," I said. "The gwyllion will have to slink away as the sun comes up."

Lyr started pacing the cave, his body tense. "What?" I prompted.

"I'm shifting more than I once did. At the wrong times. I'm losing myself."

The curse. "What exactly did you do that was so terrible?"

He glanced at me, looking momentarily startled, like he'd already told me much more than he should have. "Only the gods know."

Cloaking the truth in shadows.

"Does it have anything to do with the fuath who are trying to open up Nova Ys?" I asked.

He shook his head, his eyes mournful. "I don't think so."

My head fell into my hands, and I thought back to the fae who'd cornered me in the alley—the one with the eyes like twilight, the wings that weren't really there. He'd had an intensity that burned like a star.

"What if that man who followed me in Acre was the Nameless One? What if I lost my chance?"

"Your chance for revenge?"

"To get my power back." My words echoed off the stone walls.

"Do you think it's possible?"

"He took it away. Maybe he still has it. I actually have no idea." I heaved a sigh. "but you believe me about him, that he drowned Ys and not me?"

"Yes."

I felt my chest relax, but Lyr was still brooding. It was almost like the shadows were following him around. It felt grim in here, the rain hammering forlornly against his shield, and I wanted to draw him out of his dark mood.

I pulled out the scrying mirror, feeling the tingle up my nape as I whispered the spell to see Gina. Nothing had changed, and she still sat in a dingy stone basement. Someone had given her water at least, because it had dampened the front of her shirt. She was sleeping against the wall, her mouth open, chest rising and falling slowly. I dropped the scrying mirror.

Lyr had stopped pacing and leaned against the wall.

"What are you thinking about, deathling?" I asked.

"I don't know why, but I was just thinking about the original Ys. When I lived with my mum, before I was the Ankou. I swam on the shores, and we drank dandelion wine and ate dinner outside under the oaks. I remember the strange music. Those were my happiest memories."

"Would you like to see it again? The old Ys?"

"How?"

I closed my eyes and whispered a spell to conjure up the towering oaks from Ys. They gleamed around us, sunlight piercing their leaves. Then, I summoned the music of Ys—the soft, melodic bells tinkling over a driving rhythm.

When I opened my eyes again, I found that Lyr wasn't looking at my illusions. He was staring at me, his blue eyes wide. He looked shocked—reverent almost. It really wasn't more than a party trick, but I was glad it impressed him.

"You do remember Ys," he said quietly.

"I remember some things. The parts when I wasn't drunk." I let the images fade, but the music played on as a sort of distant lullaby. "I don't suppose you know a spell for warmth?"

He smiled and lay down on the rocky ground, folding his arms behind his head. He'd hung up his cloak to dry. "I'll allow you to curl up next to me. You'll stay warm next to my body."

"You'll *allow* me to sleep near you? Your arrogance is really insufferable."

"You can sleep on the cold rock by yourself if you prefer."

I lay down where I was, against the rocky wall, and I hugged myself. "I'd prefer the rocks, thanks."

But even as the words were out of my mouth, I knew they were a lie.

CHAPTER 31

*H*e seemed immensely cocky about the situation, like his warm body was so alluring that I'd just inevitably end up throwing myself at him during the night.

Pressed against the jagged wall, I hugged myself in my wet shirt. The sound of Ys music still chimed quietly around us, and the rain pounded hard against the cave entrance. Slowly, the golden orb of light began to dim.

Exhaustion started to claim my mind, and my eyes drifted shut. I could sleep here, even with the rain and the rocks and the freezing damp.

But as sleep took hold, I dreamt of Lyr crawling over to me like an animal. In some of my dreams, I stripped naked, while he watched on, his divine eyes burning with gold. In other dreams, he prowled over to me and ripped off my clothes. He pulled off my shorts and claimed me on all fours, my spine arched, his teeth on my throat. Our bodies were heated and ripe, moving against each other, and *gods I ached for him.* I needed him thrusting in and out of my slick body until I reached a wild inferno.

I don't know what sort of magic this was, because never in my life had I had heated sexual dreams before.

Worst of all, I woke to find that I'd moved over the cave floor in my sleep—and I'd wrapped one of my legs around his. His magic trembled over my skin, and my thighs clenched around him.

Then, to my complete horror, I realized my hips were moving against him, and I was licking his shoulder.

"Did you need warmth?" he asked, looking immensely pleased with himself. "It seems you need something else."

"I don't know what you're talking about," I said. "I just rolled over here in my sleep."

His gaze slid down my body, a sensual smile curling his lips. "You were writhing against me."

"That's just what I do in my sleep."

"We should sleep next to each other more often, then."

I wasn't about to tell him about the filthy dreams I'd had about him or my torturous state of arousal, although judging by the hardness in his pants, he was well aware. My whole body felt hot.

I couldn't stop thinking about how I wanted him to pull the shorts off me, to cup my full breasts and kiss me *hard*. I didn't feel like Aenor anymore, just a purely sexual being. I wasn't letting go of him, either. My breasts pressed against him, and my breath hitched.

But this wasn't like me. *Don't let your guard down, Aenor.*

My leg shifted on his length, and he gasped a little. He held on to my waist, his muscles tensing completely. Now, I was staring into the ancient, divine face of the Ankou, and he was looking at me with unrestrained lust.

The Ankou didn't scare me anymore.

He turned, and his arms curled around me possessively, one hand on my bum, the other gripping my hair. He gazed into my eyes with a feral intensity.

I stared back at him—this sublime, godlike being. His divinity radiated out from him, and awe filled me. This was someone who crossed between the living and the dead.

And—I reminded myself—that was why he couldn't be trusted.

I wriggled out of his grasp, rolling onto my back. My pulse raced, and I was panting hard. I wasn't exactly moving away from him.

He propped his head on his hand, eyes burning as he stared at my body. The way he was looking at me made me want to press myself against him all over again. This was, I was starting to think, a losing battle.

His eyes lingered on my nipples, hard under my wet shirt, then slid down to the tiny shorts. Every muscle in his body went completely rigid.

I had no doubt that he could feel the desire pouring off my body. Wearing these tight, wet clothes felt like a sexual torture, an excruciating tease, and I didn't even notice that my fingers had started migrating into the waistband of my shorts, desperate to pull them off.

He moved over me, planting his hands on either side of my head, knees on either side of my hips. He stared into my eyes with awe of his own—like *I* was a god.

"Beautiful." His low growl skimmed over my skin, a sensual caress. His breathing had changed, shallow and fast. "Divine."

An erotic ache pulsed between my legs, hot and slick. My tongue ran over my lips, and Lyr watched it with fascination. I didn't need to be worshipped. I just wanted him to *fuck* me hard, hands gripping my ass. I burned with sexual fire.

"I want to see all of you," he said.

My excruciating sexual need made it impossible for me to think clearly, or to remember any of my objections to fucking Lyr. I wanted sex more than I'd ever wanted anything.

I reached for the hem of my shirt and peeled it off, desperate for him to run his hands over my plump breasts. I dropped the wet shirt to the floor and looked up at him. His beauty still shocked me, even as the Ankou, and desire burned in me. His magic tingled over my body.

He pressed in, closer to me now. He gripped my waist possessively, thumbs stroking down near my hipbones, sliding under the waistband of the shorts. Warmth pounded in my core, and I let out a low moan.

He leaned down, brushing his teeth over my neck. This was definitely torture, and I needed more friction from him, needed his body sliding fast against mine. I wrapped my arms around his neck, trying to pull him down closer to me.

He managed to keep his restraint, moving slowly. When he licked my skin, my body trembled with pleasure. Then, he moved his lips to mine, kissing me with a wild desperation that slowed into rolling passion. His tongue brushed against mine, and I moaned as his thumbs flicked lower over my hips. He palmed one of my breasts, the touch too light.

With a low growl, he pulled away from the kiss, trailing his gaze over my rain-slicked body again. The cave air almost cooled my fevered skin.

"Divine," he murmured, and the word trembled over my body in an erotic stroke.

I reached for waist of his trousers. I unbuttoned them as fast as could. As I did, my fingertips brushed against him, and he let out a low sound in his throat.

Now, it was my turn to stare at his physical perfection, the muscled god before me. My body demanded fullness.

I needed the shorts off now. I pulled them off, and Lyr's ravenous gaze was locked on my body, watching as my legs fell open.

Now, the look in his eyes had gone from reverent to completely wild as he stared at me naked and aroused, his gaze lingering at the top of my thighs. The god looked like he was about to become untethered.

He lifted my wrists over my head, pinning them to the ground with one hand. The other hand palmed my breast, his thumb flicking over my nipple.

Then, his mouth moved to mine, kissing me so deeply I moaned.

His hand moved lower in a slow stroke down my sleek skin, leaving hot tingles over my ribs, my waist, my hips. But I needed him between my legs. I'd become nothing but a pool of sexual need.

"Lyr," I breathed. "Touch me harder."

Lyr seemed to be enjoying his control, drawing it out to make me more wet and ripe. With excruciating lightness, he stroked his fingertips between my legs. My legs opened wider, the slowness making me insane. The cold air on my nipples made them tighten into sensitive points.

Aching for him, I writhed against his hand, demanding more. Lyr leaned in and kissed me again, deep and sensual. His fingers still made lazy strokes at the slick apex of my thighs, a finger slipping into me to tease me some more. My hips bucked against him, and I kissed him back hard. The soft fullness of my body still ached for more of him.

I pulled my wrists free from his grasp and wrapped my arms around his neck. Something snapped in him, and he was moving with a different fierceness now, gripping me under my rear to lift me from the ground. He pushed me against the cave wall. The passion that had built in me was driving me insane.

"Tell me what you want." I was a hollow cavern of sexual need, but I wanted him to tell me.

"I want you, Aenor."

"More specific," I said.

"I want to fuck you."

"So fuck me."

He thrust into me, filling me inch by inch. My body clenched around him, pleasure rippling through me.

I dragged my fingernails down his back, pulling him deeper into me as our bodies merged. Lyr's magic pulsed around me, stroking my skin. His mouth was on my throat, teeth grazing it. I arched my neck, giving in to him.

He slammed into me harder, pace quickening, until pleasure erupted in me like a volcano. My nails dug into his back, my teeth in his shoulder like I was claiming him. I shuddered against him, my mind stilling to perfect silence.

With his release, Lyr moaned my name into my neck. Sweat and rain slicked our bodies, and he held me there against the rock as we caught our breath.

When he looked into my eyes again, I was looking at blue. Lyr again, not the Ankou.

His lips were curled in a satisfied smile.

"There you are," I whispered.

"I was here."

He lifted me from the wall, then carried me to lie on top of him, curled up against him on the floor. He wrapped his powerful arms around me, and he murmured into my hair, "Princess Aenor Dahut, rightful heir of the throne of Ys."

Curled into his arms, I feel into a deep, dreamless sleep. Quiet, for once.

CHAPTER 32

The rising sun released us from the cave, and we walked until we reached a proper road that took us closer to Jerusalem. Dirt covered my shoes, and I could have blended in well with the homeless people in the local parks. Though the plastic baggie of basil at my waist and the knife strapped to my bare thigh may have set me apart.

Even shirtless, Lyr still somehow looked like a king, and people in cars gaped at him as he walked past. My gaze kept drifting over to him, drinking him in. Last night with Lyr had been mind-shattering in a way I'd never experienced before. Every time I brushed against his arm, warmth tingled through my body, and I kept finding reasons to move closer to him.

But I was here for a reason, and I'd stay focused.

The sun stained the golden stones with tangerine shades as we walked into the old city.

Now, as we drew closer, I could tell the Winter Witch was right. Slowly, distantly, I could hear the sound of the athame —the deep, funereal song of Meriadoc. When I heard the music floating on the wind, I felt a different sort of longing.

It wasn't just power that I wanted from the athame, although I longed for that too.

I wanted my mother back.

I glanced at Lyr as we walked. When he caught my gaze, a faint smile on his lips, I felt another surge of warmth for him.

"I hear it growing louder. The Winter Witch was right. About the athame," I said quickly. "Not about how I'm going to try to cut off your head."

As soon as the words were out of my mouth, my mood grew darker. If the Winter Witch was correct about the location of the athame—did it increase the likelihood of the *Death spills from the daughter of Meriadoc* prophecy? Would I become demented somehow and try to rule a kingdom of ashes and bones? I kept wondering if the athame would poison me with its power.

The thought sent a stab of panic through my bones.

"Lyr," I began. "Are you still concerned about the Winter Witch's prophecy? The part where I'm fixing to destroy the world?"

His brow furrowed. "I can't explain why it would be wrong, but it doesn't feel right to me."

"It doesn't feel right to me either, but you said the Winter Witch was never wrong," I pointed out.

"Sometimes it can be hard to interpret things." His blue eyes reflected the morning light. "In any case, if you tried to destroy the world, I'm sure you'd have a good reason."

"Right. Like if someone next to me on the bus chewed a banana with their mouth open."

"You'd be well within your rights to send the earth into a black hole for that. Anyone would agree."

Still, sharp thoughts clawed at the back of my mind.

Something wasn't right, and I couldn't put my finger on what it was.

"Any chance we can move faster?" he asked.

"I'd love to. Except then I'd find it hard to follow the sound of the athame. It actually works better if we don't talk."

Lyr fell into silence again, but after a few minutes, I was the one to break it.

"I need to clarify something. What exactly do we do when we find the athame? Do you think it's bad if I touch it?"

"I'll take it. I'll conduct the spell to destroy the fuath."

He seemed a little too eager.

A dark part of me chafed at the idea of giving over the athame—the Meriadoc power—to him. It was *my* athame. It would direct my family's sea magic. What if he drew power from it, and he sucked it all away?

"Lyr," I said again. "Athames are used to conduct power, but they can store it, too. I mean, do you think I could get some of it back? For myself?"

A muscle twitched in his jaw. "I don't know. But that's not our primary objective."

I gritted my teeth. Not *his* primary objective. Nor was it mine, I supposed, but gods, I wanted that power.

The city seemed to grow older around us as we walked, the buildings of golden stone.

"Once I find this athame, and give it over to you—I'll be handing over something clearly very important, with the power to defeat spirits, and it belongs to my family. To me. Are you hiding anything else important from me? Because I mostly trust you now."

Thorns grew in the silence, until at last he spoke. "I will support you to reclaim the throne of Ys like you deserve. That's all you need to know. And now, all we need to think about is finding the athame. Because once we destroy the fuath, we can get Gina back."

"That's not all I need to know."

I wasn't even sure I wanted the throne. After years of

being vulnerable, I wanted my power back. I wanted to feel that soul connection to the sea once more. But did I want to fight to rule a kingdom of people I hardly knew, who thought I was an idiot? They'd been very quick to believe I was a monster, and I didn't particularly feel like expending the effort to convince them.

I didn't need a kingdom. I just wanted safety, wealth, and the power to control the seas—was that so much to ask?

Still, with Gina held captive, waiting for me, this wasn't the time to argue about a magical object. Lyr was right about one thing—we needed to keep our minds sharply focused before the fuath disrupted us again.

I followed the Meriadoc song up a stone staircase set into a hill. We were crossing inside the ancient walls that surrounded the old city. People were moving around, drinking coffee, eating pastries.

The song was growing louder, and I increased my pace, my heart racing.

Then, Lyr froze, sniffing the air. When he whirled, my stomach lurched. I turned to see four of the possessed knights running up the hill for us, swords drawn. I recognized Melisande and Gwydion among them, but I didn't know the names of the other two.

I pulled the dagger from my sheath. Then, I whispered an attack spell and magic sparkled down my arm.

Lyr shot me a quick look. "Don't fight, Aenor. Run. Just find it for me."

For me. I noted his word choice.

His shadowy demigod power curled off his body, sending a jolt of dread through my blood.

"Will you be able to track me?" I asked.

"Yes, and I'll take care of the other knights while you go."

I pivoted and took off at a run. I turned sharply off a cobbled road onto a narrow path—too small for cars, crammed on either side with shops selling coffee or scarves or baubles. A stream of people were moving up and down the street, blocking my way.

It was hard to track the athame at this pace, but I needed to get far away from the fuath. Once I'd found a place to hide, I'd slow down again until I could properly track the athame.

A shadow loomed above me, and for a moment, I thought it was just one of the ancient arches above the narrow road. But when it moved, I realized Melisande had found me. She was swooping above me in circles, her orange wings beating the air. I sprinted faster, pumping my arms.

I careened down the sloped alley, trying to dodge passersby. I veered away from a woman with a stroller, knocking into a table of sweets. The shop owner shouted at me.

Mentally, I tried to stay focused on the sound of the athame, but it was nearly impossible while I was running wildly through tiny medieval streets crammed with shoppers. Melisande hadn't come back again, but I wasn't letting up my pace.

Gods have mercy. Where could I hide here? The little shops around me were like traps.

I took the stairs three at a time, my hip catching on a stand of pistachios. Nuts everywhere. This might be the worst city in the world for Gina.

Then, Melisande circled above me again, and my blood went cold. She was following above me, swooping lower. She'd drawn a sword, and I had a feeling she was intent on connecting its blade with my body.

I chanted a spell, and my sea magic electrified my nerves. Melisande dove for me, swinging for my head. I ducked, and the tip of her sword landed in a plaster wall, just missing my skull. Her attack had missed, but she gracefully landed on the earth, and her smile chilled my blood. She pulled her blade from the wall, ready to swing for me again.

Around us, humans were screaming hysterically, running in either direction.

I flung an attack spell at her through the end of my blade. She dodged it, and it slammed into a ceramic nativity set behind her, sending tiny magi crashing to the ground.

She swung for me again, and I shifted. But this time, the blade caught my side.

"Oh, Aenor," she cooed. "You'll have to try harder."

If she hadn't been possessed by the fuath, this situation would have been worse. The real Melisande was an expert in enchantment, and she'd force me to carve my own eyes out or something. But the spirit possessing her wouldn't have learned a skill that took centuries to develop.

I flung the knife at her chest, but she blocked it with her sword. It bounced off her blade, clattering to the stones.

"Aenor," she purred. "Disgraced princess. The dethroned wretch. I'll do a better job than you ruling Nova Ys."

"What makes you think that's going to happen?" I shouted.

I flicked my wrist, sending another blast of attack magic her way. It hit her in the chest, but without the blade to direct it, the charge wasn't as powerful.

She staggered back, her chest smoking.

But I made the fatal error of looking her in the—stunning, fiery—eyes. Instantly, I could feel the power of her enchantment whispering around me. Melisande's expert enchantment... How had the fuath learned this skill from her?

"Aenor..." My fists clenched as her voice rang in my mind. "Aenor Dahut."

She kicked the dagger closer to me, and it spun over the

ground. I breathed in her scent—orange blossoms. She smelled like the goddess Melisande. Not like the fuath.

I fell hard to my knees, ready to worship at the goddess's feet.

She wasn't a fuath, of course. She smelled of orange blossoms, not seaweed. She was the morning sun, blazing with coral light.

I needed her to love me. I craved her blessing, her divine grace.

The goddess looked down at me, a smile curling her lips. "Pick up the knife, Aenor."

My hand shook as I reached for the blade, those errant, outlaw thoughts in my mind still yelling at me.

Not fuath.

Traitor.

Usurper.

Pretender.

But those words floated away like puffs of dandelion seeds on the wind.

The stronger voice was the one urging me to do whatever she wanted.

I picked up the knife hilt, waiting for my next instruction.

CHAPTER 33

She cocked her head. "The throne of Ys never should have belonged to you. Now, I will rule as queen. It is my reward."

I nodded mutely. Of course what she said made sense. She had the wings of a monarch! She was born to reign. Monarchs had been named for her.

"Hold the knife to your throat." She pointed a fingertip at me.

I did as she said, and its blade nicked my skin.

"Cut your own throat, Aenor."

I wanted to make her happy, but something stopped me. My hand shook, the blade vibrating against my skin.

"Do as I told you. You will be remembered only for drowning Ys," the goddess said. "How terrible do you have to be before the gods steal your power? What sort of a foul whore could wreck a kingdom that badly? A streetwalking little tramp?"

At her words, sadness washed over me. I'd wanted her to approve of me, but I'd disappointed her. I *was* a terrible little wretch. I gripped the dagger hilt tighter.

But a voice in the hollows of my mind shrieked in a rage...

A bubble of clarity bloomed in my mind. It was those words she used. I hated those words. *Tramp. Whore.* The friends and women I'd known over the past century or so had been called the same names—the streetwalkers and the actresses and the mistresses, the dancers and the abandoned wives. They'd all endured the words forged into blades, weapons to cut them down.

Under the wild flood of thoughts, a single name rang out.

Gina.

That single word knelled in my mind so loud it ripped me from the trance. With a wild snarl, I lunged for Melisande, slamming my fist into her jaw so hard that she spun. She landed hard on the stone, her jaw catching on a display of crucifixes on her way down.

I gripped her hair, then pressed the blade against her throat. A bit of blood spilled onto the cobbles, the scent making me sick. *Sever the head, fertilize the land with blood.*

But I stilled the knife where it was, my hand shaking with fury. Maybe I should leave her alive for questioning.

"What do you mean, Nova Ys is your reward?" I said.

"The true ruler of Nova Ys promised it to me for my help," she rasped.

What the hells?

Who would have promised her a crown in Ys?

I felt sick. It couldn't be Lyr, offering to marry her.

Could it?

"Lyr?" I shouted.

"I'm not fucking telling you." I gripped her hair, knife still at her throat. She struggled against me, wings started to beat the air. She wanted to fly away from me.

She of the poisoned blood...

I gripped her by the wings, slamming her back to the

ground. With a flick of the dagger, I sliced the blade through the delicate base of her wings, cutting them off.

"Who promised you'd be queen?"

Her screams echoed off the stone.

She wouldn't be getting up anytime soon, but she wouldn't be answering me either. I recognized the sound of that pain. It was the sound of someone cutting your soul away. Hollowness ate at my chest.

Death spills from the daughter of Meriadoc.

Gripping the bloodied knife, I turned and ran back down the winding alleyway, ignoring the stares of horrified shoppers. My breath was sharp in my lungs, and once I'd gotten far away from Melisande, I listened again for the music of my family.

Had Melisande been controlling the fuath? That man I'd met—the one with the twilight eyes—he'd been looking for a woman. Maybe it was Melisande, the would-be queen of Ys.

I was running so fast I'd lost the thread of the music, and I needed a moment to catch my breath.

I ducked into a doorway, lungs heaving. My legs still shook.

Someone had promised Melisande the crown. I didn't know who it was, and I'd just barely made it out of her thrall alive.

I wondered what Lyr would do when he saw her lying wingless in the road.

After another deep breath, the song of Meriadoc wended its way through the narrow streets again.

My chest ached with longing at the sound.

My power.

I closed my eyes. It was growing stronger. I couldn't let myself be diverted by power-hunger here. The goal was Gina.

Gina. I'm coming for you.

I walked quickly, my body dripping with Melisande's blood.

I turned off into another, smaller alley, the music pulling me as if by an invisible thread tugging at my heart.

It was coming from somewhere nearby. Somewhere *very* close indeed.

I nearly didn't see it—the small black door inset into pale stone, tucked under a stairwell. But the magical tug in my chest pulled me closer to it.

What a glorious song...

It had been over a century since I'd heard this music. I could almost feel my mother around us—like she was giving me her blessing from her watery grave halfway across the world. She wanted me to have the athame. And loud as it was, its power was immense. It was the song of my childhood, and the song of Ys's golden age. I was ablaze in an inferno of nostalgia.

And what's more, this was *my* power. I didn't really want to give it over to anyone.

I touched the door, and its surface shimmered.

"Glamoured," I whispered.

I pressed my palm hard against the door, melding with the magic. The door swung open slowly with a groan. That seemed... odd. Maybe whoever was keeping the athame wanted me to find it. Maybe fate had written this for me.

I crossed into a hall of smooth golden stones, and the door closed behind me.

The athame drew me in, as hungry for me as I was for it. On some level, I was concerned. Maybe it wasn't a good idea to wander through an open door when people wanted you dead. It was too easy. It seemed very much like a trap.

But the athame was here, the fuath were coming, and I was running out of time to get to Gina.

If this was a trap, I'd have to fight my way out. I'd lived a hundred and seventy-six years, and never once had I found a situation I couldn't escape.

As I took another step into the hallway, doubts started to swarm in my mind. Whoever lurked in here with the athame could be working with Melisande.

My pace had slowed. If I'd known a proper invisibility spell, I would have used it then.

But it was just me and the knife, and the weak protection spell I was whispering.

The hallway opened up into an enormous library—a floor of black and white tiles, and neat books that spanned two stories. Marble columns separated the bookshelves. Between the shelves, arched windows overlooked gardens outside. It looked like an English garden, full of roses and neatly trimmed hedges.

I scanned the arches opposite the window, trying to work out what to do next. Row after row of books, in one language after the next.

I turned again, listening to the Meriadoc music.

My gaze landed on an archway so dark I hadn't noticed it before—a black hole in the stacks of books. The only thing escaping its shadows was the music of the athame, pounding in time to my own heartbeat. It entranced me.

Euphoria spilled through me as I took another step forward, and the music skittered over my skin.

But my breath caught in my throat when he stepped from the shadows, his dusky eyes gleaming.

It was the fae I'd met in Acre.

Now, I heard a different song. A low, distant drumbeat—one that went with fire and smoke, and the sweet tang of pomegranates.

Shadows swept behind his back like wings. He looked completely at ease with the knife-wielding intruder in his house.

"Aenor Dahut, daughter of Meriadoc." He had the cruel beauty of a god, but the easy smile of a sensualist.

He burned like an evening star...

Blood slicked the knife where I gripped the hilt. "Are you the one who drowned Ys? Who killed Queen Malgven?"

His eyes lit up—that twilight indigo shot through with gold. "Oh yes, that was me."

The rage I felt for him nearly blinded me. "Why? *Why* did you come after us?"

His gaze flicked to the knife in my hand. "Have you come to kill me?" He seemed to find this infinitely amusing. "I must say, it seems a little uncouth to show up for an assassination with someone else's blood on your knife."

I wanted to cut his wings off, but they were made of shadows. He had no interested in telling me why he'd drowned Ys. Maybe he didn't have a good reason. Maybe he just liked hurting people for fun.

But, no. I was missing something, but I didn't think I'd get the answers now.

If I hadn't been drunk the day he'd arrived in Ys, maybe I could have stopped him. I was once the most powerful fae around.

I felt the weight of rocks on my chest. There it was. The dark truth. It *was* my fault that Ys sank. I could have stopped him, if only the dandelion wine hadn't knocked me out.

Keep it together, Aenor. Think clearly.

"Killing you will have to wait," I said in my calmest voice. "I'm just here for something that belongs to me."

With my true power, I could have pulled the water from his body and left him a desiccated husk on the tile floor. I could have crushed him into the earth, food for worms.

Death spills from her...

"Something that belongs to you?" His amused tone had a vicious edge.

"The athame. Did you destroy Ys just to get it?"

A flicker of surprise lit up his eyes.

"I know about the athame," I said. "And the fuath you're controlling."

A dark laugh from the Nameless One. "Aren't you a clever one?"

His tone gave me pause. He seemed to be mocking me, and he made me think I'd missed the mark completely.

He closed his eyes, breathing in. "Aenor Dahut. You have heard what they say about you, I assume? The whore who sank her island." Those vibrant eyes opened again, shocking in their brightness. "It's a fantasy, of course. The men who tell the story want to imagine they could have had you. They could have possessed the beautiful princess who smells like sea-foam and flowering brambles. She was available for the taking, with her silk scarves and unquenchable appetites. What a tempting thought."

His self-assuredness made me want to run away. He was completely relaxed.

"Why do you want to get into Nova Ys?" I asked.

"*Nova* Ys? They made a new one?" He sounded bored by the concept.

My mouth opened and closed. None of this was adding up, which meant I had no idea what to do next. I didn't think my magic was powerful enough to really hurt him, and I didn't understand what he wanted. "Can you tell me what you actually want?"

His eyes twinkled. His hair, his eyelashes and eyebrows, were dark as the shadows. "What do I want? You, Aenor. I have spent many hours dreaming of tormenting you. How delightful that you came right into my home. What should I do with you, now that I have you in my possession?"

His words were a cold blade in my heart.

Clearly I had to try to kill him. But I had some questions

for him first. "Why have you dreamt of tormenting me? I don't even know who you are. I'd never heard of you before you came to Ys. I've done *nothing* to you. I don't even know your freaking name."

For just a second, his beautiful smile faltered, nearly imperceptibly. Then it was back, charming as ever. He prowled even closer, and my pulse raced. "Is that right?"

The power of the athame tugged at my body, hungry for me.

This man—whoever he was—was my enemy, and I had to end this now.

I lunged, the movement fast enough to catch him off-guard. I swung for his neck with the blade. The dagger just barely caught him in the throat. Sadly, he managed to block it from going in deeply. He caught my wrist in his crushing grip.

He spun me around and twisted my arm behind my back until I was sure he was breaking it. His grip was pure steel, and he jerked my arm up behind my back. I screamed, the sound echoing off the stone.

Then, he leaned over me and whispered in my ear, "Sleep."

My muscles went limp, and darkness pulled me under.

CHAPTER 34

I woke to find myself hanging in chains, my toes dangling in cold water. The steel of the manacles cut into my wrists, and my arms ached. My feet didn't quite reach the ground.

The Nameless One stood in the shadow before me, his eyes burning with the glow of the evening star. Torchlight sculpted his perfect face.

No longer in the luxurious, book-lined apartment from before, I seemed to be in a rocky cave. It smelled of death in here—fire and charred flesh. A bit of sulfur. Water ran in a small stream beneath me, wetting my toes. There was hardly anything down here, except a slab of rock to my right. Maybe it was the sound of that rhythmic drumming, but the slab reminded me of a sacrificial altar.

I glanced behind me, and a pit opened in my stomach. Sharp iron spikes jutted from the rock, so close they were grazing my body. All he had to do was kick me hard in the chest, and the spikes would pierce my heart and lungs.

"What do you want?" I said.

He didn't answer.

My throat was dry and hot as desert sand. The sound of water beneath my feet was its own sort of torture. Gods, I wanted water. I wanted to fall on my knees and lap it up like a cat.

I glanced at the altar once more. A piece of fruit lay on it. I licked my dry lips, hungry for it. Behind the altar, dim sunlight glowed over a set of stone stairs.

I looked down at myself.

I still wore the same clothes, though oddly, he'd washed the blood off me. The shorts and shirt I was wearing were wet now and smelled faintly of soap. He'd stripped the dagger off me, and the sheath off my leg.

"Why did you wash the blood off me?" I asked.

His pupils widened for a split second, and he took a step closer. "Do you think I want animal blood all over my nice rock dungeon?"

Animal? Jerk. "Of course not. It wouldn't be civilized."

His eyes danced with laughter again. "How about I lead the discussion?"

In contrast to my wet and cheap clothes, he wore a shirt of the most exquisite fabric, a pale blue color.

Standing in front of me, he rolled up his sleeves, exposing muscled arms with thorny tattoos.

There was something distinctly disturbing about the way he did so, like he was about to *get to work*. And the kind of work people tended to do when they had a woman chained up in front of them wasn't usually anything nice.

I wondered for a moment if I could swing my legs and snap his neck with my thighs. I'd read that once in a book— the captive woman just swung her body, clamped her thighs around the man's neck, and twisted. Neck snapped.

It seemed wildly unlikely, though. And worst of all, he seemed immortal. I'd still be stuck here, hanging in chains, when he woke up and tortured me to death.

My throat went dry. Would Lyr come for me?

"Good," said the Nameless One. "Now that I've seen the fear in your eyes, and I can hear your heart speeding up, I'm sure you've become fully acquainted with the gravity of your situation, and your terror is delicious."

"Why am I here?"

"I'm sure you're up to speed by now, that despite the shocking physical beauty you see before you, I'm one of the worst people you could have the misfortune to meet."

"You really didn't need to spell it—"

He put a finger to his lips. "Shhh. I wasn't finished. You came to me to kill me, with a dagger." His voice sounded so calm and soothing. "Did you *really* think you could kill me with a little dagger?"

"I had no idea I'd find you here. I had to improvise."

That drumbeat pounded in my belly—a dark, primal invitation. It seemed to follow him wherever he went.

He cocked his head. "Do you have any idea how many women would pay to have me chain them up? This doesn't really seem a fitting punishment. You know, I could draw out your agony until you begged for death instead."

Something like panic started to climb up my throat. It was making it hard to think clearly. That, and the heat in here, and that infernal drumbeat. Phantom flames seemed to rise up around him, orange and gold flickering over his body.

The spikes that were just millimeters from my back. A droplet of sweat rolled down my temple.

The Nameless One narrowed his eyes. "You smelled of the Ankou when you first came to me. You're working with him."

Maybe it wasn't the blood, then, that had him so irate. Maybe he really hated how Lyr smelled.

"Get to the point." The chains in my wrist were cutting into my skin.

This seemed to amuse him more. "I'll give you the athame your little heart desires. But I need two things from you."

I swallowed hard. "I don't know how to get to Nova Ys."

He sighed. "I don't give a fuck about Nova Ys. Why would I need an island when I have all this?" He gestured at the stony walls. Then he turned, crossing to the rock slab. He picked up the piece of fruit.

"All I need you to do is to take a bite of my fruit, Aenor, filthy little kingdom drowner that you are."

"I didn't drown my kingdom," I said through clenched teeth.

"But that's how the story goes, and that's the part that matters."

"You're a monster, you know that?"

He narrowed his eyes. "Yes, I believe I've heard that once or twice before, over the millennia. People hate me; I hate them. Everyone agrees I'm a dick. However, I promise you, I enjoy my life anyway. Now how about *you* enjoy something for once in your sad little life."

I glared at the fruit. Eating it was definitely a bad idea.

"What's the other thing you want?" I asked.

"I want to know where your mother is."

I stared at him like he'd lost his mind. "What? You don't seem insane... Scratch that, you do seem insane because you have a woman chained up in a rocky basement," I rasped, my throat parched. "So let me refresh your memory. You killed her a hundred years ago. My mother is dead."

He tilted his head, a line forming between his eyebrows. "I did kill her, yes. But of course, she didn't stay dead. You do know that, don't you?"

A strange numbness overtook me, until I could no longer feel the burning in my arms, or the chafing at my wrists. Everything seemed to go quiet.

His sensual laugh skimmed over my skin, his eyes

sparkling. "Your *lover* didn't tell you? I smelled Lyr's scent on you, and he forgot to tell you this key piece of information? Now that is hilarious." His laughter seemed genuine. "It's a real betrayal, isn't it?" That mocking tone made me want to break things. Him, specifically.

The Nameless One cast a slow gaze over my body. "Apparently he thinks you're good enough to fuck, but not good enough to trust with the truth."

Lyr. Death god. A man who could pass between worlds. He'd committed a crime against the gods—an unnatural act. He'd killed tons of people and didn't seem to feel bad about that. And what was worse than killing people?

"Lyr brought my mother back from the dead," I murmured.

Darkness poured from my enemy's body, melding with the shadows around him. "And I need to find her."

The betrayal crashed over me like a storm wave. I knew Lyr had been keeping something from me. And *this* is what it was?

What else had he kept from me? A promise to Melisande, perhaps. He was using me to get the athame, and then he'd be gone.

A hot tear streaked down my cheek. "I don't know where she is."

"Hmm. Mayyyybe not." He held my gaze. "The athame will lead us to her."

I didn't want him anywhere near my mother. He'd already killed her once.

My thoughts whirled. Why hadn't Mama come to find me if she was alive? I didn't get it. "For how long?"

He shrugged. "Months."

"You're wrong," I said with more certainty than I felt. "She can't be alive. She would have come for me right away."

His gaze shot to the ceiling, and he let out a long sigh, like he was appealing to the gods for patience. "Oh, would she? Or maybe she doesn't love you. In any case, there is your other task. Like I said, if I'm to set you free…"

Then from the shadows—he picked up the athame. I stared at it, a deep longing unfurled in my body. The blade was the pale green of jade, but the hilt looked like bone. Gods, I could feel its power from there. My power. Sea magic.

The sight of it in the hands of the Nameless One made me feel physically sick.

He held it up. "Is this what you so desire?"

He knew it was. I wasn't going to repeat myself.

Using the athame, he started cutting into the fruit. As he did, a wild hunger ripped through my body.

CHAPTER 35

*H*e held it up to my lips, and all my worries drifted away like seeds on the wind. Lyr's betrayal—my mother raised from the grave… They were intangible thoughts I could no longer grasp. I wanted to *taste* it.

I didn't know what it would do. Maybe it was enchanted, so he could trap me in his home as a slave.

This close, I could smell a hint of whiskey on him.

"I'm not going to eat your fruit," I said. "Just so you can turn me into a mindless sex slave or whatever you want."

He raised his eyebrows. "That does sound fun, and I truly wish I'd thought of it myself. The idea of you stripping off your clothes and grinding yourself against me in a lust-fueled mania is something I will dwell on later in my free time. But that's not what I want right now. You once had power over the sea. I might need you to use it again."

"What will the fruit do?"

"It just ensures I'll be able to find you again."

"That sounds awful."

"Or you can stay here in chains as my prisoner." It was a threat, but his velvety voice promised seduction.

I didn't trust him one bit. And yet—as he'd so nicely pointed out—I didn't have a ton of options.

Wild hunger unfurled in my body. "You'll give my power back to me?"

A slow shrug. "Eat the fruit, and you might get your power back—in small doses, so you don't try kill me. What other choice do you have? Granted," he purred, "keeping you as a pet of my own does sound fun."

"Who the hells are you, anyway?" I asked. "What's your real name?"

"Salem."

A shiver rippled up my body. Lyr had said Salem was a god—the god of dusk, in fact. Maybe he had been a god at one point, but he'd since fallen from the heavens. Now, he was a fae—like me, but ancient and a billion times more powerful.

"Are you *the* Salem?" I asked. "The one who gave the city his name?"

His beautiful eyes gleamed with malice. "Ah, so you *have* heard of me. How flattering. All good things, I assume?"

"Only today. No one really knows who you are." I didn't want him to get a big head or anything.

Salem held the fruit closer to me, and I gaped at it. I could almost taste the sweet tang on my tongue, the juices running down my throat. It smelled divine, like an enormous ripe berry, ruby skin glistening in the torchlight. I needed to sink my teeth into it.

I gritted my teeth, trying to think clearly through my hunger. This was a bad idea, of course. A deal with the devil.

"You've got a simple choice, Aenor. Do as I ask, or you'll never leave here alive."

And then what about Gina? This animal was going to keep me in here until he got what he wanted. Gina would starve to death if I didn't give in.

The Nameless One cut deeper into the fruit. Red juice dripped down his fingers, and thirst ripped through me. He moved closer, his power thrumming over my skin.

He lifted the plump fruit to my face, and I wanted it in my mouth. As if by its own volition, my tongue shot out. I licked the sweet juice off his fingertips, then off the fruit's glistening skin. Its full flavor entranced me, making me feel just as ripe. Suddenly, I was acutely aware of the feel of the wet shirt on my skin, and the tight, wet shorts sculpted to my body. My breath sped up, pulse racing faster.

Salem's dusky eyes fluttered for a moment. I lapped up the fruit's juice from his fingers, savoring every drop until he pulled his hand away again. I hated how much I wanted more of it.

He flashed me a savage smile. "Why do I feel like you enjoyed that?"

I slowed my breathing. "It was disgusting."

He quirked a smile. "Is that right? That really wasn't the impression you gave me."

He was still toying with me. He'd said that he wanted to torture me—not let me go. Promising freedom and then denying it would be the best sort of torture.

He leaned in, smelling my neck. "You know, I like the scent of this fruit on you."

Of course he did. It smelled of him—seductive and forbidden. His gaze landed on my neck, and I realized a droplet of the juice was running down my throat.

Salem stroked it with his fingertip, then licked it off, flashing me a wry smile. "I should let you go, of course, but it would be so delightful not to."

Oh, *screw* you. I couldn't count on him to keep his word. I had to get myself out of this. Maybe I could try that swinging thing, and snap his neck with my thighs.

I glanced behind me, wondering if I could muster up

enough momentum to try that move after all, but the sight of the spiked rocks again disabused me of that notion pretty fast.

One inch back, and my scalp was uncomfortably close to the spikes behind me. That's when a thought ignited in my mind. A comb of iron, a stream of water beneath my dangling toes…

Mama was right—you had to count on yourself.

Lyr was a liar, and I wasn't going to wait for him to show up and find me.

And the animal before me wasn't going to keep his promises, was he?

I supposed he'd be able to find me. But maybe if I had enough power—the athame's power—I wouldn't be so easy to catch.

All along I'd been thinking, "If only I had my power back." But I *did* have some power. I had a sort of comb here, the spikes raking my scalp. I had the water beneath my feet. And I had my song.

I was done waiting for the men around me to fulfill their obligations.

I smiled at him, shaking my head slowly *no*, so the spikes dragged through my hair. Then, I began to sing.

The Nameless One stared at me, entranced as my song curled around him. He dropped the mask of amusement he wore, and his bright eyes held a sad expression.

I got a glimpse into his soul—the bubble of how he saw me: wicked and enticing at the same time.

My blue hair enchanted him, cascading down my narrow shoulders. His gaze followed the curves of my tattoos over my tan skin.

He stared at the T-shirt clinging to my body, damp from where he'd cleaned me, nipples straining against the cotton. The small shorts showed off my shapely legs with the whorls of tattoos over my thighs. He stared at the sweeps of dark eyelashes against my large green eyes. My lips looked inviting to him.

He saw power coiled in my body, ready to erupt. He didn't want to unchain me, because he liked me vulnerable before him.

He was keeping a tight leash on the wild beast inside him, stopping himself from doing what he really wanted to do.

He loathed me, for certain.

But I also made him yearn for something he'd lost, and he thirsted for me. I was like a ripe, juicy piece of fruit to him, and he wanted to touch me bad.

My pulse raced, chest flushing.

Once I knew I had him completely enthralled, I let the song fade.

He'd moved closer, and I could feel the heat radiating off him.

"Now, friend," I said evenly. "Take these cuffs off me, and tell me how to get out of here."

"I told you I'd let you go," he murmured. "And I will."

He pulled a key from his pocket and reached up for the cuffs. When the lock clicked open, my hands slid out and my feet dropped to the stone, cooled by the water.

As soon as he'd freed me, I could see some of the sharpness returning to his gaze, his muscles tensing a little. I was running out of time.

I held out my hand. "The athame," I commanded him.

Desire burned in his eyes as he handed it over to me. My hand trembled as I reached for it, then I snatched it from his grip. A jolt of its Meriadoc power shot into my veins, surging through my blood. I let out a shaky sigh, exhilarated by its power.

It wasn't what I really wanted—that glorious, innate connection to the sea. But it was the Meriadoc magic, and it was powerful and mine. I felt *strong* now. Royal once more.

I could try to kill this man now, but he still had the rest of my power—and I intended to get it back from him some day.

I started to run.

Just as I started off, Salem grabbed my arm, his grip tight. "Aenor. Wait."

I swung my free fist hard into his face, landing it on his jaw.

Then, I turned to run for the stairs. Magic spilled through my muscles, giving me speed, and I took the rough stairs two at a time.

The top of the stairwell opened up into the enormous library, right into the darkest archway. My thumb circled over the athame's bone hilt. It had a thumb-sized indentation in it that I pressed my finger into, feeling its power charge me.

I rushed for the door, the air whipping my hair around my head as I practically flew down the hall.

I nearly crashed into the door, but I managed to stop myself just in time. I slid the bolt across.

I ran out into the narrow alley, clutching tight to the athame. I wanted to keep it for myself.

Men are wolves, Aenor. Don't give them the chance to tear out your belly.

CHAPTER 36

I wanted to leach every last bit of magic from the athame until I could tear down my enemies. *Aenor Dahut, Flayer of Skins, Scourge of the Wicked.*

I whipped through markets, down narrow alleyways—no idea where I was going, just trying to get some space so I could figure out what to do next. I rushed through the streets with the athame's power beating through my bones.

My mind was ablaze.

Was it true that Mama was alive—or was Salem just trying to confuse me?

I took a pathway that curved around an ancient church, then darted into a covered market. *Get away from that wolf, Aenor. Survive on your own.*

When the fire in my mind started to calm a little, I could think more clearly.

I'd come to Jerusalem to get Gina. Getting to Gina meant defeating the fuath. When the knights were no longer possessed, they might be able to tell us where to find her.

Only Lyr knew what to do with the athame to make that happen. He'd kept that knowledge *all* to himself. It meant I had no other choice but to hand over the athame—unless he'd just been using me this whole time.

I wiped a hand across my forehead. I'd been running so fast, so wildly, I hadn't been able to track where I'd been going. I'd been on a street that curved outside the city walls, sloping down into a valley.

I stopped to catch my breath. Some of that initial rush of Meriadoc power was ebbing now.

I looked around me. I wasn't even in the city walls anymore.

I'd run into a rocky park just outside the walls, with a few trees and some tidy grass. Behind me, dark alcoves stood in a stony wall, as if they'd been worn down over time, or carved by men long ago.

Twilight was about to fall, the skies violet streaked with gold. The evening star burned in the sky, and shadows climbed over the grass like long fingers.

How long had I been in that terrible cave beneath Salem's home? All day, it seemed. No wonder I'd been so thirsty, so desperate for that fruit.

No matter where I went, he'd be able to find me now.

The sound of drums beat louder, as if the stones themselves were emitting the sound. And distantly, I heard the sound of screams.

This was *his* city—and he was a fae ancient enough to be worshipped as a god.

Why had I come here, to this very spot that sounded like his magic?

I closed my eyes, breathing in deeply. I needed to track the Ankou. I needed to get the truth out of him.

Lyr, where are you?

I listened for the low dirge of his music and tuned into it, trying to lure him to me. Trying to draw him closer with my own song, letting our rhythms meld.

It didn't take long before I could smell sea-swept stones moving closer. He wasn't far.

After a few minutes, I turned to find him walking for me, gilded in the setting sunlight.

The sight of him made my body tense. Had he really lied about my mother?

"There you are." His blue eyes searched mine. "I was tracking you all day, but your scent was gone until twenty minutes ago. Melisande is half-dead. I tore the city apart looking for you. I was losing my mind until I felt the pull of your magic again." He stared at the athame. "You found it."

I pointed it at him. "Stay where you are."

He stopped where he was, fingers twitching. "What's wrong?"

I tightened my grip on the hilt. If I really needed to, I thought I could draw more power from it. I could blast him with it.

"I met Salem."

He arched an eyebrow at me. "The god of the dusk? What are you talking about?"

"He's not a god. At least not anymore. He's a fae, here on earth. He's the one who destroyed Ys. That's how I found the athame. He had it." My whole body was shaking, but I kept my tight grip on the hilt. "He told me something kinda interesting."

"Do we really have time for this?"

"It was about how you raised my mother from the dead."

Golden light beamed form his eyes, and those tattoos started moving on his skin again. He took a step closer as his god side took over.

"Oh, is the Ankou taking over for you?" I said. "Get a tough question and you let the death god handle it."

"I raised your mother from the dead to rule as queen of

Nova Ys. I was too busy in Acre to oversee it, and I thought maybe… it would work."

My knees felt weak as understanding dawned in my mind. It was true.

"That's the crime you committed," I said. "The crime against the gods. *That's* what it was. My *mother?* And you didn't think I should know that my mother had come back from the dead?"

Good enough to fuck. Not good enough to tell the truth.

"I didn't tell you because it was a long time ago, and it didn't work. She lived for less than a day, then she returned to the realm of death. It's why I can't control the Ankou anymore. I gave up a piece of my soul when I brought your mother back. The transgression sent me into multiple hell worlds, one after another. Only a few minutes passed here on earth, but it felt like an eternity to me. I felt a part of my soul ripping from my body. It was the most exquisite agony. That piece of my soul remains missing, and it was all for nothing. All for a few hours of life."

I stared at him. "Don't you think you should have told me about something like this?"

"There was no reason to tell you. It's over. She's gone."

"If she's still dead, then why did Salem say he's looking for her? He seems like he knows things, and he thinks she's alive."

Lyr held out his hand. "Give me the athame, Aenor. We're running out of time."

Liar liar liar.

Still pointing the athame at him, I took a step back.

Could I really relinquish all this power to him? If I gave the athame to him, I had to trust that he'd do as promised—defeat the fuath, help me get Gina back.

And yet I'd known all along that he cloaked the truth in shadows.

"Did you know Melisande is working with the fuath?" I said. "*I* am the one who cut off her wings."

He froze where he stood, and anger darkened his features.

"She wasn't possessed like the rest," I said. "Melisande said she would be queen in Nova Ys. She said she was promised a crown by the true ruler of Nova Ys, and that she would be queen."

He was still holding his hand out to me, a muscle tightening in his jaw. "We can talk about this later." He glanced to his right. "The fuath are here. Look. We're out of time."

I took my eyes off him for one second, glancing at the grassy park.

Midir, Gwydion, and the rest were running for us, swords drawn. My heart slammed against my ribs.

Lyr's body glowed with gold. He flicked his hand, and the knights stumbled, falling to the grassy earth. He'd slowed them down, but they wouldn't stay down forever.

I took a step closer to him, ready to take a leap of faith and hand him the athame. But the sound of music stopped me in my tracks. It drifted from the cave just behind me—a song I knew nearly as well as my own, but one I hadn't heard in a hundred years—the tinkling of bells over a low melody. It was the music of Ys.

It was also my mother's song. She was here.

Well, crown me in flowers and call me a king. Lyr had lied. Again.

"She's here," I whispered.

He moved for me—too fast. I slammed him with an attack spell, channeled through the athame. Then, I turned and ran into the cave, athame in hand. Spurred on by the power of the athame, I moved faster than I ever had.

Knowing Lyr, the attack wouldn't set him back by much.

But I had magical speed on my side, and now the cover of darkness.

My mother's music reverberated off the walls, and I followed it.

"Aenor!" Lyr's furious bellow echoed off the rocks, interrupting the music.

Liar liar liar.

I imagined him with Melisande, sitting in twin thrones, ruling my kingdom after I'd handed them the key to Meriadoc power like an idiot. He'd promised her my throne.

That cleaving feeling in my chest was my heart breaking. For the briefest of moments, I'd thought maybe Lyr was someone I could trust. How dumb was I?

Let a man get close to you, and he will rip out your belly.

"Aenor!" his voice echoed off the stone.

A golden glow at the end of the tunnel lit the way, and I flew toward it like a moth to a flame.

Fast as lightning, I shot into a rocky hall, with torches that cast dancing shadows over the stone. It smelled of burning flesh and sulfur.

It smelled like the cave where Salem had chained me up. A shallow stream of water ran through the cavern.

A heavy wooden door slammed closed, sealing up the opening.

I whirled, and my heart clenched. My breath was coming as fast as a frightened rabbit's. A slamming door never seemed like a great omen. Especially when the torches dimmed a little.

But my mother's music surrounded me like a cocoon, calming me.

When her thin figure stepped from the shadows, my heart leapt.

My mother wore the same yellowed wedding dress she'd

always worn, stained with my father's dried blood. She wore narcissus flowers in her hair, like she always had.

Tears stung my eyes. "Mama?"

She smiled at me, her face radiant. "Aenor." Her green eyes shone in the torchlight. Her crown of pearls and seagrass gleamed on her silver-blue hair.

We'd found each other again, and everything would be okay.

Except Lyr was already pounding on the door.

CHAPTER 37

*M*y mother stood there, watching me. Maybe she was in shock, just as I was. A hundred years ago, she'd have been pulling me close, stroking my hair.

The tone of the music shifted a little, darker now. My skin grew cold.

I could hardly breathe. "Mama, why didn't you look for me? How long have you been alive?"

"A few months. But I was looking for something else."

An ache built between my ribs. "What?"

She beamed. "My kingdom."

Since I'd run from Lyr, pain had taken root in my chest. Now, the roots grew deeper, climbing around my heart. Her kingdom was so important she couldn't let me know she was alive?

"What are you doing here?" I asked. "Why are you in Jerusalem? We're nowhere near Ys."

I couldn't make everything add up. If Lyr had wanted power so badly, why bring her back at all?

BOOM. BOOM. BOOM. He was banging on the wooden door, the sound echoing.

She gestured at the cavern. "I came here because this is Salem's home. His true home. I thought I'd find him here, in this cave of blood and bones. I have a score to settle with him. I wanted the sea power. The magic you once had." She nodded at the athame. "I wanted that back, too. And then, I wanted to vaporize him into dust for what he did to us."

I still clung to the athame, like it was the only stable thing about this situation. Even the rock beneath my feet felt like it could give way at any moment. I was caught completely off guard here. "Wait. Go back. You wanted my power from Salem? For yourself?"

"Well, I am the queen." For the first time, I noticed her nails—long, shiny black nails, pointed at the tips. Like metallic claws—like Beira's claws. She'd never had them before.

This all just felt *wrong.* "I saw Salem today." I sounded unsure of myself. I'd never had that much doubt in my voice before, not with my mother. "I didn't know who to blame until today. I called him the Nameless One."

"He was to blame, yes." Her green eyes narrowed. "But he's not the only one to blame, of course."

"What do you mean?"

Her body had gone eerily still. "Don't you remember? Of course, I suppose you don't. You were drunk that day." She sighed. "You were always drunk on dandelion wine. Useless, really. The gods blessed you with immense power, and you wasted it. The day Salem came to Ys, you had the power to stop him. Maybe you couldn't kill him, but you could have stopped him. You let me die instead. So you must under-stand that you didn't deserve that power. I would wield it better."

All ability to speak seemed to desert me. I felt like she'd punched me in the stomach, but one thought was starting to crystallize in my mind. "You were in control of the fuath, then. You're the person trying to get to Nova Ys, trying to capture Lyr."

"Oh, yes."

My knuckles turned white gripping the athame, and my thumb slid into the small indent. It was the perfect size for something I'd seen not that long ago... "Which means you were watching me. You ordered them to kidnap Gina."

She shrugged. "I wanted you to shoot Lyr again and hand him over to me, but perhaps I chose the wrong tactic. Perhaps I could have persuaded you with... motherly love." Her cold laughter echoed off the rocks. "In any case, he's come to me now, hasn't he? Everything has come right to me."

"Where is Gina?" I asked. A sharp tendril of anger curled through me.

She wasn't my mother anymore. She was an abomination. It was Lyr's fault, but that wasn't the important part. The important part was that the abomination knew where Gina was. "Where's Gina?" I asked again.

Lyr's pounding on the door boomed through the cavern.

My mother sighed. "The human? Who cares? Aenor, I didn't come here to kill you. I came here to rip Salem's spine out of his throat and burn him to ash, to scatter him in the Mediterranean. I'll do that soon enough. But Lyr is more important, I suppose."

I stared at her. "Where the fuck is Gina?"

"Language!" She chided me.

"The fuath you control have been trying to kill me, you know." Slowly, the pieces started shifting together in my mind. "Did you tell Melisande she could be queen of Nova Ys?"

She shrugged. "I needed someone to help me access the knights. She wouldn't kill Lyr, but she helped me break the magical barriers in the fortress. I promised her she'd be queen. I told her that all I wanted was my athame. She believed me." She chuckled at her own genius. "I look forward to killing her. I wanted to rip off her wings first. But it seems you got there first. You and I are very similar in some ways."

My heart was twisting in two. Here before me was my mother, corrupted and warped by death. I felt like a little girl again, but one with a broken heart. "You shouldn't be alive."

She frowned at me. "What in the gods' names happened to your accent?" Her gaze swept up and down my body. "And where are the rest of your clothes? Are you drunk again, Aenor?"

I took a step away from her, staring at the brown blood-stain on her dress. Once, it had been as familiar as home to me. A gruesome comfort. This was, after all, the woman who'd soothed me when I had nightmares, and threaded my hair with flowers when I wanted to look beautiful, who'd sweetened my water with mint when I was feeling sick. And that macabre dress had always been a part of her.

Now, the stain on her dress just seemed twisted. "I don't understand why Lyr didn't tell me you were alive."

I said it more to myself than to her, but her eyes brightened. She flashed me a small, sad smile. "Well, he didn't know, did he? He brought me back from the dead, because he knew I was the true ruler of Ys. He was always loyal, Lyr. He always believed in me. He knew that Nova Ys needed me to rule. I was the true queen. But after he brought me back, he decided there was something wrong with me, the fool. An abomination. Do I seem evil to you?"

"You do, yes." I shot a quick glance at the door. Was Lyr going to break it down?

"Lyr decided I was too evil for this earth," my mother went on, "and he killed me again. He's as bad as Salem. He cut my head off. I plan to do the same to him." Her brilliant smile gleamed in the dim light, its heartbreaking beauty almost making me forget what she really was. "But I didn't stay dead, did I? The rules don't apply to me anymore. I'll rule over Ys even more brilliantly than I once did. I'm a queen with unlimited power. And it will be even better when I control the sea."

The Daughter of the House of Meriadoc.

The prophecy rang in my mind. It wasn't about me. It was about my mother. That little green stone that Lyr possessed was meant to stop *her,* not me. Lyr hadn't understood, because he thought she was dead.

"Where is Gina, Mama? She has nothing to do with Nova Ys, and you should not be using her as leverage."

"The fuath told you. If you delivered Lyr to me, I'd return Gina to you. But you didn't give him over, did you? I knew you were capable of it. You're a Morgen. You could have enchanted him and shot him with iron. Again. But you didn't. So if anything were to happen to Gina, you'd only have yourself to blame."

Her beauty hides her true nature. Her heart turns to ash, her soul infected by evil.

It wasn't my dad's blood poisoning me. It was the crime against the gods, poisoning Mama.

BOOM BOOM BOOM. Lyr's fist pounded against the door.

She of the House of Meriadoc will bring a reign of death.

The door started to splinter with the force of Lyr's pounding. She glanced at it, completely unperturbed. "Did you know that the Ankou has been ruling in my place? He wears a crown. The gall of him. I think I'll nail him to a tree like his mum." Her laugh was like two rocks rubbing together. "Let's see who's the abomination then."

"Definitely the one nailing someone to a tree is the abomination, so that wouldn't disprove it, like, at all."

Her green eyes flashed with rage. "In any case, perhaps then he'll tell me how to get to Nova Ys, when I've hurt him so much he can barely remember his name. Then I'll get my kingdom."

Mine, a voice in my mind roared. *My kingdom.*

My mother was a living nightmare, and her body was beginning to glow with a powerful, pearly magic.

Lyr's fist was fracturing the door, and she smiled at it. "I came here for Salem, and so did you, even if you didn't know his name. I came here to kill him. You came here to get your athame back. It seems he's drawn us all in, like planets orbiting a star. We've all converged. Either Salem is a force of nature, or the gods are blessing me by giving me everything I want at once."

What she wanted was to nail Lyr to a tree until he told her the truth. And he was coming right to her.

"Lyr!" I shouted. "Run!"

I didn't want to see what she'd do to him.

He didn't listen to me, because listening to me wasn't his style. The door shattered, and he rushed in.

"The stone!" I shouted to him. "I need it."

The indent in the athame's hilt was the perfect size for the stone.

Without asking a single question, Lyr tossed the green stone to me. I snapped the stone into the hilt, and power charged down my arm.

Enraged, my mother started to run for me, but Lyr stepped in front of me protectively.

Golden light beamed from Lyr's body, wrapping around her in tendrils like vines.

I started chanting in the dialect of Ys, working on the most powerful attack spell that I knew. "*Egoriel glasgor lieroral—*"

My mother cut me off, shrieking a spell of her own, and

murky magic stained the air around her, like ink sliding through water.

Her spell's impact hit me immediately, and nausea began to climb in my gut. It felt like she was making us rot from the inside out. Her magic revolted me, and I clutched my gut.

I stepped out from behind Lyr, working on my spell. I would need a clear shot at her, shooting the magic through the athame.

Now that I was closer to her, I could see her eyes weren't the same color. They were the murky green of seawater, and the light in them moved like phosphorescence of the deep.

"I should have killed you at birth," she hissed.

A flash of light filled the room as Lyr's spell strengthened, the magic wrapping around my mother's neck.

"I'm sorry that I brought you back." Lyr jerked her up in the air with his magic.

"Egoriel glasgor lieroral ban—" The spell started to charge down my arm, crackling with ancient power.

But my mother wasn't done. She threw back her head, opened her mouth, and screamed, a high pitched song— music to curdle your blood and turn your bones to ash. With her voice, my nerves exploded in pain.

Gods have mercy, make it stop. Lyr was trying to crush her throat, and his grip looked brutal, but it didn't seem to stop her shriek.

Then—called up by her shrieking song, salty water slowly began to rise up my throat, stopping me from completing my spell. I gagged as it climbed up my esophagus, and it filled my lungs. Pain spread through my chest.

I fell to my hands and knees, vomiting up rotten seawater onto the floor.

I couldn't drown—not in the sea.

And yet I was drowning here in a cave, at the hands of my own mother.

CHAPTER 38

$\mathscr{L}$ yr dropped my mother to the floor, and she fell onto her backside. Her crown slipped over her eyes, and the roar she unleashed bellowed off the cave walls. But her spell was still choking us.

Lyr was drowning too, on his knees, his eyes bulging. Somehow, his magic still spun from his fingertips, twining around my mother. Her chest started to bulge, like her ribs were about to explode.

I gagged up more seawater, desperate for air. I needed to breathe, oh gods I just needed a breath of air.

I glanced up again, and Lyr was trying to rip her heart out of her chest. I didn't want to see it, but I couldn't tear my gaze away.

Another burst of water in my lungs, climbing up my throat. *Air. Air. Air.* My lungs were about to explode, my own chest ready to burst open.

When I looked up again, wiping my mouth, I stared at Queen Malgven.

Her chest looked completely intact, and viny ropes of

magic were now spilling wildly from her, curling around the Ankou.

Lyr's enormous body vibrated with the effort of trying to move. She'd *frozen* him—the powerful demigod, the Ankou. *She* was more powerful than he was.

What kind of a monster had he created?

Her smile could wilt flowers. She walked closer to Lyr. "I want to hear what your screams sound like when I drive iron through your tendons. The trick is to make sure you don't lose consciousness, so you can tell me what I need to know. I'll peel your skin off in long, thin strips."

I forced myself to my feet, gasping—one ragged breath, one glorious lungful of air—when slimy seawater started choking me again, smothering my lungs.

Gods, I need air. I slammed down to my knees again.

"Stay on your knees where you belong, girl," she spoke to me, even as she stared at the tendrils of magic spilling from her fingertips. "I need to ask the usurper a few questions. I've got him exactly where I need him."

The thick, heavy scent of the sea pressed down on us like rotten sand. I felt trapped deep in the abyss, unable to breathe.

I kept my eyes on my mother, trying to stand again.

She lifted her fingertips—her claws—in front of Lyr's face. "I had my nails done. Iron doesn't hurt me anymore, since I recovered from death. I'll give you once chance to tell me how to get to my kingdom before I start carving into your flesh."

The magical bindings around Lyr were cutting into his skin, drawing blood. They'd immobilized him.

I was still gripping the athame, but I couldn't breathe.

One breath—one glorious breath of air filled my lungs. Then, another wave of foul seawater rose in my throat.

When I looked up again at Lyr, I saw that my mother had *draped* herself on him like a lover. Except she was digging an iron claw into his shoulder, opening his old wound. She wiggled her nail around, and I could see the pain etched on his features. The urge to save him burned through my body like wildfire. I wanted nothing more than to release him from his pain.

"You brought me back to rule Ys," my mother purred like a lover while dark blood ran down his body. "And now you won't let me rule. I believe I can help you rethink the situation. Haven't you always wanted to know how it felt for your dear old mum when she died?" She jabbed another nail into his chest—near his heart, but not in it. "Shall I strip you naked as well?"

I wanted to tear her vile head off her body. This wasn't my mother. She was a thing. An abomination that never should have existed.

I just needed her to pull her attention off the magical ropes, long enough for Lyr to get control again. That's all I needed. One moment of pure distraction from her, to stop her from hurting Lyr.

No air.

I coughed up another lungful of rancid seawater, then forced myself up, staggering, the athame in my hands. The Meriadoc power gave me strength. As it flowed through my muscles, I sucked in a sharp breath.

"*Egoriel glasgor lieroral banri mor!*" I shouted, finally getting the entire spell out.

Powerful sea magic burst down my arm, exploding from the end of the athame, slamming into her chest. She staggered back, shocked, her skin now ashen, eyes dark.

She was still standing, but she'd pulled her attention off her magic. That was all I needed, just a moment of distraction so Lyr could get control—

She shot forward fast as lightning and struck me in the chest.

The blinding pain spreading through my ribs told me something was wrong.

I thrust the athame into her body, stabbing her between the ribs. *"Egoriel glasgor lieroral banri mor!"* I rasped.

Sea magic rippled all over my body, pure pleasure with the athame's hilt in my hands. My mother's murky eyes flew open.

I read betrayal in them. My heart was breaking. Time slowed down as I stared into her watery eyes, flecked with phosphorescence. She'd once been like a home to me; she'd once stroked my hair while she told me about the apple orchards on the far side of Ys. She'd taught me to be careful, that men were wolves and a woman needed to look after herself. *Mama.*

Then, before me, her body crumbled into wet ash. With my heart ripping in two, I stared down at her remains, her pearly crown resting on top of the ash.

No, my heart was *actually breaking...*

When I looked down at my own chest, I saw that she'd thrust her fingernails into my heart—and they remained jutting from my chest, even when the rest of my mother had crumbled.

Time seemed to stretch on. All the breath left my lungs as I stared down at the iron spikes in my heart.

Lyr shouted my name, catching me in his arms. He pulled me to him, but he seemed distant, and I couldn't hear him anymore. I couldn't see him.

I wanted to reach for him, but my heart stopped, and my world went dark.

CHAPTER 39

I floated under the sea, in lifeless and dark water.

I thought maybe I'd always been here.

I'd always be here.

I belonged to the sea of nothing.

In the distance, a star burned, and milky rays of light threaded through the water. It was beautiful, but it wasn't supposed to be here. Pale, morning light strained for me. A morning star. A flicker of its power washed over me, then faded again, leaving my chest empty.

I floated in darkness again, and the cold of the water seeped into my skin and bones. So *this* was what death was like. Maybe it was different for everyone.

Pure sadness, iron-sharp, sliced into my chest—exquisite despair cut me in two. This was my death. And in my death, the cold, dead sea didn't feel like home. I needed to breathe. The god of the depths wanted me to suffer. He was claiming a part of my soul.

Briny seawater began to seep into my mouth, dripping down my throat.

I'd always been here. I always would be. Pierced with iron, drowning in the sea hell. This was my eternity.

I could feel the god of the depths pulling my soul from my body—

Then, a warm hand clamped around my arm, ripping me from the sea.

Sunlight and air bloomed around me.

I landed hard on a grassy shore, and I rolled onto my back. Power flooded me now—divine, marine power that I once possessed. I felt the sea in my soul.

I stared up at the Ankou, the sunlight haloed around him as he knelt over me. He leaned down and kissed me on the forehead, then lay down in the grass next to me. Wildflowers spread out around us, and I tried to remember their names from childhood—purple woundwort, sea carrot, creeping buttercups, scarlet pimpernel. Blackthorn, with white blossoms, climbed low stone walls around the field. Ahhhh, how had I gone from the sea hell into this heaven?

I filled my lungs with beautiful air—air that smelled of Ys: water mint, salt, the wildflowers around me.

Lyr reached for me, then pulled me toward him, lying back on the grass. He wrapped his arms around me protectively, and I rested my head on his chest, listening to his heart. It beat in time to the melodic music of Ys. Distantly, the bells of Ys chimed.

"Are we in Ys?" I asked. "What's happening?"

He ran his hand down my hair, soothing me. I never wanted to move from here. I'd been so angry at him before, but it didn't matter now, did it? Because he wanted to keep me safe, and I wanted to keep him safe, and nothing else mattered.

Except—was I still dead?

"I pulled your soul from hell."

"So where are we?" I asked.

"This is your paradise. It's very much like Ys, but you created it."

"Are you really here?" I wrapped my arms around Lyr's waist.

"Yes."

I should've been devastated that I was dead, but it was so beautiful here. It was so perfect. And Lyr was with me. I rested my head on his chest, listening to his heartbeat. Vibrant life pounded in his chest.

When I touched my own chest, I felt nothing. Stillness in my ribs, my heart poisoned with iron. A flicker of disturbing wrongness pulled me out of my joy for a moment.

"What's about to happen next will be unpleasant," he said.

Dizziness swarmed in my mind. "What do you mean?"

Without another word, his body seemed to fall away beneath me, the earth ripped out from under us. I fell, and noise engulfed me. It was the sound of Lyr's screaming, and the clanging of the bells of Ys, growing louder and louder.

Why did Lyr sound like he was in so much pain?

I landed hard on a stone floor, head cracking against the ground. Power flooded my limbs—sea magic. *My* magic. Ahhhh. Sea-foam roiled in my blood.

I pushed myself up onto my elbows. I was alive again— back in the rocky cavern.

But Lyr wasn't here anymore. Nor was my mother.

To my horror, Salem was standing over me.

My mind reeled, and I tried to figure out what the hells had just happened.

I'd died… and Lyr had brought me back.

Just like with Mama.

But I didn't feel like an abomination. In fact, I felt like I had my power back.

My heart *beat* again.

I looked down at my fingertips, which glowed with blue-green magic.

"I got my magic back." Death and the athame had returned it to me.

Queen Aenor Dahut... the sea winds whispered my name. I could smell the power on me. I could feel the waves of marine power crashing in my chest. My mind filled with the noise of the ocean's magic, the roar of waves.

Gods, I wanted to use it all at once. I had a violent urge to drown everyone who'd ever wronged me.

I'd start with Salem, the man who ruined my life.

"Well, well, well. What a time to be alive," he said.

I rose to my feet, staring at him. A smile curled my lips.

He arched an eyebrow. "You look very pleased with yourself for someone who just died."

I beckoned to him, trying to draw water to me. I wanted to suck his body dry, leave him like the desiccated hearts on my wall.

He breathed in deeply, looking disturbed. Ruffled. For just a moment, those beautiful twilight eyes looked unnerved. Then he regained his composure again, flashing me a languid smile, his posture at ease.

My power wasn't working like it should, and dizziness fogged my skull. The roaring sound of my magic was deafening me. It wasn't working.

I swayed on my feet, nearly falling, but Salem swept an arm around my waist to steady me.

I stepped away from him, baring my teeth. "Don't touch me."

He laughed softly. "A little ungrateful, isn't it? I let you come back from the dead unharmed, and the first thing you do is try to kill me. I think I feel a little hurt."

I took another step back. My head was spinning. "How did you end up here in this cave?"

The light in his twilight eyes dimmed for a moment, and he shrugged. "You tasted the fruit I gave you. I told you. It means I can always find you. And it means I felt your spirit die. I've spent a long time looking for you, and wouldn't it be sad if the fun ended so soon? Sadly for you, it doesn't seem that you got all your magic back. Just one little delicious taste."

I pressed my hand against my heart, feeling it beat beneath my palm. My chest was indented where the abomination had pierced my heart, but the skin had already healed over.

I'm here. Alive.

Lyr had brought me back. Just like he'd brought my mother back. Did that mean he'd been thrown into the hell worlds again?

"I was here with Lyr." I cast my gaze around the room. "I just heard him screaming like he was in agony. What did you do to him?"

"What did I do to him? How about we talk about what I didn't do to him. I didn't shoot iron bullets into his chest or attack him with the athame."

Nausea turned my stomach, and I clutched it. The initial rush of power I'd felt when I'd emerged from the death realm had sputtered and died out. "Tell me exactly what happened."

"You know, you make a lot of demands for someone who was trying to kill me seconds ago." He tapped his lips. "I felt you die. I felt your soul leave this world from this very spot."

My heart tightened. "How?" It took me a moment to realize the fruit I'd eaten might have something to do with it.

"Because, Aenor. You're linked to me now. Lyr was holding your wretched corpse when I came into the cave, then he simply disappeared, screaming."

Panic gripped my chest. Now, I remembered what Lyr had told me. When he'd brought my mother back from death, it felt like he'd spent an eternity bouncing through hells.

My resurrection had sent him to the hell worlds—again.

It smelled of burnt flesh in here. My muscles were tensed, ready to fight, but I didn't have the energy.

"I see you killed your mother, too." Salem crossed to the wet pile of ashes. "There. Doesn't she look nice like that? It suits her. It's a bit sad, though. I've been looking for her for ages, and it's a shame I didn't get to kill her again." He stepped on her ashes, then ground them into the floor with his shoe. "There were questions I wanted to ask her." Anger tinged his last statement, his mask of composure slipping.

Bile rose in my throat at the gesture. Maybe she'd become an abomination, but she'd once been a great queen, and Salem was stepping on her. That old hatred for the Nameless One burned in me like a star.

My fingernails pierced the skin of my palms.

I'd find a way to get all my power back from him. All of it.

He turned back to me, his gaze piercing me. His strange beauty was like a dagger in my heart.

Lyr had caused all this, with his crime against the gods. He never should have brought my mother back. He shouldn't have hidden it from me. But I couldn't be angry with him—not when he'd sacrificed part of his soul to revive me.

Everyone made terrible decisions sometimes. I certainly had.

I pressed my hand on my heart again. "How come I'm not an abomination?"

I was asking the question to myself, but Salem turned to me. He snorted with laughter. "What makes you think you're not?"

I breathed in, glorious air filling my lungs—even if it smelled a bit of burning bodies and sulfur.

"I don't feel any different," I said. "I don't feel evil."

"Nobody *feels* evil." His dark laugh echoed off the walls.

Salem's attention was rapt on me. I don't know why, but it made me feel like the center of the universe.

"In any case, I'm not done with you. I came here because I felt you die, and I was relieved to find you recovered. You work for me now, Aenor, and I don't want to lose an asset."

My heart started beating faster. "Bullshit. What do you need me for? Why aren't you trying to chain me up or torture me or something?"

"I don't need to chain you up. I'll be seeing you again in the future."

"Where is Lyr?" I asked again.

"Let's see... he journeyed with you to the hell worlds to get you and then disappeared. I imagine he's being tortured somewhere. Probably still screaming. You really are a terrible girlfriend."

Anger simmered. *"Where?"*

"Fuck knows. Death is his world, not mine. Also, I don't care. I hope that clears things up."

I glanced at the shattered wooden door, then at the athame on the floor. He didn't particularly seem to care about the athame, which was just about as baffling as everything else about him.

I turned away from Salem, looking for signs of Lyr, my hand on my beating heart. An evil presence hung in the cavern, a sense that terrible things had happened here. It was probably Salem himself, exuding menace.

"My mother said this was your home." My voice echoed. "This foul hell hole is a fitting place for you."

When I turned back to him, I found he was gone.

How did *that* happen?

I snatched the athame off the floor, and I broke into a run. I fought past the dizziness, propelled by desperation to find out what happened to Lyr. I needed him, and I needed Gina.

I had the athame now.

At the mouth of the cave, a figure loomed in the light. By the tall, spiked crown and the golden light emanating from him, I knew it was Lyr. I practically slammed into his chest.

He loomed above me in his Ankou form, and the World Key gleamed on his chest.

"Lyr! Are you okay?"

Golden eyes gleamed in the darkness, a haunted look in his eyes. "Yes."

"What happened to you?"

"It doesn't matter. I'm back now. Your mother sent you to the sea hell. I had to bring you back."

I gripped his arms. "But you turned her into a monster when you brought her back. Will I turn evil?"

"You were only dead for moments. She'd been dead decades before I brought her back, losing parts of her soul. When I found her in the death realm, she already seemed demented. When I found you in the death realm, you seemed the same. I took a chance, and I was right."

It was still a crime against the gods, and Lyr would have to pay for that.

"And what happened to you?" I asked.

"I flew from one hell to another, until finally, I ended up in the realm of the Winter Witch." He lifted the key. "She returned the World Key to me, and I opened the portal."

I slid my arms around his neck, and I pressed my body against his. His clothes and hair were soaked with freezing water, but heat from his body warmed me.

Slowly, the blue was returning to his eyes. I wanted Lyr now, not the Ankou.

I pressed my hand against his cheek, looking up into his eyes. "Are you okay?"

His eyes seemed to search mine. "I should have told you about your mother. I felt ashamed of the mistake I'd made. I thought that once I killed her again, it was all over. I had no idea she could come back. I only knew her soul wasn't in the sea hell anymore."

"We all do dumb crap, Lyr. Even divine death gods like you."

His wild magic skimmed my skin, and I felt like I was melting into him. He'd literally traveled into the hell worlds to save me. "Why did you bring me back?" I asked.

"Because I'd do anything for the true queen of Nova Ys."

"And you weren't worried that I'd come back monstrous like my mother?"

"Maybe a little worried, but you don't seem any worse than you did before."

"You're such a charmer." I took a deep breath. "Salem came into the cave when you were holding me."

"I saw him. Just before I slipped into the death realms, I saw a fae who burned like a star."

"He's gone. He was there when I woke up, and then he just disappeared, like smoke. I don't know how. He still has my power. We have to find him at some point. But not right now. We have to get to Gina. My mother never told me where she was, so she's still tied up somewhere, probably dying of dehydration. Where are the other knights? They'll know where she is."

"Still unconscious," said Lyr. "Still possessed. I knocked them out before we entered the cave. But now, we have the athame."

CHAPTER 40

*A*s Lyr completed the spell over the knights, I stared at them. The spirits of the fuath shrieked, the magic ripping them out of the knights' bodies.

Gwydion stood first, smoothing out his clothing. Night had fallen, and the moonlight washed them in silver. Stars twinkled in the purple sky.

"Where in the gods' names are we?" Gwydion grimaced. "My mouth tastes as though I've been eating vinegar crisps."

Midir retched. "I have an unsettling memory of licking a demon's horn at some point."

The other knights—not being demigods—moaned on the grass.

I rushed over to Midir, the only one who'd remembered anything. "Where is Gina?"

"What the fuck are you asking me? What happened, and why am I not wearing silk socks?" Panic flamed in his eyes. "I am wearing *cotton* socks. For the love of all that is holy, what the *fuck* is going on?"

I slapped his cheek, hoping to snap him out of it. It knocked his leafy crown askew on his ginger hair. "You

remembered something. Licking a demon's horn, which…
ew, but do you remember the rest? The fuath?"

Midir blinked. "They were coming for us, weren't they?
And we needed an athame."

He cleared his throat, looking dazed that I slapped him.
To my shock, he did not threaten to peel off my skin.

Gwydion shuddered. "A fuath inside me. My body is a
temple. It really is an outrage."

"Where is Gina?" I shouted.

"Who the fuck is Gina?" Midir straightened his crown.
"Lyr, your depraved captive is hurting my ears. Now that you
apparently have found that athame, I think it is time to do
the thing with her head on our gates."

Gwydion made a face. "We'll have to shave her head first,
at least."

"No one is killing anyone," said Lyr. "And especially not
the true queen of Ys."

They stared at him.

Gwydion touched his forehead. "Okay, what in Beelze-
bub's arsehole has happened while we were possessed?"

Lyr's tattoos moved on his skin, his eyes glowing with
gold. Now that he'd brought me back from the dead as well,
this wouldn't get any easier for him.

"Aenor didn't destroy Ys," said Lyr. "It was an ancient fae
named Salem. For just a moment, I saw him. And I
know Aenor."

Midir held his cheek where I'd slapped him. "So who was
controlling—"

"Look, we can catch you up later," Lyr interrupted. "Two
things need to happen now. One, you need to remember
where you left the human girl, and two, someone needs to
bring Melisande to the dungeon."

Gwydion heaved a sigh. "Fine. I *vaguely* remember the
human girl. I don't remember her name or what she looked

like, but she's tied up beneath a shop that sells frosted biscuits shaped like human baby faces."

"That's not vague," said Lyr. "It's very specific."

Gwydion frowned. "The bakery is memorable. It's honestly the creepiest part of Jerusalem." He waved at the rocks behind us. "Including this bit, where they used to sacrifice people."

I glanced back at the caves, a chill skimming up my spine. Salem's true home, a place of human sacrifice. Not shocking. And I'd eaten his fruit, meaning he could always find me.

Still, we were finally making progress with Gina.

"Good!" I said. "We have a location. Anyone know where this bakery is?"

Gwydion sighed, pulling his phone out of his pocket. "Hang on. Oh, bloody hell. Did the fuath have data roaming turned on this whole time? Fuck pigeon."

"Gwydion!" Lyr snapped. "Stay focused."

"Calm your tits, I'm looking it up," said Gwydion. "It's not far." He held up the phone to Lyr's face. "See? On the map. A few streets away."

I'd had no idea the knights had phones.

"I've got it," said Lyr. "Midir, I need you to find Melisande. She's recovering near the market. Just follow the trail of blood; it won't be hard. Bring her to the…" he waved a hand, "baby-face bakery. I'll open the portal there. Gwydion, you stay here and wait till the other knights wake up. Bring them to the portal also. We'll return to Acre while everyone recovers."

I wanted to get Gina back right away.

But after that? Once I knew she was safe? I wanted to come back to Jerusalem. Salem was still here, hoarding my power.

My thoughts were on him as we started running back through the city walls. He was, truly, evil to his core.

And I'd given him power over me.

* * *

GINA SAT on the stone floor in a cellar, surrounded by cookie crumbs. One half-eaten baby-faced cookie lay on the ground, with pink cheeks and a curl on its head.

Lyr was ripping the bindings off her.

Tears streaked Gina's cheeks, but she seemed to be fine. "I thought they were going to kill me. They kept feeding me those baby-face sweets, and I thought it was, like, a weird cult and maybe they were going to sacrifice me to a giant baby. Is that a thing that happens?"

I shook my head. "Spirits don't understand human dietary needs very well."

She sighed. "It's a nut-free bakery though. I made them check. They kept rolling their eyes like I was making up the allergy."

At last, Lyr had her bindings free. She shot up, with the energy of a million hot suns. She *always* had energy. "What happens now? Are we staying in a hotel again?" She glanced at Lyr. "Is he your boyfriend? He's well fit."

"Better than a hotel," I ignored the other questions. "I'm taking you to a crusader castle." I remembered the last time I was there. "Which, with any luck, is still standing after I lit it on fire."

"You *what?*" said Lyr.

"Lit it on fire, a little? It's probably fine."

"She does that when she's lying," Gina pointed to my face. "That nose wrinkle she's doing."

I grabbed her hand. "Shhh. Come with me. I have to catch you up on one or two things. We just have to jump into a pit of icy water first."

CHAPTER 41

Gina zoomed around the dining hall on roller skates, while Midir scowled at her over his wildflower salad. "Remind me again. *When* are we sending that human back to the Savoy?"

"Tomorrow," said Lyr. "Aenor just wanted a little more time with her."

Midir stopped eating, his fork hovering midair. "Aenor is not going with her? Please tell me she's not staying here."

I smiled at him. "I'm staying here."

Gwydion chuckled. "This should get interesting."

"Why?" asked Midir, his fork still suspended in hair.

"Because Salem still has my power, somewhere in Jerusalem, I think. And I want to get it back."

Lyr and I had returned to Salem's home—exactly where I'd found the door days ago. Except—the door was gone this time. We'd scoured the city once, and the cavern again. We hadn't found him, but we weren't done yet. I could still hear Salem's music there, distantly.

"And then," said Lyr, "the coronation in Nova Ys."

I sighed. If you wanted people to believe you, they had to hear it from a man.

Gwydion filled his wineglass. "I'm just shocked about Melisande. She didn't even deny it. Just confessed right away. Granted, she was always a major bitch, but…" He took a long sip of his drink. "I guess I'm not surprised. I mean, I feel like I should be, but she was just always a full-on bitch. The only time I ever saw her cheerful was immediately after banging Lyr."

Lyr put his head in his hands, like he'd been enduring centuries of his brothers' bull crap.

Gwydion put his hand to his mouth in mock horror. "Oops. Should I not have brought that up?"

Midir stared at me. "Now that you mention it, Aenor seems more cheerful now, doesn't she?"

And that was my cue to leave.

I rose from the table. "You know? I've been meaning to pay Melisande a visit." I snatched my wineglass up and refilled it before I left the table.

I glanced at Lyr, who was looking at me with curiosity. "I'm just going to talk to her," I said. "I'll meet you right after."

Gina looped around the large hall on the roller skates, her curls flying behind her. A lollipop stick jutted from her mouth.

I frowned at her as she circled round me. "Where did you get roller skates?"

She pulled out her lollipop. "Lyr found them for me. I told you he'd become your boyfriend and you two would fall in love. I have psychic powers."

"No, you said Irdion would be my boyfriend, and he remains dead after I shot him."

She shrugged. "Close enough."

"You should go to sleep soon. Tomorrow you're back to

London, and then you need to catch up on all your school stuff."

She spun in a circle on her skates. "I don't think I need school anymore. I'm going to become a knight like these guys."

"That's not even possible. You're human."

"I can become fae. There's a spell for everything." She popped the lollipop back in her mouth. "You just need to get reading."

"Go to sleep, Gina."

She nodded at the silky cloak I wore, the color of moss. "But look at you. Dressed like them. You like it here, too."

I looked down at the cloak and long gown I wore. This wasn't quite me, although the silk did feel nice.

Gina skated off again, and I headed down the long corridor. Was it only a few days ago that Lyr had dragged me out of the dungeon here? That seemed insane.

A hollow ache in my chest darkened my mood. I'd desperately wanted my mother to come back, and I'd found myself so close to her—only to find that death had corrupted her.

But maybe she'd always been a bit... off? Since the day she killed my father, she'd worn her wedding dress every day, stained with his blood.

I thought of Salem laughing at me when I said I wasn't an abomination.

What makes you think you're not?

Nobody feels evil.

I figured out what had bothered me the most about Lyr's story about his mother.

His mother was publicly executed, and even if no one spoke about it openly afterward—my mother would have known about it. But she'd agreed to marry my dad anyway.

She'd jumped at the chance to marry a king who'd slaughtered his last fiancée that way.

My entire body felt cold as I crossed down the old, dank stairs to the dungeons.

It was hard to reconcile this calculating version of my mother—the warped, slightly psychotic one—with the same woman who'd combed my hair and held me in her lap when I'd skinned my knees.

I'd had well over a century to get used to the idea of her being dead. So I don't know why I felt so sad. I was close to two centuries old, and it was absurd to think I needed someone to comfort me at this stage. I was Aenor, Flayer of Skins, for crying out loud.

For some reason, tears pricked my eyes as I crossed into the dark dungeon hallway.

I glanced into Debbie's cell as I passed. Her delicate frame lay curled up in the corner, her pink hair draped over thin shoulders. I pulled my cloak off, then slid it between the bars for Debbie.

Still clutching my dandelion wine, I crossed a few more cell doors down.

Melisande sat slumped in the corner of her cell, dirt smudged on her body. Her wing stumps and throat were bandaged, though dark blood stained the bandages.

When she saw me, she didn't even muster up enough energy for an enraged scowl. She just looked... defeated.

"Aenor," she said in a dull tone, her eyes on the stone. "You cut my wings off. You little bitch," she said listlessly.

"On the plus side, I did leave you alive."

"That's not a plus side. That was an additional cruelty."

I stared at her. "I don't understand why you'd betray everyone here for the crown of an island you've never even been to. What's the point?"

Now, for the first time, her eyes sharpened, and she was staring at me like a bird of prey. "What's the point? Have you not noticed how they operate here? They eat before us, the council of three. Three males, making all the decisions. I follow orders. I'm good enough to fuck—not good enough to consult on decisions. Not good enough to trust with all the secrets they keep among themselves. Once, women ruled the fae world. We were treated like goddesses. Your mother brought all that back. A true fae queen, just like the old days. And I was going to be her successor, reviving the old House of Marc'h, ruled by women centuries ago. All I wanted was the power I deserved."

I felt strangely sad for her. "It didn't really work out, did it?"

Her gaze went unfocused again. "I can smell Lyr on you. Don't think for a second he'll treat you as an equal. When you're drinking that dandelion wine up there in his room, don't think you'll be any different."

Her lips looked completely parched, and I handed her my glass of dandelion wine through the bars. "Here."

She leaned closer, eying me suspiciously. Then, she snatched the wine and drank it down thirstily.

"Just so you know," I said, "my mother was never going to make you queen. She wanted it for herself. She was just using you to get the fuath closer to Lyr."

Melisande wiped a hand across her mouth, glaring at me. But it seemed she was done talking.

I turned and started crossing out of the cells, but as I passed Debbie's cell, she called to me.

"Hey, you bang the meaty hands guy yet?"

"Sure did, Debbie."

"Nice one, Tennessee. Thanks for the cloak." Her large eyes blinked up at me.

I hugged myself as I reached the stairs again. Melisande had been a force of nature before I'd cut her down. Imagine how powerful we would have been if we'd joined forces, instead of trying to destroy each other?

When I reached the top of the stairs, I headed for Lyr's room.

I pushed through the door, and I found him sitting perfectly still on his bed. The breeze whispered through the window, toying with his pale hair. His powerful body beamed with gold.

He was sitting *too* still, like a predatory animal. He'd shifted again, eyes glowing gold, and his crown strained into the air above his head, reaching for the heavens...

When the door closed behind me, his head whipped toward me, and his eyes faded to blue.

"Aenor." The way he said my name sometimes raised goosebumps on my skin.

I flashed him a smile, and he rose. He crossed to me, then scooped me up in his powerful arms. Then, he dropped me on the bed. He was shirtless—again—and I let my hands linger over his muscled chest. Already, my pulse was racing.

He moved between my legs, my dress riding all the way up to the top of my thighs. I hooked my legs around him, and he kissed my neck. His mouth felt so good on me, and he was stroking the top of my lace panties—

But there was something I needed to tell him, and it couldn't wait anymore.

I wrapped my arms around his neck. "Lyr," I whispered into his ear.

"Mmmm?"

I pulled back a little, and I looked into his deep blue eyes. "I have to tell you something important."

"Is it about how much you want me?"

I had to tell him about Salem. "When I was looking for the athame, the Nameless One captured me. Salem. He chained me up, and he wouldn't let me go until I did something for him."

I felt Lyr's entire body go rigid, and rage burned in his gold eyes. "What?'

"He wanted me to eat a piece of fruit. It was enchanted, somehow. And he said it meant he'd always be able to find me."

A heavy silence fell over Lyr, and he seemed to be struggling to stay in control, to not let the Ankou take over. He looked as if he were vibrating with fury.

A muscle twitched in his jaw. "What does he want?"

"I don't know. He just said that he might need my help for something. He said he wants me to use my power."

"So he'll give it back?"

I wanted to kill Salem, but I had to be calculating. If there was a chance he'd give me my power back, then I'd wait till after he returned it to me. "That's what he said."

Lyr leaned down, grazing his teeth over my throat. There as something possessive in the gesture. He kissed my neck deeply, running his tongue over my throat until I moaned, moving my hips against him.

When he pulled away again, he murmured into my neck, "Salem is not trustworthy. He is the man who destroyed Ys. He's the one who killed your mother. You can't wait for him to give you your power back and hope that he's good on his word. I just need to kill him. I'll rip out his heart, and I won't let him get anywhere near you."

My heart sank at that thought, even though the logical part of my mind knew that he had a point.

I brushed his pale hair off his face. "Don't do anything hasty. Not without my command."

He stared deeply into my eyes. "What else is on your mind? Something else is bothering you."

I sighed, my chest heavy. "I've been wondering if my mother was always a bit warped. You know, the bloodstained wedding dress, the nighttime stories about how she murdered my dad. That kind of thing. What if both my parents were a bit evil?"

"She was never perfect." He pressed me close against his powerful body. "But nobody is. I'm not. You're not. It doesn't mean we're evil. Your mother had her flaws, and she hungered for power. But she protected the people of Ys fiercely. She protected the weak and the vulnerable like a good leader should. That's the real reason she had my loyalty. And maybe you didn't take after her in the old days, but now I see the best of your mother in you. I started seeing it after you threw that woman's husband out. You're like your mother once was."

I nestled my face into his neck, breathing in his scent.

"I thought we needed her back," he said. "And I wanted it so badly that I committed a crime against the gods. But all we really needed was you. You're the true queen of Ys. And it's now my mission to protect you."

I smiled up at him. "But why do I feel like you've been protecting me all along? Or at least, you didn't kill me when you should have. You thought that I was torturing people to death for no reason, and nailing iron into fae bodies for sadist purposes. Why am I still alive? Why didn't you throw me in prison at least?"

He shifted. "I just couldn't. When I saw you in London standing over that human body, I thought it was my duty to kill you. But the idea of hurting you made me feel physically sick. It was like iron corroding me every time I thought about it. It felt like witchcraft."

"Is that why you healed me in the prison and gave me a pillow?"

He flicked his fingers under the waist of my panties,

teasing me again with slow, lazy strokes. "Yes. That's why I gave you my cloak. And I wanted you to smell like me."

"How sweet."

"I told you. It's my job to protect you."

I dragged my fingernails down his bare back as he tugged down my panties.

Oh, Lyr.

When I got my power back, I wouldn't need protecting.

THANKS SO MUCH FOR READING. If you want an optional short epilogue, please check our website!

ALSO BY C.N. CRAWFORD

For a full list of our books, check out our website.
https://www.cncrawford.com/books/

And a possible reading order.
https://www.cncrawford.com/faq/

ACKNOWLEDGMENTS

Thanks to my supportive family, and to Michael Omer for his genius critiques and emotional support. Thanks to Nick for his insight and help crafting the book.

Robin and Stephanie are my fabulous editors for this book. Thanks to my advanced reader team for their help, and to C.N. Crawford's Coven on Facebook!

54863149R00180

Made in the USA
San Bernardino,
CA